I0764522

FOUR RIVERS

KARISA DELAY

Four Rivers

Published by *Vendera Publishing*

Send all questions and comments to us via the contact page at:
www.venderapublishing.com

ISBN: 978-1-936307-35-7 (Hardcover)

Cover Art by: Silent Shudder | www.silentshudderphoto.com

Cover Formatting and Interior Layout by Scribe Freelance | www.scribefreelance.com

Published in the United States of America

I dedicate this to all those who have been patiently waiting, and following my every post. Also, I want to thank my husband and eternal partner Dillon for his love and support.

PROLOGUE

At the base of Mt. Fuji, thick evergreens loomed over Aokigahara's dense vegetation. In the western sky, Venus followed the sun, shining brightly before disappearing into the underworld. Ben turned and looked down the long trail taken by hundreds of suicides. It was covered with pine needles and fist-sized volcanic stones. He paid no heed to the dark, dwarfed figures lingering in the shadows. The three-foot-tall creatures were robed in black vestments that covered their heads and bodies all the way to the ground. They stood behind the thick cypress and oak trees, peering at Ben through blazing crimson eyes as he made his way up the steep slope.

Ben stopped ten yards from a large red pine. The branches began arching and cracking above the pathway, showing the way to a nearby cave. The cave's entrance was concealed by faded ivy and thick kudzu vines. Beneath piles of dead leaves, human skeletons gave evidence of the evil that resided past the threshold.

Ben stepped toward the cave, but a rustling sound broke the silence. He stopped and turned to his left, his senses alert. The trees whispered and the earth growled as something approached. The dwarf figures moved out of the shadows and encircled Ben. Dried leaves crunched and crackled under a heavy tread, and stones and clods of dirt skittered and rolled ahead of whatever was coming. Seconds later a man appeared, tall and dressed in a long robe. He stepped closer to Ben, towering over him. Ben didn't move.

The large cloaked man kneeled on one knee before Ben, and the dark figures followed suit. "Master, we are humbled to be in your presence," the large man said in a voice as cold as the moon.

"Rise and face me, Son of Adam," Ben commanded.

The man stood up and pulled back his hood, revealing blood-red irises. A beam of moonlight slipped through the canopy of trees and caught bronze highlights in the chestnut hair that covered most of his exposed body. Two horns protruded three inches from his forehead, curving inward.

"How may we serve thee?"

"Where is she, Cain?" Ben nodded in the direction of the cave. "Where is your whore?"

"Do you plan to kill her?"

"My intentions are not yours to ponder. Yours is only to obey."

Cain and the cloaked figures bowed, but a soft breath moved across the air.

"Hello, Benjamin." The sultry voice came from behind him.

Ben turned and glared at the olive-skinned brunette who was leaning against the bark of an old oak tree. Her skin was smooth as satin, and her long hair flowed across her breast.

"Lilith."

"Ah, are we still holding a grudge?"

Ben stepped closer to Lilith. "I assume, based on your note at the funeral, that you know where I can find Alexis."

"I do. She has been taken to the realm with those vile Angels."

"Which one? There are eight."

"In time."

"I think you're playing games."

"I'm not." She nodded toward the small beings. "They were there watching."

"Watching? In Belize?" Ben laughed. "I didn't see any of them."

"Because she blinded you." Lilith caressed Ben's face. "You allowed her to distract you from your true purpose."

Ben grabbed her hand and moved it away from his face.

Cain began to move closer to Lilith, and the small dark figures also closed in, forming a solid black mass around them.

Lilith composed herself and straightened her shoulders. "Do something for me and I will tell you where to find your precious human."

Ben glanced around at the small dark shadows and then up at Cain. "Do you know what it feels like to lose the one you love right before your eyes? I don't have time for your schemes."

"I didn't take Alexis from you."

"No, but you will tell me what you know to get her back."

"Each apple that fell from the tree transformed into crystals. All were to be placed around the world to hide them from our kind."

"You're wasting my time. I know all about the crystals."

"The Bereishit, the one Alexis has, can take you anywhere. Like all the other crystals, the one who holds it controls it."

Ben stared at Lilith and took a step closer. "Your knowledge of this is quite detailed. Why is that?"

"Because I had its companion."

Ben frowned. "The tree only bore thirteen fruits—the one Eve took and the others that belonged to agents of the Light."

"Almost correct," Lilith said. "The tree did bear only thirteen, but the one didn't come from the tree on this planet."

"We had the Immortalis," Cain said.

"The perfect diamond," Lilith added.

Ben's frown deepened. "Adam's crystal wasn't one of the twelve? Who told you this? And when did you go back?"

Lilith shrugged. "It doesn't matter."

Ben saw her glance at the subhuman creature cursed to remain on Earth for his sins. "Why would you need it? No one knew how the crystals worked or where they lead."

Lilith grinned. "Adam and Eve knew."

"Why would she share information with you?"

"It was for my children."

Ben looked at the small dark figures encircling them. "These are not children, Lilith. These beings are merely your failed attempts to be like me, yet they still know their Master."

"The Immortalis can grant immortal life," Lilith said. "I wanted another ..."

"I'm not here to help you build a family tree. I want to find Alexis."

"Your human is fine," Lilith snarled, and she turned around to leave.

Ben grabbed her neck and slammed her thin frame against the tree. "What?"

Cain's face was full of rage. "Master!"

Ben ignored him and glared at Lilith. "What do you mean? What else do you know? Tell me the realm!"

"You know they won't hurt her."

"But she will have to die in order to stay."

"They all die," Lilith muttered. "There's something else you should know."

"About Alexis?"

"Not exactly."

"Then what? Nothing you say will be more important."

"I was ... with child—before I left."

Ben grabbed her wrist and squeezed. "A child?"

"Master, please!" Cain pleaded.

Ben released his hold and Lilith fell at his feet. "You gave birth to a human child? You're the one they should blame, not me. This is all your fault."

"My actions didn't force your hand," Lilith replied as Cain helped her up from the dirt. "You broke the laws of creation yourself."

"The laws? You mean the sheer idea of chaos?"

"Chaos that gives us both purpose to rule over Darkness."

"You were created for me, and we were to be as one. This was never meant to be."

Lilith pulled her hand away from Cain and walked up to Ben. "I have created a son of both worlds."

"You've created an abomination neither from Heaven nor Hell."

"Imagine the army we could have if I could give you more children."

"There is no *we*, Lilith."

"Benjamin, you and I are the same."

Ben stared up at the cave. "Where is he now?"

"He lives among the humans. I made sure he would be able to hide from our kind. He has many who follow him in the shadows to protect the power that runs through his blood."

"What does your bastard have to do with Alexis?"

"You really have changed," Lilith taunted. "And all because of a human? Are you truly in love with her?"

"How you weave hypocrisy, Lilith," Ben snapped.

"What I did was different. I didn't love Adam, I only wanted to corrupt him. I'd do it again."

"What you did caused everything to change. I will destroy you before this is over." A dark fog began to form, enclosing all that stood there.

Cain stepped closer. "Master."

Ben turned back to the beast. "What?"

"I willingly serve thee, for you have spared me your wrath this whole time, though I am from the house of your enemy," Cain said, bowing his head. "I will do what you ask of me."

"Tell me where to find Alexis."

"The fifth realm of the Messengers, but I don't know how to find it."

Ben grinned over Cain's shoulder at the woman standing yards away. "I will come for you when it's time. Until then, free them."

Cain nodded as Ben pointed to the small shadow figures and then disappeared, leaving a rumble below him across the earth.

CHAPTER ONE

Six Months Later

DAYLIGHT HAD BARELY made its way to the busy streets of New York City. Banners, signs, and protestors filled a block of East 91st Street, as more than two thousand people gathered in front of a stone-fronted embassy and shouted through the wrought iron fence.

"American crime, American time!"

The man they were chanting about nervously looked out the window. He had recently been given immunity after being suspected in the brutal rapes of six college girls. Several armed men stood behind the tall iron fencing, watching the protesters.

"American crime, American time!"

"American crime, American time!"

Along a side street, inches from the protest, Ben watched the crowd. He waited for the Gatherers, the darkest of his kind, to finish entering this side of our world. Of the thousands of demon Gatherers, seventy-two had been called to the presence of their Master that morning.

Cezar stood at the front next to Ben. "Would you like me to leave?"

Cezar was a part of the world of evil, but his power was not as great as the company he stood among.

"Is this not where you want to be?" Ben asked.

Cezar bowed his head. "I desire nothing more than to be a Gatherer of the dead."

Ben glanced at Cezar. "Has anything come of your efforts?"

"We've searched," Cezar began. "But we have yet to find anything leading to the Messenger realm."

Ben turned back to the crowd of protesters. "Their realm is like our own, and it will be the most protected of the eight."

"Where do we begin? It's not as if we can access it, even if we found the Fifth Realm of Light."

Ben looked at Cezar. "You're right. That is why I've sent a multitude to find me a Messenger."

"We've never been able to just find them. They're not very friendly toward us and ..."

"I need her back."

"What if she is truly gone? What if Lilith was lying?" Cezar let out a breath and added, "Forgive me."

Ben glared at him. "Your failure to understand my instructions and your questioning my ability to recognize reality sounds as if you want to incur my wrath."

"No, Master. It's that the only way we can see the Light is ..."

"During the exchange at death. I'm aware that your powers have been limited to manipulation of the living, but your presence is also required during the transition of death. As is a Messenger's."

"You want me to try to take one?"

The crowd of protestors was unaware of the negative energy being released by the shadows and how it was affecting them. The shouting became louder, and the crowd pushed closer to the wrought iron fence.

"American crime, American time!"

Ben turned to the massive group of shadow men, each of whom stood seven feet tall. "My faithful servants, from this point you have had but one concern, to take death in its time. But now it is our moment to show our hand in power and rebuild the first temple to protect Alexis when she returns. You will do this by no longer staying within the boundaries of the Light's balance."

Cezar looked at Ben, whose eyes were black as night. "Can they do that? Break the balance?"

A deep, pulsating voice came from the sea of men. "What about the Messengers? We are not ready for war. Our numbers are evenly matched, but we are not guaranteed victory."

"Since the beginning, we all have stayed within the rules set forth to maintain the order of balance between good and evil," Ben replied. "This has kept their eyes looking away as we prepare. We have been manipulating these humans into feeling powerless or trapping them in their own guilt after death. All which keeps us strong." Ben motioned to the protestors behind him. "But those who are already so close to perdition need to cross over to help strengthen us past equal numbers."

The protestors were screaming, "American crime, American time!"

"Today I free you from those chains."

Cezar asked the question that tens of thousands of his brethren wanted to know the answer to. "We can take their lives?"

"Each Gatherer that stands before me was once enslaved by a human whose purpose was to build a temple for the Light. Since the time of King Solomon, you have learned to master the elements of the dead to your advantage. With each person you gathered and kept from the Light, we became more powerful. I command you to bring more unto me. However, we still only take those who seek us."

Cezar appeared confused as the multitude of dark beings began to transform. The black masses stretched into thin creatures of death.

"Why take only the ones who seek us?" Cezar asked. "Wouldn't we grow in strength faster if they take as many as possible?"

"That would eliminate your purpose," Ben snapped. "And spoil the pot. Your men are to sway the human mind to take steps away from the path that keeps them in the Light, just as before. When they decide to turn away, that's when the Gatherers can take them without waiting for death."

Cezar stepped back.

"I have released many evil beings across this earth, but today the demons of Solomon will walk among the living," Ben said.

A hollow roar came from the Gatherers.

"Will the humans be able to see us now?" Cezar asked.

Ben turned to him. "Fear is like faith. If they see the Darkness, they will only hope for the Light. No matter what humans try to hide, they're all made of greed."

Cezar nodded and turned back to join his new ranks, realizing his place was far from where he stood, but all the men transfigured into dark silhouettes and passed through the walls, leaving him alone.

"Cezar, it takes more than desire to join their fold," Ben said. "Find me answers, and then that power I will grant you."

Ben looked again at the crowd, which was no longer peacefully protesting. Ben let out a deep growl and a great roar passed through the crowd. The wind stood patient as it waited to be released from his grasp on the thousands of vulnerable individuals. Before anyone could ask what was happening, the ground rumbled and violently shook. Ben vanished, leaving chaos in the streets.

CHAPTER TWO

MARCIA ZEN TOOK a deep breath as she entered the old country church, whose walls, floors, and pews were made of wood. She walked to the front, where her daughter Rebecca had saved her a seat. The scent of flowers from enormous arrangements of ruby red roses and ivory peonies filled the chapel, and the soft light of candles sitting in front of one of the floral swags glowed across the altar, creating the illusion of a hillside. Marcia remembered a similar hillside near her parents' home, where Alexis would often go to pick clovers in search of one with four leaves. The memories rushed through her mind so rapidly that she didn't notice the pews beginning to fill behind her and that the chatter had turned to whispers.

"Red was Alexis's favorite color," a strong male voice said quietly.

Marcia woke from her reverie. "What?"

He leaned in closer. "The roses were Alexis's favorite color."

Marcia looked at the young gentleman sitting next to her. The brim of his fedora cast a shadow over his glasses. "The bride changed the colors in her memory," she said

"Rightly so," he said, looking straight ahead. "She really wanted to be here today."

Marcia tried to look at the man's face. "Did you know my daughter?"

"Yes. It's a great loss."

"We all miss her very much."

"It's too bad you didn't tell her that more often while she was here."

Marcia frowned. "Excuse me?"

"Sometimes people are taken before they know they are loved."

"Do I know you, young man?"

"Our paths crossed years ago."

"Is that so? Were you five?"

He leaned close to whisper in Marcia's ear. "Our Alexis isn't dead."

Marcia glared at him. "Who did you say you were?"

"I didn't."

"Well, I don't appreciate ..."

Marcia jumped when she felt a hand on her shoulder. She looked up to see Rebecca looking at her.

"Mom?"

"What?"

"Who are you talking to?"

"This jerk," Marcia said, and she pointed to the space beside her. No one was there.

Rebecca gripped her mother's hand. "Are you OK?"

Marcia's heart was racing. "Yeah, I'm OK. I thought ... never mind."

The door at the back of the chapel opened. The music changed and the guests turned to watch. A procession of four bridesmaids and five groomsmen made their way to the front where the groom nervously waited. The guests stood as a bride adorned in a vintage lace dress was escorted down the aisle.

Rebecca put her arm around her mother and whispered, "Adriana said she couldn't replace Alexis."

The members of the wedding party took their places. The place next to the bride, where the maid of honor, Alexis, would have been, was empty.

CHAPTER THREE

ALEXIS SAT ON A smooth grey rock outside the blue cottage. The landscape of the realm of the Messengers wasn't much different from the world she knew and loved, except everything appeared as though it had been airbrushed perfectly, like her dreams. The greens were a perfect mix of avocado and jade, the pebbles were polished smooth, and the dirt beneath her bare feet felt like velvet powder. It was all so inviting.

Alexis sighed. *I don't want to be here.*

The moon peeked over her left shoulder as the sun warmed the right side of her face.

How long have I been here?

Her body felt empty but she wasn't hungry or tired. Something was different.

She heard something and turned to see a tall, well-built ebony man standing to her left. "May I sit with you, Miss Zen?"

"OK, sure."

Alexis looked back at the beautiful scene in front of her, hoping something would begin to make sense.

"A bit overwhelming?"

Alexis nodded. "A little."

"We are here to help you."

"Help me with what? You haven't told me anything."

"It's complex and not easily explained. It has taken others years to comprehend."

"What others? And I thought my coming through that portal was a big mystery to you."

"The mystery is how you survived, given that we didn't bring you here ourselves."

"Who are the others?"

"Some were great men who completed their tasks on Earth and were spared death. Others were brought here to see and then return as witnesses of the Light."

"It's like a bad dream."

"This is very much real, and your absence has put the universe in danger." The man stood up and offered his hand to Alexis.

Alexis stood up without assistance and chuckled. "I doubt my absence has caused the universe to spin out of control. Not many people knew I existed, and those who did weren't the type for world domination."

"It only takes one to change things. And he knows who you are."

"Who is *he*?"

"Alexis, know that we are not trying to deceive you, and we want to explain how this is possible, but the complexity would be too much all at once. Allow the precepts to come unto you as a child learns."

She folded her arms. "I'm not a child. And deflecting the question isn't winning me over."

"I'm approaching the subject in the way I am directed."

The man was clothed in a white linen robe and pants, with his chest slightly exposed. He wore no shoes. He started walking across the pebbles, and Alexis followed.

"This isn't the first I've heard about this mysterious person," Alexis said. "Why mention it if you weren't planning on telling me who it is?"

The man turned as they came to the edge of the stream. "We are not to mention him by name."

She rolled her eyes. "Of course."

"We can only guide you to understanding the difference between good and evil so you can choose what is right."

"I must have missed the guidance part. I'm no closer to knowing why I'm here than I am to knowing who's on the naughty and nice list."

He grinned and made a slight nod. "With great enlightenment comes great personal discovery."

"Is there anyone who can answer my questions?"

"Alexis, I would like to show you something." He offered his hand to help her across the narrow stream.

She ignored the gesture and jumped over the stream. "Do you have a name?"

He crossed the stream and faced her. "My name is Aharon."

Alexis followed him through what seemed like miles of forest. The scenery was similar to that which greeted her when she arrived, except there were no people in white surrounding her. But the smells were the same and the path appeared to be the same.

They left the forest and entered a lush green meadow strewn with vivid blue coneflowers and bright copper poppies. The tall oaks bowed their branches once Aharon and Alexis were clear of the tree line.

Alexis stopped abruptly and gazed past the emerald field to a distant hilltop. Her palms felt clammy, and her heart began to beat faster. "Is this a joke?" she asked.

"No, why would you ask that?"

"I've been here before."

"Yes, this is where you entered our world."

"No, before that—in my dreams."

"What exists here also exists on your side, so it's likely you saw something similar."

"The place was in my dreams, and it had an unwelcoming force on the other side of that hill."

"You have nothing to fear. This place is of peace. No evil has power here."

"But there is so much darkness on the other side."

"Trust me."

Alexis began walking toward the hillside. Perhaps, as before, she was in a nightmare and only needed to wake up. As she neared the top, she paused to take in a deep breath.

Aharon placed a hand on her shoulder. “Open your eyes.”

CHAPTER FOUR

A CERAMIC KETTLE WHISTLED on top of the gas burner. Mrs. Prollofsky grabbed the handle with an orange crocheted potholder and walked from the kitchen into the dining area. She placed two tea balls, each filled with dried chamomile, into two delicate gold-lined cups before pouring the boiling water.

Suddenly, the table rumbled and the teacups began rattling on their saucers. Mrs. Prollofsky set down the kettle and held the teacups by their handles to keep them still, but the glassware and dishes in the cabinet were clattering. The vibrating stopped, and Mrs. Prollofsky let go of the teacups.

"Those aftershocks keep coming."

Baba glanced at the guest sitting in the chair across from her. "I think it might even snow."

James Mitchell turned to look out the window at the heavy clouds rolling in from the northeast. "Sure looks like it."

"Sugar?"

"No, thanks."

Stacks of photo albums were spread out on the round oak table. Several of the edges were worn and falling apart, and some of the photos were hanging by the last bit of adhesive.

"I have been going through some of these old pictures," Baba said.

James touched the top of her hand. "I would love to see some, if you don't mind."

Baba smiled and took a sip of tea. "I don't mind. We don't get much company up here in the winter."

"That's why I didn't bring my sports car." He pointed over his shoulder to the black SUV parked outside.

Baba and James began a journey through old memories, starting with her wedding day, then on to various places the Prollofsky family had lived, the numerous summer vacations, and most of the holiday gatherings. Baba shared stories of each of her children and remained composed when she spoke about the death of her oldest daughter, Sarah.

"She was a stubborn child, with a lot of challenges. We didn't know which direction she would go. We had prayed that God would save her from her burdens."

"I am sorry. You have suffered a great loss this year."

"Thank you, but to be honest"—she lowered her voice—"I didn't expect to have Sarah as long as we did."

"I don't quite understand. Was she ill?"

"Sarah was a free spirit. Between the drug use, failed rehab, hitchhiking, and proclaiming love for many men, we never knew where she would end up."

"I thought she worked at the truck stop off the interstate."

"Yes, but it wouldn't have lasted. I cried many nights, afraid of where she was sleeping, not knowing if she was hungry, if she was hurt, or if she was still alive." Baba flipped to a page with Sarah's high school picture. "Her innocence was evident, and many people took advantage of it."

"That had to be hard."

"It's still hard, knowing I won't see her face until I, too, pass, but I sleep better knowing she is better off now."

James watched as Baba continued to flip through pages of photos, eventually coming to one of Alexis's baby pictures. The photo was discolored and worn on the edges. Alexis was bundled up in a pink and mint floral print blanket while snuggled in her grandfather's arms. Baba slipped the photo out of the sleeve and turned it over. On the back was a handwritten note, *Alexis age 6 months.*

James leaned closer. "Does she look like her mother or father?"

"Her father, but Alexis didn't know her birth father," Baba said. "She knew him only through pictures."

"What happened to him?"

Baba shrugged "He just vanished one day. The police found his car abandoned but never a body." Baba flipped the pages. "I think I have a picture of him, such a great guy."

"Poor Alexis."

"I know. My daughter remarried shortly after Mikel went missing, but Marcia's second marriage didn't work out, and after a few years, she married Matthew. It was as if he filled the void for both Marcia and Alexis. When she was old enough, Alexis made it known she wanted to be remembered as Matt's daughter, so she asked him to adopt her at fourteen."

"What else did you know about her father?"

"He was European, Scandinavian I think, with beautiful eyes, like Alexis. Marcia was so in love with him, it crushed her heart when he left. But none of that matters now."

"All of us at the base miss Alexis. She had a brilliant mind."

"She was like a daughter to us growing up. Her mom often left her with us while she worked out of town. I thought Alexis was the one ..." She cleared her throat and put the picture back.

"The one?"

"Nothing. I just want answers about her death."

"I wish I could give you that peace, but my hands are tied."

"You could tell me how she really died."

"I don't know how I can."

"The truth usually works," Baba said.

"That's not what I mean. What I'm saying is that I can't share classified information."

"Ann!" A little man came shuffling from the bedroom. "Ann!"

"What is it, DziDzi?"

"You must see what is happening all over the TV," he said as he looked for the remote. "It's starting."

"This is Alexis's grandfather," Baba said to James.

"She mentioned him. Quite the Scrabble player."

"More like quitter." Baba stood. "The clicker is on your chair, dear."

James stood up and the three walked from the dining room into the sitting room. The room was ten by twelve and wrapped with windows, exposing a beautiful view of the hillside behind the house.

"What is going on that you're in such a fuss about?" Baba asked.

"New York City is like a war zone," DziDzi said. "The earthquake this morning has everyone crazy." DziDzi sat down in a creaky rocking chair close to the TV.

James stared at him. "Are you saying New York had an earthquake, too?"

"Yes. That's what we've been feeling," DziDzi said.

He turned the channel to the local network, which was showing live coverage of New York City. The camera zoomed in behind the reporter, to the people raging through the streets, smashing store windows, looting and destroying anything in their path. Many buildings and abandoned cars were ablaze.

DziDzi muttered in his native tongue, "*Poważnie! Nie rozumiem (Seriously! I don't understand.)*"

Baba grabbed the remote and switched the channel to a cable news station.

James was on his phone searching the live feed. "It says here it began when a sudden earthquake measuring nearly seven on the Richter scale brought down the gates of the Russian Embassy early this morning in New York. A peaceful protest turned ugly when the protesters tried to force their way inside and later took over some city streets by force. There's a video from someone's phone."

James and Baba watched the amateur video of one of the protestors. It began with chanting, *American crime, American time*. Then the video panned across the crowd, showing the homemade signs waving through the air. The chanting slowly changed to shouting. When the ground shook, the video wobbled as the person holding the camera phone fell to the ground.

"A second earthquake?" Baba questioned.

"I told you," DziDzi said.

Baba returned to James's phone. The screen showed pieces of the surrounding buildings beginning to fall. The video focused on the front of the crowd, where people were pushing their way toward the embassy gates. The rumbling stopped and everyone stood completely still as an eerie silence fell.

After a few seconds, someone shouted. "The gates are gone!"

Someone else yelled, "We need to bring him out to be judged."

The crowd of over two thousand people began to spread through the embassy grounds.

"Oh my God, are they killing that guard?" Baba said.

James turned it off. "This is nothing we need to see."

The news coverage on TV began showing a live feed of the police trying to barricade the blocks near the embassy, while other officers shot canisters of tear gas into the center of the crowd. Their efforts didn't faze the mob of people.

Baba shook her head. "I can't believe people are acting like that."

"The sad part is, this is nothing compared to what people are capable of doing," James said.

"But it's terrible to see such violence."

"I'm sure the police will get it under control soon."

"We need to pray for those people and the families there," Baba said. "I'm thankful we don't live on a major fault line. It's bad enough that the small vibrations we get shake my china."

"You're safe out here in the woods," James said. He glanced at his watch. "I should head out. I've got to be at work early tomorrow."

"Are they going to release Alexis's personal items yet? It's been six months."

"I'm not involved in that decision. But I know most everything is still being processed to ensure there was no government information on her computers." James headed to the hallway leading to the back door. "Is there anything in particular you need?"

"I would like to have her things when it's all done, especially the journal I gave her for her birthday."

"I will see what I can do, Mrs. Prollofsky, but it will probably go to her next of kin."

"Please, let me know when they release everything."

"I will. And thanks again for inviting me over."

"You're welcome. It was nice to talk with you. Please, promise you will come back."

"I promise."

James left and Baba shut the door and watched through a window as he walked to the SUV. A small dusting of snow had covered the vehicle. DziDzi walked up behind Baba.

"Do you think he knows?" he asked.

Baba pulled the curtains closed. "No, but it won't be long before he or someone else figures it out."

CHAPTER FIVE

AHARON AND ALEXIS stood atop the hill, gazing down the opposite slope.

"You appear to be disappointed by what you see," Aharon said. "Please share what saddens your heart."

"I'm not sad," Alexis said. "This wasn't what I expected."

"What were you expecting?"

"In my dreams there was a city off in the distance that had been destroyed and left for scavengers." She motioned to the valley below. "While this was nothing but a sea of shadowy men clothed in suits of black."

"You could see they were men?"

"Yeah. They had faces."

"As I mentioned, your side has the same ground. However, our side is not taken over by cities. But your dreams are different."

"How so?"

"Dreams exist between two realms, the physical and the spiritual. That is how we can enter your mind to guide you, and that is also how your loved ones who have passed can visit you. Through dreams they share the realm of the spirits with you."

Alexis pondered the idea. "And the evil that I saw?"

"Someone was sending you a message."

"But who?" A quick flash came, reminding her of the hand she saw reaching over the hilltop in her dream and the voice calling for help. "Do you think it's someone not of the Light?"

He didn't answer but his eyes showed concern. "Follow me," he said and turned away.

"Wait. Can you give me a moment alone?"

"I will wait for you by the trees."

"Thank you."

He nodded and headed down the hillside.

Alexis took in a deep breath and closed her eyes as she exhaled.

I don't know where to begin, but from what I have seen, a higher intelligence does exist, so if you are listening, please guide me. I pray that you will show me the way out, that I may return to the world I know.

When she opened her eyes, the sun had caught the edge of the crystal inside her pants pocket. She took it out and rubbed her fingers across the inscriptions. Images of it falling to the ground replayed in her head, and she relived the horrifying feeling of being sucked through the portal.

I'm here because of you. This hunt for your meaning has left me nowhere but lost and alone. Alexis drew her arm back to throw the crystal over the edge of the hill.

"You shouldn't do that."

Alexis jumped and turned to see Aharon back at her side. "How'd you do that?"

"The crystal has a purpose."

"To cause me nothing but confusion, and now the loss of everything. I think its job is done."

"In time you will see that your destiny has always been where you are."

"Right, to be stuck in a place without any guidance."

"That crystal has great significance, but its true purpose is not for all to know, including the Messengers."

"It opens portals to realms."

"As do many other crystals. And they, like this one, have other purposes. It will serve you when it's time."

"If you don't know its purpose, how can you be sure it will serve me later?"

"The same way you trusted physics before you ever picked up a book. Faith without knowing every answer is not only the province of churches but also of the Angels who bring the message." Aharon began walking. "We know there is a reason, but we don't always know the plan."

"I've never been one for metaphoric leaps of faith. I find the tangible facts more grounding."

Alexis followed Aharon back down through the field. The sun was as bright as when she crossed into this world.

"Everything has its place and everything will have its time," Aharon said as they arrived at the tree line.

"I don't accepted predestination. It's like watching a movie with someone who already knows the ending."

"Your destiny for eternity is not decided, that choice is yours alone. Nevertheless, each person placed on earth has a purpose for that time. Even those who walk in the dark have significance."

"OK, answer me something easy."

"I will try."

"How long have I been here?"

"You came to this realm six months ago."

Alexis stopped walking. "Six months? How is that possible? I feel like I got here yesterday. My family has probably given up hope. Poor Ben and James, what I put them through."

Aharon put his arm around her shoulder. "We do not live in darkness, and the mind's perception of time can be lost. Worry not about those you have left behind. A time will come for you to see them again."

They continued through the forest down to the edge of the stream.

"Tell me more about the others," Alexis said.

"The other Messengers?"

"No. The others your kind brought here."

Aharon crossed the stream and put out his hand. "I told you they were great men who completed their tasks or were brought here to be witnesses of the Light."

"But who were they?"

"In time I can show you."

"Show me what? You keep photo albums at the cottage?"

"Alexis, if you're patient, maybe you will meet one of them."

"They're still here?"

"Not here, but close enough." Aharon waited for Alexis to cross the stream. "Come to the cottage where we can talk more about this."

CHAPTER SIX

ABOUT AN HOUR'S drive from Tel Aviv, Israel, in a building wiped from all known databases, sits a stone edifice with a lone watchtower. Weeds and chrysanthemums compete with olive trees to take over the ground inside twelve-foot-high fencing. A building with three-foot-thick walls contains tiny rooms where Arab and Jewish militants were interrogated during World War II. More than two hundred Palestinian prisoners are held in secret in those rooms.

"Please! Someone's in here!" cried out a young prisoner being held for the murder of several woman and children.

The other prisoners, seized by paranoia, joined in. *"The darkness is moving! Someone help me! Who are you?"*

Outside, in the tall watchtower, guards continued to watch the night vision monitors that showed the length of the prison's outer perimeter and each of the four interior hallways. Everything appeared normal.

"One more day of this and we get to rotate out," a guard named Joseph said, leaning forward and putting his thermos on the table near the phone.

"It's been a long, cold, wet three months," another guard added. "I can't wait to be somewhere warm and dry."

Joseph, his eyes trained on the monitors, gave a laugh. "Agreed."

Since the prison was top secret, none of the guards knew each other nor would they work together again. Each quarter, a new set of guards, all blindfolded, was brought in at night to replace the current guards, who also were blindfolded before they were driven away. The journey to and from the secret prison required stops at four checkpoints, and at each one, a new driver would take over. No one except members of the Israeli government knew exactly where the prison was or how to get to it.

"In the time we've been here I've never heard them all be paranoid at once," one of the guards was saying.

"Must be the full moon," Joseph said.

"Except they can't see it."

"Radio over and have them check the cells one by one," Joseph told the guard sitting behind him.

"Save me!" a prisoner yelled out.

An older guard named Ezra sat silently listening to the screams. His brow was furrowed, and his head was turned slightly so he could hear the audio monitor on the control panel.

Joseph nudged him. "What's your problem, Ezra? Are we not funny enough for you today?"

Ezra was a short, potbellied man with a large flat nose and wiry grey hair. His concentration broke for a second, and he gave Joseph a lopsided grin before returning to the control panel. Most days Ezra would be the willing butt of the other guards' jibes, but at that moment he was focused on the prison building, the security cameras, and the screams from the cells coming through the speaker, his eyes constantly shifting from one to the other.

"Ezra?" the guard behind him yelled. "Are you still alive, old man?"

Ezra stood up suddenly, knocking the chair behind him out of the way. He leaned forward, peering at the equipment. "Are you seeing those guys on the monitors?"

"The prisoners?" Joseph asked.

"No, the men walking in the prison yard."

"Levi and Roth are supposed to be on patrol in the yard," a guard said

"Not Levi and Roth," Ezra said in a quavering voice. He pointed at the monitor. "Them."

Joseph looked and saw men entering the perimeter one at a time and then disappearing on the other side of the stone fortress.

"Mik'nas! Poretz!" Joseph shouted into a microphone. *"Poretz!"*

He slammed his palm down onto the large red button next to one of the audio speakers. The button was there to sound the alarm if a prisoner broke free, but now it was warning of someone breaking in.

No one in the tower had responded to Joseph's verbal alert. There was no movement, no sound, except for the ringing alarm. The guards below weren't responding, either.

Still keeping an eye on the intruders, Joseph gave a command to Ezra. "Call Roth and find out what's going on."

There was no response.

Joseph turned around and saw Ezra and the other two guards lying on the floor. He felt the blood drain from his face, and he bent down to place two fingers on the side of Ezra's neck. There was no pulse and his skin was ice cold.

A cracking noise sounded only inches from Joseph. He unholstered his sidearm and slowly stood up. He turned around and came face to face with the dark shadow of a man with black inset eyes. Startled, he stumbled back and tripped over Ezra's body.

"Who are you? What do you want?"

CHAPTER SEVEN

A QUARTER MOON PEERED inside the master bedroom as the Zens slept. Marcia lay away from the center of the bed, facing the window where a solid black figure stood watching her breathe.

The guilt you feel is the pain she lived.

The eerie whisper crept into Marcia's dream. She took in a deep breath and let it out in a long sigh. Her eyes tightened and she pulled the heavy comforter closer. This night, like all the other nights since her daughter's death, she found herself lost in a world of darkness with no way out. Like the other dreams, she started in an abandoned warehouse with dirt floors, accompanied by a broadly built man who lingered in the shadows. Marcia always searched for a way out but never found one. Panic would seize her and she would awake terrified.

Tonight was the first time she could hear a voice, but it didn't make sense. It wasn't coming from the man she was seeing in her dream.

Marcia called out to the blond figure, "Please, what are you saying?"

The man stepped into the light, revealing his pale skin and strong jaw line. He was holding a small book. "I haven't spoken."

She left this earth not knowing your love, how can you dream in peace? Again, the voice was overpowering and was coming from someone else, someone Marcia couldn't see.

"Show yourself!" she demanded.

The man with her in the warehouse seemed to be looking around for the voice as well. "There is no one else with us. Let me take you from here."

"Where?"

"Let us finish the journey we started last night."

In her dreams, Marcia never felt safe, never knew or understood the places she ended up. Her guide through the dreams never spoke to her and didn't tell her the reasons for taking her so many places. But tonight she was willing to return to her nightmares.

"Tell me who you are."

The man leaned close to whisper in her ear. "My name is Azure."

Outside her mind, the moonlight dimmed behind the black being that stretched forth its arm and traced the outline of Marcia's body. The figure placed its long black fingers over Marcia's temples, pressing its darkness across her face.

I will take it all away. Your pain will belong to me. And your soul will be mine to control.

Marcia gasped as she sat up.

Matt turned over, still half asleep. "Are you all right?"

She was breathing heavily, but she nodded. "Just a strange dream, that's all."

Matt sat up. "About Alexis again?"

"Not exactly."

"What do mean?"

"This time instead of me being in some dark place and having Alexis there right at the end to be ripped from me, I am in an open building talking to someone."

"The same person you've seen before?"

"Yeah. All the other times this guy kept pointing to a little black book and trying to tell me something about it, but these dreams never had sound."

"You could hear him tonight?"

She shook her head. "I thought he was telling me something, but it was another voice. I didn't see anyone else until we went to ..."

"Went where?" Matt was lying back on his pillow with his eyes half open, looking toward Marcia as she spoke.

Marcia grabbed her phone from her night table. The brightness of the screen illuminated the room. She quickly typed something and waited for the search to bring up an image.

"The Internet isn't working."

"What are you trying to find?"

"I'm looking for what I saw in my dream."

Matt kissed Marcia on the left shoulder. "It was only a dream, you're safe now."

She let out a breath. "It felt very real, like I couldn't breathe, and then I saw these red eyes. That's when I woke up."

She got up and walked toward the bedroom door, her heart still beating fast as she thought about the last image from dream. The house was lit only by the moonlight coming through the windows in the front. Marcia stepped into the hallway and felt along the wall for a light switch.

Marcia.

"Yes?" She waited for a response from Matt.

Marcia.

"Matt?" She turned and looked into the bedroom. Matt was asleep.

She proceeded to the kitchen and went to the refrigerator to fill a glass with ice water. Marcia moved to the sink and glanced at her reflection, sighing at her appearance. Her eyes had small bags beneath the dark circles and the grey was no longer easy to hide.

She took a sip of water and heard a hum in her ears.

Marcia.

She put the glass down and waited, hoping her husband would appear, but all was quiet. She felt a chill run down her spine and felt the air around her go cold. Her stomach knotted.

Marcia—you deserve to feel her pain.

Marcia grabbed a small medication bottle from the basket near the sink. Her hands were shaking as she spilled her last three anxiety pills onto the counter.

Those can't help you.

She popped one in her mouth and took a gulp of water. She leaned over the sink and tried to control her breathing. The past six months had taken a toll on her. Hearing voices was more evidence of her weak mental state, and talking to people who weren't there was even worse.

"It's all in your head," she murmured.

The room was quiet. Cool air brushed across her shoulders and up the back of her neck. It was gentle and swept across her cheek. Marcia took in a deep breath. Suddenly her heart jumped as Oslo began barking outside the kitchen window. She looked, but there was nothing out there.

She sighed. *It's only in my head.*

"No it's not," a deep male voice uttered into her ear.

The window reflected the perfect outline of a tall man standing inches away from her. Marcia spun around, grabbing her chest as she lost her breath. She could barely get her husband's name out before falling to the ground.

CHAPTER EIGHT

INSIDE THE SOUNDPROOF walls of Lab 11, Sublevel 6, James unpacked crates of material on top of the white table next to where the computers once sat. Anything Alexis had put in there was gone, and the space had reverted to a sterile white room. The crates held only some of her belongings—a laptop and camera, three unused VEs, a digital recorder, the holo recording system Alexis had used to see the bottom of the ocean, and a small red flash drive. But something was missing other than her personal effects. James searched the crates marked for private storage but didn't find what he was looking for.

James picked up the phone on the desk and dialed.

"Colonel Logan's office," the secretary answered.

"I need the speak to the colonel."

"I'm sorry, but he's in a meeting. Can I tell him who's calling?"

"Elizabeth, this is James Mitchell."

"Hold please, Mr. Mitchell, he told me to alert him if you called."

"Thank you."

James rustled through a stack of papers at the bottom of a crate. Most of the papers contained the details of Alexis's atmospheric device. He found an invoice lying on the desk next to one of the crates and skimmed over the inventory.

"It's not here," he murmured.

"What are you looking for?" Colonel Logan asked.

"Sir, I apologize for interrupting you."

"Never mind. What do you need?"

"I was just going through Alexis Zen's effects, and something is missing."

"What is it?"

"Her tablet."

"Why do you need her tablet?"

James hesitated. "She had some pictures of us together, and I wanted to have them for a keepsake."

"If it wasn't government property we sent it to her next of kin after we scrubbed it of any classified info."

Relief washed over James face. "Thank you, sir."

"Mr. Mitchell?"

"Yes, sir?"

"I saw the photos in Japan, on the boat. And I listened to the recording data from over there as well as the audio from the temple in Belize."

"Sir, I apologize that I failed to report our findings. After Alexis ..."

"James, I want answers about that ship you two saw. I will have the data sent back over to you. Comb through those photos and whatever data Miss Zen gathered on her devices. Find evidence of why those craft are becoming more visible. I want to know if they're the same as the others."

"Yes, sir."

"I have one of your lab techs on Six going over the audio from Japan. She will report her findings to me directly."

"Who, sir?"

The colonel cleared his throat. "Miss Anderson."

"Paige? Sir, she can't be trusted anymore. Ever since she ..."

"James, she is a valuable asset to Level 6. I don't care about her actions outside the base."

"She put people in the hospital because of her irresponsibility. She comes to work smelling like a liquor cabinet."

"Mr. Mitchell, let me remind you that you're extremely under-qualified for the job position I've placed you in."

James sighed. "I will send her what I gathered from Belize."

"Don't worry about Belize. I want the data from Japan analyzed first. That's our priority."

"What about finding Alexis? The data from Belize could help us."

"James."

"Sir?"

"Someone else is looking into what happened in Belize. If she can be found, you will be brought in to assist, but until then I need to find this UFO."

"Understood."

James hung up the phone and then reached inside his lab coat. He pulled out a small leather-bound journal, the one given to Alexis on her birthday. He sat down, staring at the first page. The characters were far different from anything he'd seen before. He pictured Alexis smiling, felt the memory of her peace begin to warm the room. His cell phone rang. The caller ID was blocked, but he took the call.

"This is James."

"Status?" a male voice asked.

"Slight problem," James said. "I don't have the tablet with the inscriptions."

"Where is it?"

"The Zens have it now."

"Get it."

"I will."

The caller ended the call, and James returned to the first page of the journal. *What am I not seeing? Why have a treasure map with no key to decipher it?*

CHAPTER NINE

AHARON GUIDED ALEXIS past the multitude of Messengers gathered near the cottage. They walked inside the cottage's small white room and Aharon shut the door. The wooden table with intricate detail around the edges was still in the middle of the room, but only one map-like page was laid out.

Alexis walked to the table and pointed at the odd pattern of circles on the page. "This is the one I asked about when I first came here."

"What did you want to know?"

"I was told this was a map, but I've seen something like it in the Voynich manuscript, a book I've frequently scoured."

Aharon joined her at the table. "You've seen a replica. This is one half of the original. But it was never a book."

"In my world, the manuscript is a mystery of language and symbolism. And this was found in it. I have a copy for light reading when my brain is having trouble sorting things out." Alexis remembered changing her bank password to VOYNICH, ensuring no one could access her accounts.

"I can attest this has never left our realm, but there is another like it."

Alexis was too involved in the page before her to hear him. "The Voynich manuscript is an amazing discovery, and I always assumed it was compiled data versus a straight read. My guess is that this was some secret society's handbook."

"I can't speak for the book you mention, but this is no part of a secret society," Aharon said.

Alexis looked closer. "It didn't make sense that someone of that time could have come up with something so complex and indecipherable. Why create it if you weren't planning on sharing it?"

"Those who know the language of God take it with them to their death, but those who speak the tongue of Evil will live in death."

Alexis glanced up at him.

Aharon pointed to a few of the words inscribed at the top. "The writing you see is that of the gods, but the one you saw is not of the Light."

"Right, you said the one I saw was a replica."

"Not just a replica, but the replica to the other half to this one," Aharon said. "The Scrolls of Dimensions."

"Never heard of it."

"There are no humans alive who have."

"Then who made the replica?"

"An eager explorer from your world who inadvertently changed the human point of view. His follies opened doors despite his hope for personal gain."

Alexis laughed. "I know that scholars carbon-dated it to the fifteenth century and it was thought to be written by an Italian. Not that I trust in carbon dating entirely."

"This time you can trust its accuracy."

"All right, so it was a man from the fifteenth century, an Italian, an explorer out for personal gain."

"His travels across the ocean in a fleet of three led to the expansion of man's mind and the proliferation of government across the lands."

"Columbus," Alexis said.

Aharon nodded.

"Where did he get the original other half?"

"Not where, but who."

"So who?

"That question I cannot answer. The original has been with us since the gates of Eden were sealed. The two halves haven't been brought together."

"Maybe those in the shadows are responsible."

"It's possible, but their knowledge is not like ours. They no longer have guidance from the Light to know things of foresight, and so they cower in the darkness, afraid of their own shadows."

Alexis frowned. As a child, she was never one to accept the stories of angels and demons waging war against each other behind the scenes. "How would Columbus get this?"

"It would have to come from someone that was present in Eden, someone who saw the original, which could be someone from either side." Aharon thought for a moment. "As with many others who walk the earth, understanding comes from perception."

"Perception is not always reality." Alexis looked at the page. "The page I've seen is a very real likeness to this."

"That's why it had to be one of the four placed in Eden."

"Four? If memory serves, there were only three, Adam, Eve, and the Devil." Alexis rolled her eyes then exhaled. "But I'm sure you can't explain that to me."

"Yes, you're correct. It's best we take it one step at a time." Aharon pointed back to the page with circles.

"If I can think of the question, don't you think I could comprehend the answer?" Alexis argued.

Aharon smiled. "Even if you could understand it, it would stop further questions. This universe, like all other complex systems, is filled with so many wonders that the human mind can't take it all in. You will get your answers, I promise, just not at the present time."

"So asking if God exists would be redundant."

Alexis considered the page with nine circles in three rows of three, noticing their similarities and differences. Each of the eight outer circles was connected to another, either by a bridge or a convex line of sorts. She focused on the one in the center. It was different, and only four outer circles connected directly to it.

"This one in the center is larger. Why?"

Aharon motioned to the entire page. "Wouldn't you like to know what this is first?"

"I feel the answer to my first question will solve that mystery."

"Clever you are."

Alexis smirked.

"I will show you."

Aharon waved his hand over the center of the page. The inner circle bulged, and then it expanded and lifted from the page. Aharon turned the translucent image in the air, making it rotate rapidly. The two-dimensional circle was now a three-dimensional sphere with two inner core areas.

"The entirety of this holds all that exists, while the two inner parts keep life until it moves on. Most beings wait to be guided through to one of the inner cores."

"Therefore, the outer one must be larger to hold the mass of the rest," Alexis said softly, transfixed.

"That is correct."

Alexis studied the circles, focusing on the innermost one. "You said *beings*. Meaning other than human?"

Aharon slowed the rotation of the sphere. "Yes. Not all that exists within this world are human."

"This world being Earth, I presume."

Aharon nodded and then pointed to the large page rolled out on the table, where eight circles remained. "These are all a part of Earth, too."

Alexis glanced through the suspended image to the circles on the page. "Will you bring all the circles together so I can see them as a whole?"

Aharon made a motion with his hand, and the other eight circles lifted from the page and spiraled together with the rotating sphere, putting them all on one invisible axis. The eight circles moved into the first circle, making it glow. "This is much to comprehend all at once," he said.

"No, on the contrary, this makes perfect sense."

"Understand that these are only part of what exists in your world."

Alexis continued to gaze at the rotating sphere. "Since you said this was half of the original, I assume there is an equal number for the Darkness."

"Not exactly half. The core realms, which were the three circles that lay in the center of the page, are the same on both maps." Aharon pointed through the sphere and the original three became brighter. "But the Dark can only access the middle layer, or their own eight realms. We in the Light can access all three core realms plus our own eight."

"But you can't access the Dark realms?"

Aharon looked at Alexis through the rotating sphere. "Not unless we step away from the Light. This is merely a fragment of the realms that exist in this universe."

"I've always felt there was more than humans, and that creation didn't just happen. Even science proves this, we just don't except it. It's asinine to assume we are the only planet with life and that complexity was an accident." Alexis looked away from the sphere and gazed at Aharon. "My own close encounter convinced me that we're not alone."

Aharon smiled. "I am aware of what happened in Japan."

"It freaked me out, but it also excited me. What do you know about that UFO?"

"I only know where they are from, their intentions are not my charge. But they appeared harmless from our perspective."

"Where are they from?"

"A planet called Apexia, millions of light years from Earth." Aharon turned to the sphere.

"How could they travel here without ..."

"Alexis, the Apexians are not important at the moment, nor are they a threat to humans. I would very much like to hear your theory of how you see this all as Earth."

Alexis turned her attention back to the rotating sphere. "When I first came here I was told this was a map. I didn't see it as a map, because I had seen the Voynich manuscript. Since then, I figured that this world and my own were divided simply through frequency changes. That's how the crystal opened the portal in the first place"—she pointed to the small center circle, which was glowing intensely—"making the other eight circles represent different dimensions, or layers within my own world. Plus, the bridges drawn here are metaphoric in a way. With your explanation of two equal parts, I see them as protected pathways for the Light and Dark."

"I can see why you are able to be here."

"Why exactly?"

"Your high intellect combined with your ability to cut through to the heart of a matter is unique," Aharon continued. "Most don't shift their perspectives so easily. The counterpart to this map has been in your world for many years, in the presence of a multitude of intelligent people, but not one has come close to unlocking its real meaning. You have put a mere glimpse in a new light and see its wonder for what it is." Aharon moved his hand over the sphere and placed the nine circles back onto the page.

Alexis shook her head. "In my world these circles don't suspend themselves into a mobile."

"You still adapted your beliefs in the face of reality," Aharon said. "Trust me, not everyone is as easy to convince."

"It's useless knowledge if it doesn't get me any closer to home."

At that moment, another man walked in from the white walls. "You can't leave."

Alexis glared at the newcomer. "What do mean I can't leave?"

"Alexis, this is Dathan," Aharon said. "He means you can't leave yet."

"We've met before," Alexis said.

Dathan stepped closer and nodded. "I helped to welcome you here. And I meant you can't leave."

"You're the one who told me this was a map," Alexis said.

"You need not worry about that at present," Dathan said. "You will understand in time how it is truly a map."

"She sees it as the Earth," Aharon said.

Dathan frowned at him.

"On her own," Aharon said.

"Sort of," Alexis chimed in. "Which should earn me some real answers. So let's start with why I can't leave."

"It's not possible for us to take you back. No human has ever been brought here and then returned."

"You also said that before I came it wasn't possible for anyone to get here without you bringing them, yet here I am."

"A valid point," Aharon said.

"Why do you want to leave?" Dathan asked. "Are you not at peace here?"

"It's not what I'm feeling, it's what I'm missing," Alexis explained.

"Life wasn't perfect for you there," Dathan replied. "Here we can be a haven from your trials."

"Dathan, she is no longer a small child," Aharon said.

There was an awkward silence for a few seconds, and then Dathan bowed his head to Alexis, turned, and disappeared through the white marble wall.

"Where is he going?" Alexis asked.

"To get answers."

"What's through the wall?"

"A passage to our home."

"Home?" Alexis looked around the small, white cottage. The lone chandelier looked elegant above the plain wooden table. "Is your home not here?"

"In a sense, yes."

"Where is your other home?"

"Maybe we can discuss this more later," Aharon said. "One precept at a time."

"Later? Do you have somewhere you need to be? It looks like I'll be here for a while."

Aharon sighed. "Fair enough. If I told you all beings were extraterrestrial to their own planets, would you find it offensive?"

"I'm not sure."

"Imagine we all started in one place, and as that place expanded, the beings were placed throughout the universe. One male and one female of each order."

"Are you saying every planet started with an Adam and Eve?"

"In a way, yes."

Alexis gave a small laugh. "Did every Eve eat the forbidden fruit?"

"No, only yours. And that is what makes your planet very different from the others."

"What was different?"

"This is as much as I can tell you now. The rest will have to come later."

"Why?"

"Knowing those details may change your mind in the future."

"What's that supposed to mean? How is an alien version of Eve going to change my future?"

Aharon frowned. "I don't know what is going to happen in the future. I can only say that your decisions have to be brought through your heart and mind. My telling you too much here could tip the scales."

CHAPTER
TEN

MATTHEW ZEN HEARD his wife sobbing and found her sitting on the floor of the spare bedroom near the back of the house. Several cardboard boxes were lined up along the wall and two more were on the floor in the middle of the room. Each was marked with Alexis's name.

Matthew knelt down at her side. "Marcia? Are you OK? What did you see?"

"I'm fine. I didn't see anything."

Matt grabbed a tissue from the box on the dresser and handed it to Marcia. "Are you sure you're OK?"

Marcia wiped her eyes. "The dreams were bad enough. But after last night and seeing things, I thought I would look through Alexis's belongings. I wanted to feel her presence in a positive way. Find something to ground me."

"I understand. It's hard when you lose someone you love." Matthew put his arm around her. "It's OK to cry. I still can't go a day without shedding a tear."

She sniffed and patted away more tears. "Yes, but you're not constantly having nightmares about Alexis being ripped away. You're not seeing ghosts or talking to people who aren't there."

"No."

"Last night was so vivid. I'm not really sure what part was the nightmare."

"Maybe we should talk about it. You could have been sleepwalking."

"I don't want to think about it, I want to forget it. That's why I came in here—I was hoping to remember the good things." Marcia held out a pale purple book with a celestial moon faintly sketched on it. "I found this."

Matt took the book. "Alexis's diary?"

"From when she was a teenager. I didn't even know she kept one."

Matt grinned. "I'm sure there are things about you that your mom never knew. Plus, she was a teenager when she wrote this stuff."

"I could've been better with her. I wish I could tell her I was sorry—and that I loved her." She rested her head on Matt's arm.

"Marcia, she knew you loved her."

"Alexis was so smart—I felt like I couldn't connect."

"We've all have had issues with our parents when we were growing up. Heck, I still find myself getting frustrated with my mom, but I know she loves me."

"I did some things I regret—because I was selfish."

"Like what?"

"I had her committed when she was five."

Matt looked surprised. "You never told me about that. Why would ... what happened?"

"I was embarrassed."

"No one in this room is judging you. Tell me what happened."

"When Alexis was about four, she'd wake up at night screaming. She said there were shadows staring at her in her bedroom. I would check everywhere, but nothing was there, of course. Night upon night, she would imagine either shadow men or these things with red eyes standing around her bed."

"Go on," Matt said softly.

"She was always telling me stories like that. I had already had about all I could take from her overactive imagination, and then one night she said her dad was standing outside her window while she slept."

"But Mikel was gone by then."

"Yes. Alexis had only seen him in pictures, which I have since hidden."

"Kids have nightmares. I don't see why you would fault her for ..."

"The last straw was when she claimed she could also see herself sleeping, and that it was a game her dad taught her to do in order to hide from the demons."

Matt let out a slow breath. "Where did you take her?"

"At the time I partied with some people who worked at the hospital, and they knew of a female doctor willing to help. She was kind to us and I knew Alexis was safe."

"How long did you leave her there?"

"She came home after a month."

"I've never heard Alexis talk about it."

"Dr. Gevira said she might not remember anything that happened and that future stressful situations might also be blocked." Marcia fidgeted uncomfortably on the floor. "I'm sure that's why she never had success with psychiatrists."

"That's a lot for anyone to go through, let alone a five-year-old girl."

"She died hating me."

Marcia buried her head in her hands, sniffing. Matt pulled a tissue from a box on the table next to him and gave it to his wife.

"You said she didn't remember. Besides, Alexis was a kind and forgiving person."

"I know, but there's more," Marcia said through quivering lips.

"I'm listening."

"I forced her into therapy when she was twelve. But it was only because I convinced myself she was still screwed up and the rest of us were perfectly fine. Now look who's crazy and seeing things that aren't there."

"Marcia, Alexis grew up to be an outstanding young woman. You should be proud of who she was. As for those voices and the other stuff, they're caused by stress."

"It's not just the voices I'm hearing, Matt. I saw someone in our kitchen last night. He was standing behind me. I could feel him."

"Honey, I believe you experienced something. But you haven't been sleeping well since we lost Alexis. What you saw last night is probably either from sleepwalking or because you're sleep deprived."

"I know what I saw."

"I still think maybe we should ask Doctor Armstrong for something to help you sleep."

"I'll think about it." Marcia wiped her eyes and got up from the floor. "I'll be back." She stepped into the hallway and headed toward the mudroom.

"Where are you going?"

"To see my parents. I'll bring home dinner." She took a coat from the coat closet and put it on.

"Be careful, the roads will probably be slippery."

Marcia nodded, grabbed her keys, and walked out the door, pulling it shut behind her.

Matt heard his wife pull out of the driveway, kicking gravel as she backed up. He looked down to his hands at the tear-stained cover of Alexis's diary. He hesitated just a moment and then opened it.

April 17

Everyone in the house is in peaceful slumber as he just leaves my room again. I stare at a bottle of pills, pondering my choice to live or die. I can't do this anymore. I feel disgusting when he's near me. I tried pretending to be asleep, but he insists I be awake to enjoy his touch. There is no use in screaming, his lies trump the truth. I'm done lying there being still, I'm done crying. I'm done. I wish I could leave my body and not see him touching me. I wish I could run away. I wish it would all go away.

Matt closed the diary. He knew when he married Marcia that Alexis had been through a tough situation, but he was overwhelmed by tonight's revelations. He heard the dog barking outside and then the sound of a car pulling up the driveway. It was too soon for Marcia to be back, so he walked into the room across the hall to peek out through the blinds. An unfamiliar silver sports car was pulling in. Matt went to the door and opened it. A gust of wind sent a whirl of snowflakes into the house. The driver of the sports car got out and headed toward the house. Oslo snarled at him.

"Good dog," Matt said.

As the man came closer, a motion sensor turned on the porch light, revealing a brown-haired man approaching.

"Can I help you?" Matt asked when the man was ten feet from the door.

"Mr. Zen?"

"Yes, and you are?" Matt gave a quick glance toward the twelve-gauge shotgun sitting within arm's reach of the door.

"Mr. Zen, my name is James Mitchell. We met briefly met at your daughter's funeral."

"I remember. You were her supervisor."

"I was also her friend."

"What can I do for you, Mr. Mitchell?"

"Is it asking too much if I could come in to talk with you and maybe ask some questions?"

Matt sighed. "No, you can come in."

CHAPTER ELEVEN

"NEW HOBBY?" Cezar brushed the ivory keys of the white grand piano sitting in the middle of the vast empty room that opened onto an enormous balcony.

Ben was leaning against the rail, looking at a star-filled sky. "Alexis told me the room needed one."

Cezar walked out onto the balcony to join his Master.

"I forgot about the world when she was here," Ben said, absently brushing away the snow that had blown off the trees and onto his sleeves.

"We noticed. But now that you have the Gatherers taking more souls, the world will soon be at your mercy and it will be as ..."

"Mercy?" Ben shook his head. "This is nothing more than child's play."

"You want her back, but ..."

"But? There is no *but*, Cezar!"

"You know Alexis is safe where she is, so why not take this time to find Eden? Then you will control everything on this planet, including the Fifth Realm."

"Ever since Lilith did what she did in Eden, I have deepened my desire for a companion. Even with Alexis, I tried to deny the connection until she forced me to feel it. It was clear something was between us. I can't leave her there." Ben dropped to his knees, his hands still gripping the railing.

"You will have her back."

"Do not waste my time with your empty words."

"I'm not." Cezar started to take a step forward but couldn't. The house began shaking, and a growling sound rolled across the valley.

Ben turned to Cezar. “If you can’t do as I asked and find me a Messenger, then I will have to trust the Gatherers. They’re making progress, and the power within me is growing. It won’t take long before the veils separating the worlds are weak and I can release all the power I’ve gained.”

“Then the Messengers will have no choice but open their door,” Cezar said.

“Exactly.”

“Master?”

“What?” Ben loosened his grip and the vibrations stopped.

Cezar could move again. “I have another idea that may speed the way to finding Alexis.”

Ben stood up and gazed at the moon’s reflection off the glass balcony. “Tell me.”

“We’ve been having trouble finding the Messengers because they’re absent during the Claiming. It’s as if they know we trying to get to them. When the dead who the Gatherers haven’t claimed finally pass, Light is present but not an actual Messenger.”

“The light is there, but no guide to give comfort on the journey.” Ben smiled and took in a breath of air.

“Why does this please you?”

“They’re aware we are looking for Alexis, and if they’re hiding, then there is more we don’t know. Something more valuable.”

“Alexis took the crystal,” Cezar said.

“I know. I also know that their absence has given us more opportunities to welcome more of the dead into the Darkness, increasing our numbers and my strength sooner than anticipated.”

“You knew they would cower?”

“They’re not cowering, they’re waiting.”

“For what?”

“War. They have no plans to let Alexis leave, because they know I’ll come for her, and when I do they will be waiting for me,” Ben replied. “Finish telling me the idea you spoke of.”

"James Mitchell," Cezar said. "He may be able to help get the machine that Alexis built, the one that locates atmospheric disruptions but also finds electromagnetic alterations."

Ben slowly nodded. "That's perfect, but I have someone else in mind."

"Who?"

"The Omiens." Ben moved past Cezar to the other side of the balcony, where the large telescope was placed. He peered through the lens up at the sky.

"Is that not suicide, Master? They could find you."

Ben pivoted to face Cezar. "The Omiens don't care about me."

"They're all the same to me," Cezar said. "Why do they come here?"

Ben leaned back against the rail. "They come seeking something else. I witnessed the Omiens interacting with a human once, and I realized they must have the equipment to detect high frequencies and strong electromagnetic sources in order to enter the atmosphere undetected."

Cezar grinned. "We can also have them find the other crystals."

"And the Keepers who protect them. But first we try to find the Fifth Realm."

"How do we find the Omiens?"

"Omiens enter where there are high amounts of electromagnetic activity, thus their detection equipment."

"Are we sure they are not seeking us?"

"No." Ben began to walk away. "Have your men waiting in the valley of Visoko in the next week."

"In Bosnia?"

"Is there a problem?"

"No, Master, I apologize."

"Notify me and keep the Omiens at bay if they arrive sooner. They normally come near the change of the moon."

"How do we bind them?"

"They're merely humans with grey skin. Get inside their heads."

"Master?"

"If you have any doubts, I would be glad to replace you."

"I can do this. I'm just wondering about the ones who are looking for us."

"What about them?"

"What if they show up instead?"

Ben gazed at the sky. "Two thousand years ago, before the realms holding the dead had a bridge between the Light and Dark, they always entered from above. "

"And now?"

"They come up from below."

"The ocean? Is that what Zavdiel and Ellory encountered in Japan?"

"Yes."

"Why didn't they take them? I thought that's why ..."

"Apexians would never risk that with humans watching. But something must have thrown them off, because they would have definitely abducted either Alexis or James."

"You think it was Alexis? Or the crystal?"

"Maybe. The mysteries behind that crystal reach far past this world."

Cezar sighed. "That would have made things easier."

"What?"

"Abduction. I mean in regard to Mr. Mitchell. Humans become easier to sway after an abduction."

Ben frowned.

Cezar laughed to himself. "Paranoid humans are fun to push, and ..."

"Cezar, you're wasting my time," Ben snapped.

Cezar bowed his head. "I apologize. How do you know the Omiens will come specifically over Bosnia?"

"I'll take care of that. You just have everyone there."

Ben had no sooner spoken, then he disappeared. Cezar was alone on the balcony, peering out at the distant city of Dayton. Then he, too, disappeared.

CHAPTER TWELVE

MATT SAT ACROSS from James at the oval dining table. Matt, with his flannel shirt and worn denim, his calloused hands and beet-red face, was staring at James's expensive dress shirt, platinum watch, and exfoliated skin.

"Mr. Mitchell, is there a reason I should care about the military needing to look through Alexis's personal things?"

"Not all of her things," James said. "I just need to see the tablet."

Matt crossed his arms and leaned back against his chair. "You know, the military hasn't been very cooperative with us about what happened to my daughter. I'm not sure why you think I would willing to help you."

"I apologize, really I do. But ..."

"Save it. We know she didn't jump from an airplane. You people should have gotten to know her better." Matt leaned forward. "Alexis hated flying."

"Sir, I did get to know her, and she was an amazing person, but"—James paused and took in a breath—"you're right, I have to be honest. The military doesn't need her computer; I do."

"Why? What's so important on there that you would lie?"

James glanced out at the night through the two French doors leading to the backyard. The snow had accumulated over half an inch on the patio railing and glistened in the light of the full moon.

"Sir, even if you don't believe me, I truly miss Alexis, and that tablet has some pictures we took together while we were in Japan. They're the only photos of us together, and I was hoping ..."

"I see," Matt interrupted.

"I meant no disrespect," James explained. "I really wasn't sure how to approach you."

Matt put his arms on the table and leaned in. "Tell you what—if you answer one question, I will give it to you."

"Give him what?" Marcia asked as she entered the dining room. She looked at James and then at her husband.

Matt stood and kissed his wife. "Babe, this is James ..."

"I know who he is," Marcia said. "Why is he here?"

"He was about to answer a question—a kind of trade."

"I know what you seek to know," James said to them both. "But I can't give details."

Marcia sat down beside her husband. "What trade?"

"Alexis's computer thing," Matt said. "It has pictures of them together."

Marcia frowned, unaware of what her husband was talking about.

Matt looked at James. "Where is our daughter's body?"

Oslo began barking outside the glass doors.

Matt scooted his chair back. "I need to put the dog in his pen. I'll be right back."

As Marcia waited, she nervously rotated the ring on her right hand. Finally, she said to James, without making eye contact, "My daughter used to talk about you a lot with her grandmother. She said how attractive you were. Alexis always had great taste in men."

James smiled. "There was a time I thought about asking her to dinner, but Ben beat me to it. He truly cares for your daughter."

"You mean cared, past tense."

"Right, I'm so sorry."

Before Marcia could speak, Matt swung open the patio door. "I have no idea what that dog is barking at. There's nothing on the porch."

Marcia nodded. "He does that a lot."

Matt sat down. "Now, Mr. Mitchell, where's our daughter's body?"

James shook his head. "I don't know for sure."

"What do you mean, you don't know for sure?" Matt demanded.

"We were in Brazil running tests near the Mayan ruins," James said. "The weather turned bad. She got caught in the storm and we got separated. She was never found."

Marcia stared at him. "You mean Alexis could be out there somewhere, alive?"

"Not likely."

"I don't understand," Matt said. "Why tell us she jumped from a plane?"

"I've already told you more than I should. This information is beyond even my clearance," James said, avoiding their eyes.

Marcia put her head on Matt's shoulder, and he pulled her close. "Matt, I can't bear to think about her out there all alone."

"It's OK. The military is probably still looking," Matt said as he glared at James.

James nodded. "But that's classified."

"Why would they tell us she's dead?" Marcia asked.

"Because ..." James started, but he hesitated.

"Because if someone is missing, there's no closure. Their story was meant to give us closure."

"It didn't," Marcia said. "Now I want to join the search efforts."

Matt took Marcia's hand. "Honey, that's not a good idea. We don't know the area and people go missing in Central America all the time. If something happened to you, Rebecca and I would be alone."

Outside, Cezar stood on the porch, hidden in the shadows. He had been listening to the half-truths James told and the bold lies he used to get access to Alexis's tablet. He watched the charade until Matt got up and walked James to the hallway toward the backdoor. Then Cezar vanished onto the shadows of the cold night.

"Wait here," Matt said after James stepped out into the bitter air without a coat.

A minute later, Matt returned with Alexis's smart tablet.

"Thank you, sir."

"Don't thank me. I have half a mind to shoot you right now."

James accepted the tablet and backed away. "I will return it soon."

"Whatever." Matt waved him on and shut the door.

James got in his car and brushed the melting snowflakes from his dark hair. He smiled as the tablet powered up. The bright light was intense against his blue eyes as he entered the password he had seen Alexis type many times—*Oslo6117*.

James scrolled through photos of crystal inscriptions. He knew he couldn't sit in the Zen's driveway much longer. When he placed the tablet on the passenger seat, the light caught a glimpse of a dark figure sitting in the back seat.

"I'll take that."

James was startled by the voice, one he had heard many times on the phone.

"Mr. Bekhor—how did you get here?"

"The tablet, Mr. Mitchell."

CHAPTER THIRTEEN

ALEXIS SAT AT the table, looking at the map of Earth's realm system for the Light. The details would be mind numbing for most, but it allowed Alexis to understand many unexplained occurrences in her own world. She could account for the supernatural world with a scientific explanation.

"Aharon, why do only four of the portals have direct paths to this center while the others are only connected by these bridges? Metaphorically speaking, if they're all a part of Earth's Light, wouldn't they also have direct access to each other?" When she received no response, she turned around. "Aharon?"

"I'm here." His voice was softer than usual, but he was standing to her right. "Alexis, these portals are connected, but some can only be opened from within and accessed from each other."

Alexis glanced quickly at her pocket. "Why do you not want to answer my questions?"

"Alexis, I know this must be surreal and hard to fathom. Most people in your world believe in some kind of God or creator, while others hold tight to science as the almighty solution, but almost no one sees the inner workings. This has to be overwhelming for a science-minded person who struggled with faith. Plus, answering what you may already know instinctively seems pointless."

"Although my heart has always leaned toward the notion that something greater than man is in control, I am a person who needs proof," Alexis said. "I value hard data. And, yes, seeing this was hard to swallow at first. But I'm ready for more."

"I will try to be more forthcoming with what I may know."

"Good."

Alexis put her elbow on the table and rested her chin against her fist, thinking about what Aharon had said earlier, after Dathan left. *Home. Where is their home? Are we all aliens on our planets?* She recalled the unidentified craft she and James had seen in Japan. The memory of the large, triangular craft humming just above their heads sent chills through her body. She remembered the last time she saw James, could still see Ben holding onto James and trying to keep her safe. It was her last memory before being jerked through the portal. *Focus. There has to be a way back, a way home.*

Alexis pointed to the circles on the page. "I assume the dark realms look and operate much as these do."

Aharon shrugged. "We cannot open their world, and they cannot access ours. Without knowledge of where their portals exist, or a key, we all are blind to each other's placement. This keeps a war at bay and Earth ..." Aharon saw Alexis staring blankly at the map. "Are you all right, Alexis?"

"Fine," she said. She pointed to one of the outer eight circles, which had a small circular area inside it, with scalloped edges that looked like small mountains. "Why does this circle have an inner one?"

"That one represents where you are right now, the Fifth Realm. That small circle is a topological shortcut to our home."

Alexis stared at him, a smile playing on her lips. "A wormhole. But what about the other half of this map? Obviously, the Dark doesn't have this."

Aharon hesitated, but Alexis's eyes were boring into his. "Correct," he said at length. "They cannot return home, therefore their portal takes them to the opposite side of the spectrum. One of the darkest places anyone could ever travel."

"I thought Hell was all fire and brimstone."

"Once again, perception trumps reality in your world." Aharon sat down across the table from her. "Hell as you know it exists in one of the other eight Dark realms on Earth. This dark place I speak of is worse than Hell, and one cannot return from there."

"I'll be sure to steer clear of creepy wormholes."

"That would be wise."

She pointed to the last of the four circles with a direct path to the center. "What is the purpose of this one?"

"I do not know."

"How could you not know?"

"Some things must be hidden from the world and from us until the time is right to reveal them." Aharon smiled. "We are not able to travel to all the areas, nor would we want to."

"Why not? Are you not trusted to venture out on your own?"

"Keeping us from those places is for our protection, not because of lack of trust."

"Why do you need protection? I thought you were immortal."

"Yes, we're immortal. But our choices are still our own. And we still can be tempted. Our purpose cannot be distracted by other realms."

"So the realms are hidden, not locked, correct?"

Aharon frowned. "I don't understand what you're ..."

Just then, Dathan came through the wall with several other Messengers, mostly men, but a few women were with them. Aharon stood straight and bowed his head to greet the ivory-skinned man. Though Dathan's hair was white with age, his skin and features were those of a young man. Like the other male Messengers, his chest was exposed near the top, showing a glimpse of his muscles. Alexis glanced up at the group.

"Alexis," Dathan said, giving her a warm smile. "I want you to meet someone."

Alexis stood and waited as a dark-haired man approached. His build was muscular like the others, but, judging by his features, he was at least ten years older than them. His cheekbones were sharp, and his eyes reflected the same blue-green of her own. The man stepped closer and smiled at Alexis. She sensed something familiar about him.

"Have we met?" she asked.

"No, not personally," he replied.

"What does that mean? Are you one of the Messengers I saw when I first arrived? Or one from my dream?" Alexis stared at the man standing in front of her. He was beautiful. His brows were thick, but they suited his face.

Everyone gathered closer to the table. Alexis looked at them, trying to read their faces.

Dathan interrupted the silence. "Alexis, your questions have raised quite a stir in our realm. We never anticipated that one could come through the gate to our realm without us guiding them, and now we wonder if you could leave."

"And?"

The man who Dathan wanted Alexis to meet turned to her and said, "When Dathan asked to know how all this was possible, I was brought forth from a realm in the Light."

"I do not have all the answers," Dathan said. "But part of the knowledge I do have is of things that have come to pass, and this gentleman was once a part of your world for a time."

"You lived on Earth as a mortal?" Alexis said. "You're not a Messenger?"

The man nodded. "That's right."

"Are you one of the ones they spoke of, one of the few humans they've brought here?"

"Yes, Alexis."

"That's incredible. But how does bringing you to me answer how I was able to come through the portal safely or would be able to return home? Especially since the circumstances of our arrivals are different."

"The only way a portal can be opened is through setting off its own unique signal," the man replied. "You did this when your friend dropped the crystal. As immortals, we can manipulate the realms we are set to pass through. The only way a person could survive entering such a portal is through transfiguring their own frequency."

"But I obviously got here without the needed frequency shift."

"You didn't need it."

"Why not?"

"In the very moment the portal was about to take your friend, you stepped in to try to help and ended up sacrificing yourself. That act of selflessness brought out the connection we are all born with."

"I'm confused. What connection are we born with?"

"Maybe you should tell her who you are," Dathan said.

The man nodded and smiled at Alexis. "Alexis, we are related. Your father is my son."

Alexis stared at his face. He bore not a wrinkle or scar, only a strong bone structure to outline his charming smile. She frowned and shook her head at what he said. "I'm sorry, what did you say?"

"I'm your grandfather."

For the first time since Alexis had come through the portal, her mind was blank. She had already figured the math wasn't right. This man was too young.

"I never got the chance to know my father, or any of his family. He disappeared before I was born." Her tone was hushed. "My mother never spoke of them. I assumed everyone had passed."

"I realize that meeting me like this must be strange."

She nodded and gave him a rueful smile. "Strangeness has become my way of life recently."

The group of Messengers laughed to lighten the mood of the room.

"Does that mean your home is in the realm where the spirits of the dead live?" Alexis asked. "You don't look like a ghost."

Dathan stepped next to Alexis. "We know you have many questions."

"You think?" Alexis looked at the man she had just learned was her grandfather and then at the group of Messengers clothed in white. "I'm in the middle of an inner dimensional wormhole with no way out, I've been trying to grasp your labyrinth of portals and maps, and you decide to bring an ancestor back from the dead for me to meet. I don't see the point."

Aharon spoke up. "Alexis, they had no choice."

"We have no control over how the answers to our meditations are manifested," Dathan said. "I truly sought answers for you, and that's when he was brought forth. And he's very much alive."

Her grandfather placed his hand on her shoulder. "Because your father is my son and I am ..."

"Maybe we should refocus," Dathan said to the man. "She is meant to figure out much on her own. We cannot interfere."

"You're not the ones interfering. I assume that's why they sent me, to help her get back. The best way to do that is by understanding how she got here."

Alexis tilted her head for a quick recap of what she had just heard. The words weren't confusing, only the situation. "If you came here through them changing you, I still don't see how that would affect me. My father would have been born before you were brought here—unless you went back and then he was conceived."

Dathan and the other Messengers also seemed to be waiting for the answer.

"Alexis," Aharon started. "We have all desired to know the answer to this question, and trust me as I tell you that what he says next would also open our eyes, but this is something you both should discuss privately."

"What?"

"Alexis, it's a misconception that the angels of Dark and Light know everything," Dathan said. "This is not how it works. Our purpose is different within each realm, and in here, the Messengers have two main tasks. The first is to help remind humans of the gift of peace and then to guide them toward the paradisiacal Realm Two after they pass, if that is where they want to be."

"Why wouldn't they want to be in the Light?"

Dathan grinned. "I thought about asking you the same thing."

"Alexis, let us step outside," her grandfather suggested.

As Alexis walked toward the door, Aharon lightly touched the top of her arm. "He can answer many things that we cannot—spare no questions."

Alexis nodded and then continued to follow behind her grandfather.

At the door, he stopped and turned to her. "Are you ready?"

"Yes." Alexis looked back at Aharon and then at the Messengers standing in front of them. Dathan smiled at her and then went to the door to open it. Alexis turned back to her grandfather. "What's your name? It would feel weird calling you grandpa."

The man smiled. "My given name is Michael, the same as your father's."

"And your second name?"

The door swung open, and they heard Dathan gasp. "Something is not right!" Dathan said.

"What is it?" Michael asked.

He and Dathan looked out at the skyline near the forest and remained silent. Alexis stepped outside to join them.

"What's going on?" she asked.

"Alexis, what have you noticed about the sky here?" Dathan asked.

"Other than the sun never rotates, never sets, and always shares the daylight with the moon, not much. Why?"

"Do you notice anything different today?"

Alexis moved out further from the doorway and followed their line of sight straight out toward the treetops behind the cottage, on the opposite side of where the sun lingered. At first she saw only the cyan backdrop, but it didn't take long to see a disturbing difference. "It looks like ... it looks like blood."

FOURTEEN

JAMES WAITED UNTIL he was a mile or so down the road from the Zen home before pulling the car over. When he switched off the lights, they were plunged into darkness, the only light coming from Alexis's tablet resting on the back seat.

James peered into the rearview mirror at the man he had known for the past two years as Mr. Bekhor. "I told you, Alexis encrypted everything."

"And I told you to stay clear of a relationship with her."

"Sir, it wasn't that simple. Anyone who knew Alexis would find her hard to resist. Besides, I wasn't the one she wanted, so there was never a relationship."

"Not wanting doesn't mean not caring." Mr. Bekhor handed James the tablet. "You became a distraction to what she was needed to do."

"Did you find what you were looking for?"

Mr. Bekhor glanced up into the mirror and made eye contact with James. "I need one more item from you this evening."

James shifted his glance out to the cold road. "Whatever you need."

"The journal."

James returned to the rearview mirror. "It's at the lab, I can't ..."

"You can take me to the base and I will handle the rest."

"We can't take anything from Sublevel 6 without authorization," James said. "And the colonel doesn't like surprises."

"I don't need the actual journal, I only need to see what's inside."

James saw the man's intense green eyes staring directly back at him. He didn't wait to put the car into gear. He pulled onto the grey, snow-dusted highway.

"Can I ask you something?" James asked.

"You can ask."

"What good are the journal entries and the inscriptions on the tablet if we no longer have the actual crystal? If we find the other crystals we won't need all this stuff, right?"

Mr. Bekhor took a few seconds to respond. "If there was an easy way to find all the crystals and not cause a disturbance with the ones who keep them, then I could open portals unseen by both the angels and demons. But those crystals are at the top of the watch list of many who seek them, because even individually they open certain gates, but the Bereishit crystal contains information the others don't."

"What information?"

"Everything the gods know. Or so go the stories I've been told."

"I have searched my life for at least one."

"You need all twelve to locate the Garden of Eden, but hopefully with the journal that won't be necessary."

"Once we find its location, won't a crystal be necessary to open it?"

"Only a certain frequency can open the gates to Eden, which only comes from the Bereishit and ..."

"But Alexis has that one."

"There is a companion crystal to the one Alexis has."

"What?" The car swerved, but James kept it on the road.

"Just get us to the base safely. We can talk more about this there."

"Sorry," James said. "It would be nice if we knew where to find that one."

"It's pointless to have it unless we solve the clues inside the journal. That's the difference between finding all twelve or just one, as Alexis has. Though you need only one of them, you also must solve the clues to know the location of Eden."

"It sounds like a wild goose chase to me," James said as he turned onto Route 844.

"It's kept the crystals safe this long, so it's more of an intricate scavenger hunt."

James sighed. He knew that the vast majority of historians and archeologists believed the crystals were pure myth, but a few zealots who were experts on religious artifacts continued to seek the truth, and James belonged to that small group. It had been almost five years since he had been approached by Mr. Bekhor, who claimed to be an archeologist who had stumbled onto a significant clue to finding the sacred Garden of Eden. He had asked James to find out everything he could about what the government knew concerning the crystals.

"We are planning on searching for Alexis at some point, right?" James asked as he turned into the gate near Area B.

"We can discuss that when the time comes," Bekhor replied. "For now, let's solve the journal so we can find Eden."

James pressed the button to roll down the window as the car approached the guard shack. Three guards stood outside checking IDs while one guard stood with a German shepherd near the passenger side of the vehicles. The dog was sniffing for illegal or hazardous materials. James handed his ID to a guard.

"Good evening, Mr. Mitchell, is everything OK tonight?"

"Yes, thank you. My passenger has his ID as well." James pointed to the backseat after taking back his own ID.

The guard bent down to see inside the car and flashed his light over the empty front passenger seat. Mr. Bekhor leaned forward, holding out his ID. The flashlight beam caught the emerald flecks of his eyes, but Mr. Bekhor didn't flinch from the light.

"OK, you're clear." The guard stood back and waved James through.

He pulled in past the guard unit and turned left. He waited until the guard shack was no longer in sight before saying to Mr. Bekhor,

"How is it that you have a military clearance that allows you access to this area?"

"I know a lot of people."

"Government people or military?" James asked.

"A little of both. I served for many years."

"What branch? Were you here at Wright Patt?"

The man leaned forward as they pulled into the parking area outside the research lab. "That's not important right now."

"We're here." James got out and slid the driver's seat forward, releasing the seatback. "You could have sat up front."

Bekhor was putting what looked like a cell phone into his pocket. "I know."

The two men headed inside and took the elevator down to Sublevel 6. As the elevator door opened to a large metal door that looked as if it belonged on a vault, James turned and smiled. The fluorescent lights in the ceiling hummed.

Mr. Bekhor frowned at James. "Why are you waiting?"

"Sorry, this is kind of exciting for me."

"How so?"

"If everything you've told me is true, along with what I have seen in the past year, then we will discover the location of the true cradle of life."

"Mr. Mitchell, nothing is ever discovered. All that exists is merely uncovered."

"Interesting." James placed his hand on the scanner and then opened the door. "That reminds me ..."

"What?"

"The crystal you mentioned that is like Alexis's, do you know anything about where it might be? Is it protected by the same men?"

"Why is that important to tonight's task?"

"It's not. I'm just curious about how you would come by knowledge of something supposedly so rare and hidden."

A faint grin crossed Mr. Bekhor's face. "The best way to hide something is in plain sight."

"Ironically, that's what happened with the other crystal. Alexis hid it in plain sight in her lab and it ended up finding a way out—and taking her with it to Hell."

"I'm sure the crystal and Alexis are safe. Besides, we need to concentrate on translating the journal and figuring out how the crystals operate."

"They open portals, but I have no idea where they lead." James opened the second lab door, marked "11." The two walked into the room.

"I know what they open, I just need to open the right portal and figure out how to use the crystal to do it. We can't assume that all the portals open up to utopia."

"Good point." James looked over his shoulder. "Alexis believed it was caused through the vibration when it was dropped."

"Yes, but you said it didn't open a portal inside the temple in Belize when you dropped it the first time." Mr. Bekhor walked over to the white desk and picked up a framed picture. It was of Alexis and Oslo. He rubbed the dust off the glass.

"No, it didn't."

"I'm surprise she trusted you the second time."

James nodded his head as he looked through a couple of boxes that were stacked on the floor. A clear acrylic box marked "Box 143" was inside one of them. This was the same box Alexis had shown James to demonstrate how vibrations altered the placement of the object inside the box.

"The cave must have created too much chaos," James said. "Alexis thought the vibrations had to be the stronger force, that's why she did this experiment in a closed box. The cavern walls bounced the sound and alternated the original frequency."

"If she was right, we need to find what makes these areas more sensitive." Bekhor looked inside the box. "That must be where the crystal inscriptions lead—points where the portals can open."

"Who told you about the crystal and the Eden myths?" James asked.

"Stories that began when I was younger. James, the journal please."

"It's inside the lab coat, hanging on the back of that chair."

Mr. Bekhor leaned over and pulled out the leather-bound book. He closed his eyes and took in a deep breath as he opened the pages. He walked to the white work table and motioned for James to assist.

Mr. Bekhor pulled a small rectangular device from the pocket of his dress pants. "Hold each page open and I'll take a photo."

"Nice flip phone. You find that on a dig site of ancient relics?" James joked.

Mr. Bekhor waved his thumb over a small black square in the middle of the rectangular device, and a beam of blue horizontal light shot out of it. "James, flip the pages."

James didn't hesitate. He began turning the pages one by one, watching the man scan them with the device. Once they were finished, Bekhor laid the device on the table and pushed a circular outline in the lower corner. An interactive hologram of the journal appeared.

"That kind of looks like the H2E Alexis developed," James said. "She showed it to me in Japan. Hers looked more like a miniature flying saucer."

"Go ahead, turn the pages on the hologram."

James flipped through the three-dimensional hologram. "You would have loved Alexis. Her creation wasn't this advanced, but very close."

"She has a brilliant mind," Bekhor said. "It never ceases to amaze me."

James looked at him. "You never told me you knew Alexis personally."

"My knowing her had nothing to do with what I sent you here to do."

"Why wouldn't you ask her about the crystal or the journal instead of me?"

"I wasn't sure she believed in it enough, and I knew that her grandmother hadn't told her everything. Besides, I haven't seen her since she was five—she may not remember me."

"I met her grandmother," James said. "Quite the interesting woman. Definitely hiding some secrets."

"From what I remember, she was very keen on spending a lot of time with Alexis. Mrs. Prollofsky was continually telling her stories and making her memorize ridiculous landmarks."

"Is that where you heard the stories about the crystals, from Alexis's grandma?"

"Not all of them," Bekhor said. "Nevertheless, Alexis's grandparents are very well versed in this, that's certain."

"She seemed interested in getting the journal back as well," James said. "But her grandfather didn't seem to care about anything she and I were discussing."

"A blind man turns his cheek in order to hear."

James nodded.

"You can give the journal back to her now." Bekhor moved his thumb away from the device and the image disappeared. "I have everything I need from it."

"What's next?"

"We finish this." Bekhor gestured toward the journal and then his pocket, where he placed the holo recording device. "We find the truth."

James shook his head. "This stuff came so easy to her. I wouldn't know where to begin to find all the landmarks, let alone realize the journal was referencing geographical spots."

"You failed before because you weren't exactly sure what you were looking for, but she has opened our eyes. Now we know that these symbols correspond to specific points." Mr. Bekhor headed to the door. "And with the journal entries we can start where you left off. I'll be at your place in couple of days."

CHAPTER FIFTEEN

MARCIA SAT NEXT TO Matt, biting her nails and fidgeting on the cold metal chair in front of the sterile metal table. The walls of the room were painted slate grey, and a twelve-inch-wide off-white band ran along all four walls at a height of four feet. On the wall opposite the Zens was a rectangular mirrored window.

"What is taking so long?" Marcia muttered.

"Honey, we've only been here for fifteen minutes."

"Feels longer."

"You're on high alert, which makes every second seem longer." Matt looked down at his watch. They had been there forty-five minutes.

Out in the lobby, an orange beam of sunlight moved across the floor between silhouettes of people as the glass door to the Fairborn Police Department swung open. A group of detectives walked in together holding Styrofoam cups labeled with a local coffee shop logo.

"Hey, detectives!" An officer called out from behind the dispatcher's desk. "Can one of you speak to the Zen family?"

As the detectives looked at one another, a young detective pushed forward from the back of the crowd. "I can."

"Thanks, Detective Lindsay, they're in Interview 2." The officer handed the detective a sheet of paper as he passed by.

"Thanks." Lindsay began to walk around the corner but stopped and took a step backwards. He was flipping the sheet of paper front to back. "Hey, Wallace, did they say why they were here?"

"Only that they wanted a detective to help find their daughter."

Lindsay scratched his head and proceeded to the interview room.

"Finally," Marcia said when Lindsay entered the room.

"Good morning, Mr. and Mrs. Zen. I'm Detective Stuart Lindsay." He shook their hands and sat down across the table from them. Lindsay pulled a pen and notepad from his pocket. "Officer Wallace mentioned something about finding your daughter."

"Yes, we believe she is still alive," Marcia said.

"Well, to be clear, her body was never found," Matt explained.

Lindsay looked up from his notepad. "You're talking about Alexis Zen, correct?"

"How did you know her name?" Marcia asked. "We never told the dispatcher. I didn't want anyone looking her up before we spoke to you."

"My wife was afraid no one would listen to us if we told them it was Alexis," Matt added.

"I was under the impression she died when her parachute didn't open near the Gulf of Mexico. I went to her memorial service."

Matt squeezed Marcia's hand. "Detective, my wife and I need complete confidentiality. What we were told is classified information, so we've told no one about this part."

The detective stood up and put his finger over his lips. He backed up toward the corner, reaching up behind the video camera, and unplugged it from the wall before exiting the room. The Zens looked at each other.

Detective Lindsay returned with two cups of water. "Sorry. The last time something happened involving your daughter, men in black showed up with military escorts to take all of our data about a case she was a part of."

Marcia stared at him. "Why was our daughter involved with a police case? She never said anything."

"Mrs. Zen, let's talk about what new information you have first."

"But the police case could be connected to her disappearance," Marcia said.

"Tell me what happened. If I think there's a connection, I'll tell you about the case," the detective offered.

"All right. Last night Alexis's supervisor from the base visited us, and he confirmed that she never jumped from an airplane. He said she was technically missing, not dead."

"Why would they tell you she was dead if they knew differently?" Lindsay asked.

"We have no idea. Marcia said. "That's why we came here,"

Lindsay leaned forward on the table and rubbed the back of his head. "I have no jurisdiction over anything concerning the military, let alone the clearance to visit the base and find out what the military knows."

Marcia looked distraught. "Detective ..."

"I'm not saying I won't help. This may have to be off the books."

"Thank you, thank you." Marcia began to sob.

"Do you know where your daughter went missing?"

"Belize," Matt said. "She was with her supervisor, James Mitchell, and her friend Dr. Asael."

"The shrink?"

"You know him?" Matt asked.

"Not really. My partner and I met him at Alexis's apartment. Why would he be there? Wasn't she there for classified military stuff?"

"We have no idea why he would still be there. He called us days before her birthday and said he was surprising her during the layover in Japan and wanted to know if there was anything special we wanted to send." Marcia was wiping her eyes with a tissue. "I sent her a book by Pastor James Wolf, not because she needed money advice but because I wanted her to see she was doing everything right."

"We haven't seen Dr. Asael," Matt added. "He wasn't at the memorial service."

"I'll try to track him down," Lindsay said. "Did she happen to tell you what she was working on?"

"No. We knew everything was classified, so it was never a topic of conversation," Matt said.

"My mother was very close to Alexis," Marcia said. "I can give you her phone number. She may know something."

The detective stood up. "I'll get on this immediately."

Matt stood and extended his hand. "Thank you, Detective Lindsay."

"Don't mention it."

The three shook hands, and Marcia handed the detective a slip of paper with the Prollofskys' phone number and address. The Zens made their way down the hallway to the front lobby and left the precinct building while Detective Lindsay made his way through the maze of desks.

"What was that all about, Secret Agent Man?" Detective Carter asked.

"Those people believe the government is covering up the disappearance of their daughter," Lindsay said.

"Really?" Carter snickered. "If we investigated every conspiracy that walked through that door ..."

"Their daughter is Alexis Zen."

Carter stopped laughing and sat up straight. "Where do we start looking?"

"The shrink."

CHAPTER SIXTEEN

CEZAR OBSERVED Ben, who was standing in the center of a group of twelve dark Gatherers, twelve of seventy-two. They stood openly in the daylight as the Necropolis of Giza reflected the desert heat onto their black suits. People moved past them, yet paid no attention to them, despite their height and their cold black eyes. Regardless of their ability to blind others to their presence, they attracted all the dark energy buried deep within and drained all emotion from the humans. Before long, the noise of bickering tourists and overbearing guards rose up.

"If this doesn't work, and the Apexians or the Messengers find us instead, this will all be in vain," said a disembodied voice from the enclosed circle of Gatherers.

"If this doesn't work," Ben said, "I will ensure your death."

"The fate of your human pet is jeopardizing our existence," a Gatherer replied.

"All humans interfere," said another dark voice. "We should spare none."

"Enough!" Ben's voiced carried across the desert, and the multitude of tourists and workers looked up.

Ben took a deep breath and exhaled a white mist through the crowd. The people quickly forgot whatever they thought they heard and went about their business of pushing their way through the pyramid site. Silence fell about the Gatherers.

"My plan gains us two purposes, and the fact that I seek the return of Alexis should weigh on none of you," Ben insisted. "Because once I've destroyed the beacons, there will be only one left. And there our energy will be most powerful."

Cezar stepped as close as he could without becoming a part of the circle. He was dwarfed by the Gatherers' stature and darkness.

"How can we trust that Cezar and his kind will succeed?" a voice said.

"Your trust should never be with them, but in me alone," Ben said.

Cezar lifted his eyes to the Gatherers.

The dark being from the center appeared enraged as he spoke to Ben. "That's until they find you. Then we are all powerless."

Cezar looked to Ben, who appeared calm.

"All of you are valuable to me, and the dark energy you bring unto me cannot be matched by anything currently on this Earth," Ben said. "And that power will continue with me even if you fail to exist, but your individual abilities are almost at a peak, making you expendable. I implore you to reconsider your lack of faith. I show no mercy to those who stand in my way."

As one, the members of the group bowed their heads. Cezar had been witness to millions upon millions of human deaths, but only a few deaths among those of his own kind. It was something he feared could come all too soon to himself if he couldn't keep the Omiens under his control once they entered Earth's atmosphere.

"What does he mean by *powerless*?" Cezar asked a Gatherer on the outer circle. "Isn't our power eternal?"

The Gatherers parted in unison, forming an open path as Ben walked toward Cezar. Ben's eyes were flooded with blackness.

"It will always exist, but it can only be where I am found," Ben explained. "That is why you hide from the Apexians and Messengers. They desire to find and bind me elsewhere, on another planet or another portal I cannot control."

"Like the one Alexis ..."

"They would never take me inside their walls, because Darkness cannot exist in the Light without chaos." Ben pivoted around, looking at all the people. "As it exists here on Earth."

"So why do you not stay in the shadows with us?" Cezar elbowed a man passing by, who fell against another man.

The second man glared at the one Cezar had shoved. "Watch it, buddy!"

Ben came up behind the man and placed a hand on his shoulder, making him drop to his knees. "They can only beat us if they stop believing in fear."

"That's why you cast out the others before?" Cezar asked. "Because they stopped fearing you and wanted unlimited power for themselves?" There was a brief flash, and Cezar caught a glimpse of Samuel being pulled into a dark portal.

"No, their inability to listen brought that on." Ben stepped past Cezar and out into the light. "Let us refocus. We know the beings of Apexia have made a home on Earth in hopes of finding me. I'm certain they are no closer to finding me, or our kind, regardless of where I walk."

"No disrespect, Master." Cezar lowered his head. "But how can you be certain?"

"Because whatever it was in Japan that changed their course also changed their actions. We are not on top of their list at the moment." Ben turned back to face the people walking around them. "While you and your own have been helping to lead this world off course throughout the millennia, I have searched for a way to find Eden without changing the balance. And we have been able to remain undetected by the Messengers and all the alien visitors. Plus, it brought us the direct lineage of the family that were keepers of the Bereishit. Now, with the loss of Alexis, my purpose is twofold, and the Messengers have what I want. And so I no longer walk with caution in the valley."

"Keeping the balance of everything was your idea?" Cezar asked.

"Of course not. Do you think for one second I made a promise to the powers of the Light? I said from the beginning of all this that giving humans freedom to choose wouldn't bode well."

Cezar grinned. “I guess not. What’s next?”

“I’m going to start showing these humans what their faith has failed to give them. Starting with Giza and down the Nile, I will remake this world to what it once was, a desolate planet begging for life.” Ben glanced at the Gatherers. “Continue to take the souls of the dead.”

One of the Gatherers nodded.

Ben then circled around to face the crowd of tourists who were bumping into each other as they flashed their cameras toward the massive pyramids of Giza. Guards were arguing with one another over who was in charge and who should give orders to keep the tourists from getting too close to the structures.

A loud roar exploded across the sand, shaking the ground and throwing people off their feet and into one another. Archeologists inside the pyramids streamed out, trying to make it to higher ground. An enormous cloud of debris gusted out of the largest pyramid, disseminating through the air and into the faces of the crowd.

The sky turned a deep blue-violet, and smoky clouds gathered and swarmed. A strong wind picked up sand and sent it cutting across the fleeing people, blinding them. Their frenzied screams rose.

The sound of sudden cracking and wood breaking hushed the crowd, and everyone turned. White electrical charges, visible through the film of dust in the air, were shooting out of dark clouds hanging overhead. The crackling charges were being drawn toward the largest pyramid and pulling the cloud formations into a downward spiral from every point, like the start of a tornado. The people were immobilized by the bizarre events occurring in the distance. One of the ancient wonders of the world was beginning to transform into a giant resonant transformer of electricity, like a gigantic Tesla coil.

“Power is pointless if there is no one left to witness it,” Cezar said, looking at the trembling humans who were only two hundred yards from Ben’s path of destruction.

Ben smiled. "Allowing witnesses shows weakness." Ben raised his arm, and the six-million-ton structure rose three hundred feet in the air. Small pieces crumbled and slipped from the sides, falling to the ground as the Great Pyramid of Giza floated high above the Egyptian horizon. Ben lowered his arm, and the grand structure fell straight down onto the pyramid directly behind it. People cried out in horror and fear as one ancient pyramid smashed the other to the ground, sending tremors and a tidal wave of sand spreading across Giza. The remaining ancient structures, including the Sphinx, were soon laid waste.

Ben turned away from the destruction and walked past Cezar, who was watching the Gatherers, enthralled. The seven-foot beings were ravaging throughout the lifeless bodies lying in the rubble and taking their souls.

"Notice the Messengers have somehow already taken some of the dead," Cezar said. "How is that?"

"They already know who will choose the Light, just as we know who walks off the path," Ben said. "And they, too, are no longer waiting for complete death before they claim the soul."

Cezar grinned. "They're acting out of fear?"

"No." Ben slowly closed his eyes. "Cezar, why are you here?"

Cezar looked behind Ben and saw that the Gatherers had disappeared. "I have many men in Bosnia awaiting the entrance of the Omiens. I didn't need to be there at this particular moment."

"The question remains, why are you here? There are still people you need to pull away from the Light."

"I've been watching Alexis's family."

"I don't want you near them. They're not a part of this."

"Everyone is a part of this. But I tell you this only because I wasn't the only one watching them."

All of a sudden, everything was still and quiet. The sand had settled and the ground no longer shook. The screaming had ceased. All signs of human presence were gone.

"A couple of nights ago I went to see ..."

"I know you've been going to the Zens, Cezar. I've had a Watchman there since Alexis was taken through the portal—just in case she came back."

"It wasn't one of us. I could sense something different."

"What was different?"

"The other night, while I was watching Marcia Zen from the outside, someone or something else was there. All I saw was an outline of a man walking behind her, and it looked as though he touched her."

"Was it a spirit?"

"No, because it happened again when I saw the Zens talking with James Mitchell."

Ben frowned. "Why was James there?"

Cezar shrugged. "I heard him ask for Alexis's tablet."

"Why does he want her tablet?"

"I'm not sure, but ..."

"I suspected that Mitchell had a secret when I first met with him—something about him wasn't normal." Ben started to walk away but then spun around. "But why take Alexis's tablet?"

"I don't know."

"Tell me more about what you sensed around Marcia Zen."

"It wasn't completely human," Cezar explained. "It was like a dark energy that I've never experienced from any of our own, yet it felt like it could ..."

"Could what?" Ben snapped.

"I can't explain it. It was as if it wasn't there and then it was, somehow turning the dark energy off."

Ben thought for a moment as the sound of emergency sirens echoed throughout the city.

"You said you experienced this a few nights ago—are you sure it's not a dead spirit trying to haunt the Zens?"

"Yes."

"Lilith!" Ben exclaimed.

"Master, it wasn't a female."

"Have you ever wondered how I know certain things or show up without you knowing?"

Cezar's eyes widened. "Of course, that has always puzzled many of us."

"It's because I am in control of the power I have and can camouflage it as something else."

"You think James can do that?"

"Lilith can and so could her spawn." Ben stared up the sky.

"And James has never seemed entirely human," Cezar said. "You think James is Lilith's son?"

Ben vanished. Cezar scoured the rubble spread out across the desert. His eyes locked onto the distant dark Gatherers, who were also leaving. As Cezar focused, he could see a blanket of people lying on the ground. The Gatherers had taken their prizes.

CHAPTER SEVENTEEN

MARCIA ZEN LAY sleeping. The house was empty of dark energy, but her mind was not. Her dream was taking her to an unfamiliar field of tall grain-like stalks. Her view was restricted by fog. Tentatively, she began walking through the field toward a grey stone structure in the distance.

"Hello, Marcia."

She turned to see the man who had been coming to her in her dreams. He was tall and solid-looking.

"Follow me," he said in a clear tenor voice.

"Where are you taking me?" Marcia asked.

"To the top of that knoll. It's not far."

In the blink of an eye, Marcia found herself at the top of the hill next to a stone circle formation. She took in the panoramic view, but when she looked down, a black haze masked the scenery below.

"I know this place," Marcia murmured.

"Yes, most recognize it."

She pointed to the endless fields of grain with patterns of bent stalks. "And those fields?"

"They're only points of reference." He directed her attention back to the stone circle formation.

Marcia was pulled in closer to the massive stones towering over her.

"This place has significance for finding lost things." He stepped through the spaces between the stones and walked to the center. "This is where I changed my mind about where I wanted to be, and this is where you can begin to find Alexis."

Marcia's heart began to race. "What"

"You can bring things back through this gate. Start here and I will bring her home."

The horizon began to brighten as a light broke through behind the stones. Suddenly the stones blurred along with the circles in the nearby fields. Everything was spinning into a vortex of clouds, and she could feel herself drawn toward the light.

"Where do I find her?" she asked, but the man was gone.

"Where is she?" she shouted and sat straight up.

"Marcia," Matt said. "Who are you talking to, babe?" He put an arm around his wife's trembling body.

Marcia took deep breaths, trying to slow her breathing and calm her racing heart.

"It was a dream," she said. "A very real dream."

Matt began rubbing her shoulder.

"Sorry, I didn't mean to wake you," she said.

"It's OK. You want to talk about it?"

"I wish I could." She looked at her husband. "But I don't understand what I just experienced."

"You were talking in your sleep, but it was like you were talking to someone."

"Yeah, the same guy keeps showing up in my dreams. But tonight was the first time I felt protected by another presence." She turned to face Matt. "I think Alexis was there, because it was so warm when the light shined through the stones."

"What guy? And what stones?"

"I don't know who he is, and this may sound weird, but Alexis ... I think she's at Stonehenge."

"And this guy told you this?"

"Kind of. He said something to the effect that Stonehenge is the beginning of where to find her or that it would bring her there. The details are fuzzy."

"People have dreams like that all the time," Matt said. "Besides, she wasn't anywhere near England when she went missing, so it doesn't make any sense that we would find her there now."

"I'm telling you there is something about that place that's important to finding Alexis."

Matt let out a breath. "Babe, you have been on edge since we were told her body wasn't found. We still need to prepare ourselves that she may never come home."

Marcia jerked her arm out her husband's grasp. "Don't patronize me right now."

"OK. You said the details were fuzzy. So why would she be there and not Belize?"

"I have no idea."

Matt got out of bed. "I'm going into town to get the newspaper. Do you want anything? Maybe some doughnuts?"

"No, I'm just going to relax and wait for the news to come."

Matt grabbed his jeans and T-shirt that were lying over the chair near the bed. He grabbed his keys and wallet from the dresser before kissing Marcia. She could see the slope of the driveway and waited until Matt was on the road before reaching for her purse. She pulled out a slip of paper from the inside pocket. There was a local phone number scribbled on the top, above the logo. She took the phone from her nightstand and dialed the number.

The phone rang and rang, but no one answered and the voice mailbox was full.

Marcia listened to the news as she watched the dawn slowly come through the frosted windowpanes. A tear slipped from her eye. The phone rang.

"Hello."

"Mrs. Zen, did you call?"

" Detective Lindsay?"

"Yes, ma'am. What can I do for you this morning?"

"I have a lead for you about Alexis."

CHAPTER EIGHTEEN

A PERFECT LAYER OF snow was melting across the warm asphalt of the parking lot. Detectives Lindsay and Carter had been waiting for thirty minutes in their car, keeping an eye on the small brick building.

"Thanks again. I will call you if I find out anything more." Lindsay put his cell phone back inside his coat pocket.

"What was that about?" Detective Carter asked.

Lindsay rubbed the side of his head. "That was Mrs. Zen. She was saying something about a dream she had and how the government covering up what happened to Alexis is tied to England."

Detective Carter shook his head. "We might as well search the Bermuda Triangle while we're at it."

"I know." Lindsay sighed. "She just wants her daughter back, so she's grasping at straws."

"But clear across the ocean is a stretch, no?"

"Definitely. I told her at the precinct we would do what we could, but that doesn't involve Scotland Yard."

"Or getting thrown in jail here for trespassing on government property," Carter said before taking a sip from his thermal mug.

"Speaking of overseas, did you see the news this morning?"

"Egypt?" Carter nodded.

"People are crazy," Lindsay said. "Can you believe they found people buried in the sand miles away?"

"When that pyramid imploded, or whatever, it supposedly released some airborne toxin that was carried via some kind of sand tsunami."

Lindsay shook his head. "It's tragic."

Carter shrugged. "Not everyone will think so. A lot of the bodies they found outside the site were from radical groups."

"That's odd. Maybe they caused the explosion."

A fluorescent light flickered on inside the building, and a short feminine figure unlocked the front door.

Carter grinned. "And the doc is in."

"He seemed like the type to charge us for his time, so let's make this quick."

Carter chuckled as he got out of the car. "That and I have last night's paperwork to finish."

Lindsay locked the doors. "You told me you were done. I thought that's why you left early."

"I did say I was done, but I wasn't finished." Carter opened the glass door to the office building. "The wife made beef tips, and I wasn't about to miss that."

Lindsay smiled as they stepped inside. The waiting room was filled with the scent of warm vanilla, and the walls were decorated with bold paintings of lighthouse landscapes. Detective Carter looked at the name plaque next to the sliding glass window. *Mary Willard, Executive Assistant.*

"Can I help you gentlemen?"

"Yes, Mary," Carter said. "We need to speak with the doctor, if he's in."

"Sure thing, sweetie. Can I tell him what this is regarding?" She picked up the receiver and waited.

Lindsay pulled his badge from inside his coat and put it through the window. "We have a few questions about a missing girl."

"Oh, OK." The receptionist dialed two digits. "One moment, detectives."

Carter moved away from the reception window and sat on the burgundy couch. "Wonder what the hourly rate is here."

Lindsay laughed. "Probably more than my truck payment."

"You still pay for that piece of crap?"

The door opened, and a short thin man with curly brown hair emerged and extended his hand. "I'm Dr. Schaffer, how can I help you?"

The detectives glanced at each other.

Lindsay shook the psychiatrist's hand. "I'm sorry, we were expecting Dr. Asael."

"He's not here right now."

"When could we catch him?" Carter asked.

Mary chuckled. "If you can find him is more like it."

"I doubt Dr. Asael would know anything about a missing person," Dr. Schaffer said. "He hasn't been here for almost ..." He paused and looked at Mary.

"It's been at least seven months," Mary said. "And not even a phone call."

Dr. Schaffer nodded. "I was called in to temporarily replace him six and a half months ago, but it's become more of a permanent placement."

"Do you have a last known address for him?" Lindsay asked Mary.

"I only had his cell number and email. He hasn't responded to either one, and I have no other way to find him."

"You said he hasn't been here for seven months," Carter said.

Mary nodded. "Yeah, he went on vacation and never came back."

Detective Carter leaned in and whispered to Lindsay, who nodded.

"Thank you for your time," Carter said to Dr. Schaffer.

"You're welcome, Detective."

The two detectives turned toward the door.

"By the way," the doctor said. "Who's the missing girl? In case I hear anything."

"Alexis Zen."

"Zen?" Dr. Schaffer turned to Mary. "Wasn't she the patient you said Dr. Asael was dating?"

"Yes, but I read that she died. Over six months ago." She looked at the two detectives. "You think he killed her and went off the grid? I warned him to not mess with her. Never mix professional with personal. Wait, but they buried her, why are you looking for as if she's missing."

"We're just following some new leads," Carter said.

"Would you allow us to see her files?" Lindsay asked Dr. Schaffer.

"According to the papers, the girl is deceased, so I see no harm in breaking confidentiality. Mary will give you everything we have on her. Now I need to get ready for my first patient, so if you'll excuse me."

"Sure. And thanks for your help, doc," Carter said.

Mary opened the file cabinet behind her and searched the short section of last names starting with Z. She pulled a thick file and turned toward the detectives. "That whole situation was strange between them."

"Did he tell you he was dating her?" Lindsay asked.

"Not exactly. But I could see it on his face." Mary flipped through the stack of pages. "He saw her more than any of his other patients."

"Ma'am, may we see that?" Carter asked, and she handed him the quarter-inch-thick file.

"I was never to enter her file into the database, it was always locked in his office. When Dr. Asael didn't come back, Dr. Schaffer brought the file for me to put away." Mary looked thoughtful. "Beautiful girl, always pleasant when she came in, unlike most of the people we see."

Lindsay looked over Carter's shoulder as he flipped through the pages of indecipherable script and mysterious sketches.

"Mary, where was Dr. Asael from?" Carter asked.

"I have no idea. He didn't have an accent, and he never mentioned anything about his personal life until he and Alexis started hanging out."

"Were all of his files written like this?" Lindsay asked tilting the edge of the pages toward Mary.

"No."

The two stared at a sketch of a woman with what appeared to be a dark, black-eyed figure with its arms wrapped around her body, pulling her down.

"Wait!" Mary rolled her chair back to the file cabinet. "There was one other with that odd writing, but he only saw that patient once."

"Do you remember the name of the patient?" Lindsay asked.

She pulled a thin file from the middle of the row and handed it to the detectives. "You're not supposed to see this," she whispered.

"What made this guy different?" Carter was looking at a single page with strange writing. There was a small sketch of a triangular object in the lower corner.

"This guy was Miss Zen's supervisor at the base, and he requested Dr. Asael."

"Mary, will you copy these for us?" Carter handed everything to Mary.

"Yes, if you want to have a seat I'll do it right now."

"Thanks."

As Mary took the papers to the copy machine, Lindsay looked at Carter. "We need to speak with this James Mitchell. Something's fishy."

Carter sat on the white suede couch. "Yeah. And so much for this being quick."

CHAPTER NINETEEN

"WHERE ARE WE going?" Alexis asked as she followed her grandfather up a pathway paved with smooth slate. They were heading to a nearby ridge.

"I thought you might want to go to a different area to take a break from everything."

"A different dimension would be nice," Alexis said.

"I'm positive this place will help you find yourself."

"I know who I am, no offense."

The path was lined with large rocks covered with green moss and bright purple hibiscus. The slate had changed to loose pebbles as the path wound past thick tree trunks and across a narrow stream. The two began climbing up a gradual incline.

"What happened back at the cottage, with the sky? It's no longer blood red."

"Something must be changing within the balance of all our worlds. Something not of the Light." His long white robe brushed across the dirt yet remained perfectly clean.

"I take it this was unusual. Not some seasonal thing."

"It's never happened before."

Alexis stopped walking. "Then why are you so calm about it? The others seem ..."

"Nervous?"

Alexis nodded. "Why aren't you?"

"They're not nervous in the way you assume, but they don't like what's ahead. But I trust in you."

She looked skeptical. "Me? You're joking, right? I can't even find my way out of this ... place."

When she glanced up, she saw a beautiful place, one different from the path she had been following. It was a place hidden in the back of her dreams.

"When did the scenery change?" When she turned around, she was surrounded by lush tropical plants and towering palms.

"Every point on your side exists on this side, you just don't need to walk as far," her grandfather said. He pointed to the path that led down over the ridge. "Mere thought can take you where you want to go, if you can control your mind long enough."

"How is that possible? Distance is still distance."

"As immortals, we can cross oceans at light speed."

"Yeah, but I'm not an immortal so ..."

"I brought you with me for that last jump."

Alexis hurried down the embankment to a white beach. She shook her head. "Of course you'd take me to my personal utopia to try and convince me to stay."

"Not my intention. This is to inspire, not to divert." He sat along the water's edge.

Alexis waited a few seconds before sitting down. She raked her fingers through the white sand and dug her toes into it. She held a single grain up to the sunlight. "If the Earth were a grain of sand, the sun would be the size of an orange."

Her grandfather nodded. "And for every grain of sand you see, a hundred stars shine throughout the universe."

She gazed out at the blue tide. "This place reminds me of Ben and how much I want to be back on my side and in his arms."

"You speak of the one in your heart?"

She smiled. "He isn't like anyone I've tried to know. He feels different—he is different."

"You think you love him?"

"I'm halfway there."

"Love will test you, and it requires sacrifice from both sides, remember that. And sometimes that sacrifice means not loving back the way it is expected."

Alexis nodded. "Story of my life. My relationships with family and friends have always been a struggle. Even my own mother doesn't love me the way one would expect. I fault myself for expecting everything to be equal. I should take it for what it is, not how it's given."

"I had many children, and I loved them all differently. That's because each was different." He looked out at the sunlight. "Not because I loved any of them less."

"It doesn't matter. I'm not even sure if what I felt for Ben was real. Our time was cut short right when we were starting to connect, and he probably doesn't know what to make of all this. I'd guess he's seeing a shrink of his own by now."

"I have no way of looking into the hearts of others. Our abilities are only to feel or see energy."

Alexis shifted her feet, burying them deeper in the sand. "Will you tell me about your son?"

"Your father?"

"Yes." Alexis smiled. "I never knew him. The only picture I have is of when he and my mother were married."

"I didn't know him in your world. He was raised by his mother. But once I passed through to the realm of the Light, I could watch him grow and eventually find love with your mother."

"Do you know what happened to him?" Alexis asked.

Michael sighed. "He was always searching for something, and eventually he got lost. I hope he will find his way back to you. I know he loves you very much."

She made a halfway laugh. "You mean *loved.* I'm sure the dead don't find their way back that easily. On the other hand"—she looked around—"this place has changed a lot of my previous perceptions of death."

"First, the dead walk among the living all the time. Second, your father isn't one of them."

She furrowed her brow. "I don't understand. My father is dead. My mother told me he ..."

"She told you he left and that he was probably dead. But he is very much alive."

"Why? And how can you say he loves me if he chose to leave and never look back?"

"Alexis, I cannot defend him, nor will I try to explain his reasons. But I will tell you that by staying away he protected you from more than you can understand. People in his life may have found you and caused you harm."

"What kind of people?"

"When your father met your mother he was already searching for answers, the same answers you have sought, except he found himself on the wrong path. He chose to walk away from the darkness before he and your mother married, but I saw him look back, for what reason I don't understand. As I said, I cannot see into the hearts of others."

A tear fell from her cheek. "Regardless, my life was far from being protected."

"I'm sorry you suffered many trials. You feel as though no one was there for you, but please believe that someone has always watched over you."

"I feel as if watching is all anyone ever did for me."

Michael sighed. "We cannot interfere, only try to guide. That is said for both sides, yet it appears the beings of the Dark have changed the rules."

"The past is the past. How do I go forward and get back to my side?"

"The same way you came, through a gate. But you'll need to find a different way."

"The map of portals," Alexis murmured. "I'd have to find a way to open one of them."

"You already know how." He stood up and offered her a hand. "But you need to uncover exactly which one."

"I'm pretty sure the crystal won't reopen a portal, but maybe it can detect one." She went to brush away the sand but found nothing on her clothing.

"Think of the first time you realized the power of the crystal."

Alexis pulled the amber-tinted quartz from her pocket and tumbled it around in her hand. "In my lab. The sound vibration created the frequency to open the portal in my lab. I need to reverse the vibration—but how?"

"You can come with me to ask the Intelligences within the walls," Michael said, but Alexis wasn't paying attention.

"I just need to find the right frequency. In my lab the portal opening was small, but it opened the one in Belize completely. Maybe it was the surface."

"Find the right location," he said.

"Exactly what I need to do." She got up and looked around at the soft surfaces. "Where's the right location?"

"Alexis, before you can leave ..."

She waved her hand. "Hold on before you say anything else. I don't want any more confusion. After being thrown in the middle of an ancient crystal secret, yanked through a portal, meeting a deceased grandfather, finding out my real father is still alive—not to mention that some dark being wants me dead—I can't balance anymore until I get some real answers."

"Fair enough." Michael joined her as she walked away from the beach. "One thing for certain is that you wouldn't be here if the Master of Darkness wanted you dead. He is very powerful and has taken life many times before. Your soul would give him unimaginable power, which is why I'm certain he doesn't know your value to us or to the world."

She jerked her head around. "If he doesn't want me dead, then what's the big deal with him causing me suffering, like the others said? And why not tell me who it is?"

"We travel with thought because it tunnels only our own power, which is the same reason we do not use or say his name on either side. Sound is traveling energy." His eyes glanced toward the crystal in Alexis's hand. "Don't let that fall into the wrong hands. You still need it."

"Trust me, if I ever get out of here, I'm not coming back." She tumbled the amber piece of quartz in her palm. "I'm only keeping this because Aharon said I should."

"He must be able to feel its energy." Michael pointed to the crystal. "May I?"

Alexis put it into his open palm.

Michael held the crystal up, looking at the inscriptions. The sunlight caught the top and shot out four red-orange reflective lines. As Michael twisted the crystal, the light disappeared.

Alexis peered at the crystal. "I've never seen it get that bright."

"This particular crystal can open a portal into this realm from almost anywhere on your side of the map that creates uninterrupted sound vibration. Yet there is a crossing point you'll find that can open a portal to what is hidden."

"Points? Hidden? I'm not interested in opening any new points." She took the crystal back. "Which reminds me, you still haven't explained the big deal with this opposing force. If this Dark Master has no intention of harming me, then why all the worry?"

"That crystal has been their intention, and your family has been charged with protecting it. After seeing the blood sky, I feel their motives are to destroy all that is in the Light to get what has been brought here."

The soft air blew across her ivory cheek and pushed her toward the path away from the beach. Grains of sand sifted between her toes and then melded back together into a silky smooth white sheet.

She took one last look at the beach behind her before letting out a deep breath. "Why did this stupid crystal have to fall in my lab?"

"In the lines of lineage, this was supposed to go into your Aunt Sarah's care. But your grandmother felt it needed to skip a generation to keep it protected, and so far it remains safe. But you will have to take it with you when you leave here and return it to where it came from."

Alexis inhaled. "That means I have to find out where it came from."

"Most of the things we seek are hidden in plain sight. When we return to the cottage, I will ask Giah to play a song for you. Her voice will comfort you and give you peace of mind."

"For once, I think that's a great idea."

The two slowly strolled up the side of the bank toward the pathway atop the hillside. Deep green palms that seemed to sway apart as they approached offered shade. When they came to the top, Alexis took in the last hint of cocoa bean mixed with coconut in the air.

"Alexis, take your time and follow this path toward the cottage," Michael said. "I will be along shortly. I need to meditate upon a few questions of my own."

"OK." She turned and continued into the thick woodland.

Michael stood silently until she rounded the bend and was lost to his sight. "Dathan?"

The tall man came out from behind the knee-high purple foliage.

"I sense your concerns, and they're not warranted," Michael said. "Alexis is safe and she will do what is needed."

"You sense correctly, but my concerns extend beyond her being here. If they break the walls between our worlds, and she's not ready …"

Michael glanced to his left. "She has to go back. We may not know the reasons, but we have to keep our trust in the outcome."

"Why throw her back into the hands of those monsters? And should you be telling her everything?"

"I'm her grandfather, and what I keep from her is to protect her from the other dark company. Adding more fear to this situation could tip the scales away from the Light."

"They will find Alexis, and the whole truth may save her."

"I have faith that Alexis will do what she was meant to do. Our concerns could change the future if we interfere too much."

Both men looked around. The ground cover below and tree branches overhead were completely still. A calm fell from every direction. Soon an intense glow dominated the sky, penetrating the forest with white beams through the canopy of trees. Michael and Dathan looked at each other.

"Alexis?" Dathan asked.

"No, but someone opened a portal."

CHAPTER TWENTY

MARCIA ZEN walked up the concrete path next to the gravel driveway and past an off-white motor home to the back steps of her parents' home. The three inches of snow from the past few days was long gone, leaving only a frigid chill in the air and bare wet ground cover.

Marcia noticed five white kitchen trash bags piled outside the back door, so she grabbed them and tossed them over the edge of the porch into the large garbage cans. Three were heavy and looked to be filled with normal household trash, but the last two were easier to carry even though they were stretched full. She looked closer and saw several empty containers of disinfectant and cloth rags.

She opened the back door and wiped her boots before heading to the kitchen. "Mom?"

"Marcia sweetie, give me a minute, I'll be right out," Baba called out from the spare bedroom in the back of the house.

Marcia made her way through the kitchen toward the dining room. The old blue laminate counters were covered with stacks of canned vegetables, dry honey-roasted nuts, boxes of dehydrated milk, and cans of tomato soup. To the left was a sink full of plastic dishes left soaking in sudsy water. She moved into the dining room and saw more stuff on the floor and table. Three boxes of fiber cereal bars and six gallons of purified water were beside an open atlas.

"Mother, where are you going?" She looked around the room while picking up the atlas, which was open to a map of Pennsylvania.

Baba entered the room carrying a worn wooden case. "Hello, dear."

"Are you and Dad going somewhere?" Marcia pointed to the atlas, then to the three suitcases, two heavy blankets, and a large box filled with smokeless fuel containers sitting on the floor.

Baba grinned. "After all that has been happening, we're heading to the rocks to find solace."

"The rocks? In Pennsylvania?" Marcia raised her left brow. "Are you talking about the Ringing Rocks?"

"I'm surprised you remembered." Baba walked past Marcia, placed the wooden case on a chair, and then moved to an old cherry cabinet.

"Are you kidding? You practically brainwashed all of us kids with your ridiculous stories of magical rocks that aliens moved to the tops of mountains."

"I never said aliens, I said other beings. And, my dear, as crazy as it may sound, those stories are true." Baba opened a drawer.

"Why now? It's not really vacation season. And what do you mean by *all that has been happening*?"

"When I told you those stories, I said a day would come when we might have to go there."

"I thought you were talking about taking us on a family camping trip. It's not safe for you guys to go up there alone."

"We won't be alone."

"Who else is going?" Marcia demanded.

Baba glanced up over her wire-rimmed glasses. "Is there a reason you stopped over? Other than making me feel old?"

"Sorry."

"It's fine, you kids just need to realize that your father and I are not going to be around forever."

"Yes, but we'd like to keep you ..."

"And we want to still enjoy what we have left on this planet." Baba started taking out the silverware and putting it on the table. "So why did you stop by?"

"I wanted to talk about Alexis."

"What about her?"

"Do you think there's a chance she ... I mean that she ..." Marcia hesitated, trying to find words that wouldn't make her sound crazy.

She saw her mother open a hidden compartment in the back of the drawer. "What is that?"

Baba had pushed a button concealed by the burgundy lining of the drawer. It opened a small compartment, and she reached back and took out a small brushed-metal box. "This used to hold the crystal I gave to Alexis. I need it to hold something else now."

"I never knew that was back there. What else do you have hidden?"

Baba shrugged her shoulders. "A lot of us who grew up during the Depression would hide food and other things. I just got in the habit of hiding my valuables."

"You consider that crystal you gave Alexis valuable?"

"I thought you said you were wanting to talk about Alexis?" Baba wiped off the box.

"Um, yes." Marcia looked away. "Her supervisor finally told us that they never actually found her body."

"Are you surprised by this? saw right through that boy's lies."

"Who's lies?"

"Mr. Mitchell, he came to visit with me one day last week, and I could tell he knew more than he'd led us to believe."

Baba opened the wooden case. It was divided by thin wood slats into fourteen spaces of different sizes. Each was lined with black velvet, and all but three were empty.

"You're taking those with you? I thought Alexis had those."

"She did. I gave these to her when she turned sixteen." Baba placed the small metal box into one of the empty spaces.

"How'd you get them back? The Air Force gave us back her stuff a few weeks ago and I never gave that to you."

"I stopped over one day last week to visit and you were gone. I asked Matt for a couple of things that had meaning for me, and he gave them to me."

Marcia frowned. "He never mentioned it. What else did you ask for?"

"Doesn't matter, it's not a big deal."

Baba made her way to the sink. The kitchen was long and no wider than the interior of a school bus, which allowed little room to maneuver. The elderly woman leaned against the counter to pull open a drawer and grab a dishrag.

Marcia followed her mother. "Mom, I worry that Alexis is still out there, lost."

"She is a strong girl and very resourceful. I believe if she survived she would find her way back home eventually."

"So you believe she's alive? I was beginning to think I had lost my mind."

"Sweetie, leave the insane conspiracy plots to your father." Baba stuck her hands into the dishwater. "In the face of uncertainty, it's better to keep a positive outlook."

"Here, let me do that." Marcia rolled up her sleeves and took her rings off, setting them in a small dish on the windowsill. A single tear fell from Marcia's cheek as she bumped the framed picture of her sister Sarah that was next to the dish.

"Thank you, dear."

"You're right, I guess. The idea that she died so terribly has haunted me, but now the hope that she could come home has lifted me a little, even if it's not true."

"It's hard either way you look at it." Baba stepped back. "But your father and I choose to believe in what gives us peace in life. We try not to be sad. We will see her again, we will see them all one day." Baba looked at the picture of Sarah.

Marcia wiped the tears from her face. "How do you find that kind of peace and keep it?"

Baba smiled and then hugged her daughter. "Our dreams can allow us to be close to loved ones who aren't with us."

"My dreams are of a man sending me on a scavenger hunt around the world."

Baba gazed at her. "What man? Describe him."

"Why?" Marcia cleaned the suds from her hands before rinsing the cups off.

"Is he an angel?"

"No, definitely not. He's more like the devil's advocate. Light hair and dark clothes. My dreams are always hazy, but he's not angelic."

"Where do your dreams take you?"

"Take me? Usually nowhere. Why would you ask that?"

"You said your dreams had a man who took you on a scavenger hunt around the world."

"Whenever he's in my dreams we're in darkness, and I can make out where we are. One time I was in an empty warehouse. Another time I found myself alone in a cave." Marcia paused. "This last time I was at Stonehenge."

"Stonehenge? You're positive?" Baba headed toward the suitcases.

"Yes, why?"

Baba chuckled as she started to lock the suitcases. "Because you're not that good with landmarks."

"That's true, but I know what Stonehenge looks like. A circle of huge stones is not that common."

"More common than you think. But tell me more. What did he say to you? Did he tell you how we open it?"

"Open what? The only thing I really remember him saying was that I could begin to find Alexis there. There was no mention of opening anything."

Baba was organizing the food and putting them into cardboard boxes. "The portal of Light couldn't be there."

"A portal?" Marcia started to laugh. "Mom, you need listen to yourself sometimes. Magical rocks that sound hollow when you hit them, crystals that Eve passed down to us that we're supposed to protect, and now portals of light."

"Or a blond man in a black suit with piercing black eyes talking to you in your dreams, telling you where to find your missing daughter," Baba said. "Maybe crazy is hereditary."

Marcia was staring at her. “I didn’t say anything about his eyes—how did you know that?”

“I have been dreaming of a similar man. That’s how I knew it was time to head to the rocks.”

Marcia slumped onto a dining room chair. “I don’t understand.”

“There is a lot you don’t understand, and it’s much too late for me to try and explain. But it’s clear there is some force wanting someone to go to Stonehenge.” Baba took the wooden case and put it on the counter above where the suitcases sat. “But it won’t be us.”

“I can’t do this. Please, no more talk of this paranormal science fiction crap. If Alexis is out there, I need to find her without a ouija board, magic crystals, or dream interpretation.”

“Child, you should probably go home to your husband and prepare for the storm, maybe find shelter. It’s going to get worse before it gets better.”

“I think you and Dad are too old for this.”

“I have raised you kids to know there is more than what you can see, and now those things are starting make themselves visible. And your father and I were entrusted to protect these things until our death.” Baba sighed as she smoothed her hand across the wooden box.

“Don’t talk like that. This family has suffered too many deaths.”

“And we will suffer a great deal more, but it’s for a purpose more grand than our eyes can see.”

“We just need to find someone who can go overseas to help us locate Alexis.” Marcia wiped tears from the corner of her eyes. “The local cops can only do some much.”

Baba squinted toward Marcia. “Is there anything else you remember from your dreams?”

“No.”

“Nothing? No other structures or other people?”

“There was a field with crop circles, which probably means aliens have Alexis. Now I see why Matt was so skeptical—it really was just a dream. I probably saw that guy on TV or even at church.”

Baba walked over to her daughter and put her arms out. Marcia leaned in and hugged the small Polish woman. Marcia took in a strong smell of Baba's favorite No. 5 perfume as she patted her on the back.

"I won't burden you anymore with stories of angels and demons. Not everyone accepts so easily, and I know your heart feels the spirit of truth."

"I do believe in the spiritual stuff, but not all of the folklore about the secrets." Marcia released her grip. "I've read the Bible on occasion and never found mention of aliens or portals, or that Eve left a crystal to the Prollofsky family."

Baba gave her daughter a polite smile but behind her expression was a heart filled with determination and conviction. Her mother had given her the crystal when she was only twelve, when her mother was putting her on a boat headed for America. The crystal held many sad memories, because she never saw her parents again. But it was her mother's faith in the truth that kept Baba holding on to it.

"Do you really need to go to Pennsylvania?" Marcia asked.

"Yes. We are leaving as soon as your father gets back and I load the RV."

"All right, but will you please use the cell phone we got you to call us periodically?"

Baba nodded and gave Marcia a vague smile. "Yes, I will try to remember."

CHAPTER TWENTY-ONE

JAMES WALKED ACROSS the hardwood floor of his studio apartment, following the path of the morning sunlight. Modern accents in brown and orange warmed the space, relieving the harshness of exposed vents and beams, but they clashed with the second-story view of historic storefronts.

Mr. Bekhor looked out at the vintage antique store across the street. “Did she know you lived here?”

“No.” James sat at the table with the smart tablet he had retrieved from the Zens. “I’d drive the long way home and go through my back alley. I always kept the blinds closed.”

Mr. Bekhor turned from the window and looked at James. “Were you here the night she was attacked inside her apartment?”

“Yes.”

“Did you help her?”

“There wasn’t anything I could do. By the time I saw what was happening, the guy was running through her apartment. And with her coming down to Sublevel 6 the very next day, I couldn’t chance her knowing I was here.” James looked away. “I should have called the police.”

Bekhor joined James at the table. “At least someone took care of it.”

“Yes, they did.” On the tablet, James scrolled to a picture of the crystal. “I’d like to meet that person and shake his hand.”

“Not if it meant you’d end up a human popsicle.”

“Good point. But I don’t understand who could have done it. I watched her place, and no one left that night except that creep.”

Bekhor shrugged. “Does it matter? The guy who attacked her is dead." Bekhor watched James aimlessly scroll through the images on the tablet.

"No, I guess it doesn't."

"Stop!" Bekhor pointed to the picture of one of the inscriptions on the tablet. "Which one is that?"

James stopped scrolling and looked down. "This marking?"

"Yes."

"It should correspond to the eighteenth page in the journal. It's Spanish. I remember seeing this one when Alexis first began flipping through the journal on the plane to Hawaii."

Bekhor pulled out the small rectangular hologram device and sat on the table. He moved his thumb over the half-inch-square lens, and an illuminated hologram of the journal appeared. He turned the transparent pages.

"It's definitely Spanish." Bekhor skimmed the text. "This is talking about a massive structure in the East that caused the people to spread across the land after being near to Heaven."

"Heaven?" James pulled a slip of paper out from under the tablet and marked a red dot near Spain. "Not quite sure how this marking or that entry plays into all this. It looks more like an aerial view of a circular stone formation."

"Let me see. There are many ancient circular formations, temples, sacrificial sites. Goseck, Germany, for example, has something very similar to Stonehenge." Bekhor pulled the tablet closer and then glanced at the illuminated image suspended above the metal device. "There are usually two of everything."

"I've never seen another Sphinx," James joked.

"You've never been deep-sea diving in Bermuda." Bekhor was still looking at the journal. "It goes on to say *Great cities will fall away lost but always remain.*"

"What cities have fallen away lost?"

"Many come to mind. Tikal in Guatemala, Machu Pichu in Peru

but …" Bekhor studied the image of the crystal inscription on the tablet. "This might be referring to Atlantis."

"Plato's mythical city of Atlantis? How about Neverland? Or …"

"Or Troy" Bekhor said. "Most thought it didn't exist either, until 1871, when a self-taught man followed the clues."

"All right, but why Atlantis?"

Bekhor held the tablet so James could see the image. "Because there is a swampy area north of Cadiz, Spain, that looks like this from above. Of course, it's buried under water."

"Like you said, there are many replicas. How do you know this refers to Atlantis? To me it also looks like Stonehenge."

"I don't know for certain that it is. I said it might refer to Atlantis, Mr. Mitchell."

James pored over the map. "No surprise that it stays consistent within the areas of Alexis's findings. It'll be nice to see where this actually leads."

"What others haven't you translated?" Bekhor asked.

"These three and the very first one." James showed him the printouts of the crystal inscriptions with writing along the side. "I've made notes on these pages, but nothing definitive."

"Hold on, go back to the second one." Bekhor watched James flip through the small stack of papers. "That one, with the three triangles."

James shrugged. "I've about chalked this one up to be a repeat."

"The crystal doesn't repeat." Bekhor turned to the corresponding page on the hologram journal.

"It really looks like a symbol for pyramids?"

"No, this is the tongue of the Sumerian people. More specifically, *eme-sal*, the language of the women. Which makes sense if women have been the ones in charge of writing these entries."

"Do you know how to translate it?"

"Enough to fill in the blanks, I hope." Bekhor began writing on the printout of the inscription.

"I don't understand why some of these are symbols for dead languages and others are just reference points?"

Bekhor looked at James. "How many have been just reference points?"

"Maybe ten or so, why?"

There was a knock on the door.

"Are you expecting someone?" Bekhor asked.

"No. "

James got up and headed to the door. He peered through the peephole. "Can I help you?"

"Mr. Mitchell, we're detectives with the FPD, and we'd like to ask you a few questions," Detective Carter said.

"Sure, give me a second." James shot a worried glance back to the table.

Bekhor turned off his hologram device and turned over the pages of pictures and notes. James waited a few seconds before unlocking the door. The two detectives had their badges ready.

"Mr. Mitchell, I'm Detective Carter and this is my partner Detective Lindsay. We're following up on the death of one of your coworkers, Alexis Zen."

James ran his hand through his dark hair. "It was a terrible loss."

"Were you close to her?" Lindsay asked.

"I was her supervisor after she was promoted to my floor."

"So, you two never socialized outside of work?"

"No, we didn't get much time outside of work."

"Even living so close to each other?" Carter said.

"I realize we were neighbors, but plenty of people who work on base live close to it."

"Who else do you know that lives around here?"

James hesitated a moment and then said, "I can't think of anyone right off hand."

"But you knew Alexis lived right across the street, and yet you never suggested carpooling?" Carter asked.

Lindsay didn't give James time to respond. "Was her death a surprise to you?"

"Yes, of course," James said.

"Interesting you say that, Mr. Mitchell," Detective Carter said. "We were told you never found a body and that you believe she could still be out there."

"The details of Alexis's death are classified."

"Mr. Mitchell, were you with Alexis Zen on her trip out of the country over the summer?" Lindsay looked through his notes. "To Japan and Central America?"

"I'm afraid this subject is classified."

Carter took a step forward. "Did you tell Mrs. Zen her daughter could still be alive?"

"Not exactly, but ..."

"Why give her false hope?" Carter asked.

"I wasn't ..."

"So, was her body found?" Lindsay asked.

James sighed. "No, no, I was trying to give them answers. I didn't realize she would take it to you. I told her and her husband that information was classified."

"That poor woman is having nightmares about her daughter being trapped," Carter said.

James heard a voice inside his head.

You give things too freely ... the enemy will soon find you.

"What?" James said, his eyes refocusing on the detectives.

"I asked you where Miss Zen was last seen," Lindsay said.

"I don't know, she ..."

They would never believe you.

"... she went on her own a lot, recording data. I was only with her to help carry things, so I was asleep when she left the hotel. I didn't see her again."

"And you have no idea if she was with Dr. Asael?"

James shook his head. "Not a clue. Why?"

"Thank you for your time, Mr. Mitchell," Carter said.

"No problem."

The detectives turned to walk away, but Lindsay stopped and turned back to face James. "One more thing, Mr. Mitchell."

"Yes?"

"Where can we find your friend Dr. Asael?"

"I haven't seen him. And we're not exactly friends."

"Really? Then why did you request an office visit with him?"

"My psychiatrist wasn't able to see me when I was available, so I had to find another one."

"Quite the coincidence that he happened to be Alexis's shrink, too."

"Not the only coincidence," Carter added. "A lot of common things between the two of you."

James made no response.

"Let us know if you do see him," Carter said.

"Will do," James said, and the detectives left.

James took in a deep breath and closed his eyes. A vision of Alexis streamed through his mind, her blonde hair blowing in the wind, her soft skin reflecting rays of sunlight from the treetops of Belize as they walked to the Cahal Pech Temple. Another vision interrupted it, of her reaching out to help him before she was pulled into the portal. The sound of Bekhor talking broke his reverie.

"Send him. I will take care of the rest," Bekhor was saying into his phone. "No, that's your job."

Bekhor ended the call and started organizing the pages of loose papers. He put them into a leather binder and then grabbed the tablet.

"Are you leaving?" James asked.

"Yes." Bekhor took everything off the table and slipped it into a thin metal briefcase. "You should answer that."

"Answer what?" James's cell phone began ringing. "How did you ...?"

"Because I knew they would be calling." Bekhor locked the briefcase. "Really, you should answer that."

James stepped to the side, allowing Mr. Bekhor to pass. Bekhor waited by the door as James answered the call.

"Can you repeat that, sir?" A moment later, he said, "I don't understand how they are able to keep spontaneously imploding, unless you think this is a terrorist act." After another pause, he said, "I see why you called me. I'll be on the first flight out."

James ended the call and looked at Bekhor. "Did you know about this? Was it the lieutenant that called you before my phone rang?"

"I know what has happened, but it wasn't the lieutenant who called me," Bekhor said.

"How could you possibly know what's going on? And how did you know my phone was going to ring?"

Bekhor opened the door. "You don't have time to stand here and question my source. As far as more pyramids being destroyed, it's streaming online as we speak. And many are saying they saw UFOs in the area, so when I saw your phone light up through your pants pocket, I assumed you were the first they would call to investigate it."

James looked puzzled. "Why did you wait for me? Are you planning to come with me?"

"Not at the moment. However, I need you to drop me off somewhere on the way to the airport."

"Where?"

"I need to grab some personal belongings." Bekhor turned away and walked out the door.

CHAPTER TWENTY-TWO

ALEXIS WAS SURROUNDED by a bright light that warmed every inch of her body. The trees and ground no longer looked like flowing watercolor but instead were bathed in white, with spears of gold replacing the shadows. The wind was still, but her name vibrated from somewhere in the light.

"Alexis."

She peered out, shading her eyes with her hand. Just above the horizon, to the left, Alexis saw a glowing ball of light.

"Hello?"

As the light moved closer, she saw the outline of person. She peered at his bare, marble-colored chest and saw silver waves framing his face, but something larger and more majestic held her attention. The mysterious man was adorned with two wings across his back. He was clothed in white silk-like pants, but his feet were bare.

Alexis was mesmerized by his pure white beauty and the iridescent feather-like texture of his wings. "Who are you?"

"I'm Uriel."

"An angel?"

"I am one of the seven most high, but we're all angels after we pass through the Light of Kolcep."

"Kolcep? Which realm is that?"

"Most haven't heard of it, and it's not one of the realms on your map. It's not even on your planet, only the portal was left here. Therefore, beings like myself can travel faster to planets with life."

"So that's what's through the wall in the cottage, the portal home."

"Correct." Uriel came closer, revealing pale grey eyes. "Excuse me for taking you by surprise, but I don't normally interact with beings in your world."

"That's OK. Why are you here now?"

Uriel smiled. "Because you are no longer in your world."

Alexis frowned. "Why are you here?"

"Alexis, you will not survive here much longer as a human. The part of you that allowed you to pass through the portal cannot sustain your needs nor your physical life."

"What part is that? No one wants to answer the simple questions around here." Alexis turned to walk away, but Uriel was blocking her path.

"I am here to help," he said.

She sighed. "So says everyone else."

"Your heart weighs heavy because your mind tries to stay on course with this unseen journey even as it seeks to understand its purpose."

"I just want to go home. And for once, I'd like real facts." She wiped away a tear. "None of the smooth psychological lingo that everyone passes off amounts to real answers."

Uriel put out his hand. "I will show you the way."

Alexis hesitated. "I have no room for false hope."

"I can't take you through the gate you desire, because your body is not prepared, but I will take you where you need to end up."

"I want real answers, not vague abstractions."

"I will try to be more specific."

Alexis nodded and placed her hand into Uriel's. The orb behind him started to enlarge and open. "Where are we going?"

"We will need to walk through the valley that is burdened by death."

She pulled back her hand. "This would be a good time for specifics."

"Did you not ask to be guided? Did you not ask to be shown the way out to return to the world you know?"

"Yes, but ..."

"I am the answer to part of your prayer. But I must take you to the center realm where both Light and Dark reside after death. Then I will show you inside the world which you need to find."

"Why must we ..."

Before Alexis could finish her question, the small ball of golden yellow light behind Uriel began to pulsate. It started to oscillate and stretch open. Streams of violet and alabaster broke through the center and shot past her face.

"A portal," Alexis murmured.

Uriel turned to her. "A gate."

CHAPTER TWENTY-THREE

MARCIA SQUINTED AGAINST the bright sunlight as she pulled up the driveway to her home. She stepped out of her car into the scent of white oak and wet dog. Fatigued from helping load the RV, she slowly made her way up the gravel path to the steps of her back door. When she stepped inside, she heard the television blaring.

"My gosh, Matt, are you deaf?" she muttered to herself.

She walked to the bedroom, but her husband wasn't there. She shut off the TV and searched the entire upstairs but didn't find Matt.

"Matt?" Marcia called out. Seconds later, she heard movement in the basement. "Matt? Are you down there?"

"Yeah," came his muffled voice. "I'm in the back room."

"What are you doing?" She made her way down the carpeted steps and headed to the back of the basement. A white door opened to a separate storage room with cinderblock walls. Four rows of metal shelves were stacked with boxes of bulk food, old paint supplies, and decorations for each season. Several boxes overflowing with Christmas decorations were stacked near the door.

"Matt, why is all this stuff out?" Marcia asked. "I just finished putting it away."

"Sorry," Matt said, reaching for the top of one of the shelves. "I'm looking for the camping gear."

"Why? It's still too cold to go camping."

Matt stopped what he was doing and turned to her. "Look, babe, your dad just left here fifteen minutes ago and said they were going camping. He said this was always supposed to be a family trip when you all were kids. So I called Rebecca and she's headed here this evening so we can leave first thing in the morning to meet up with them."

Marcia raised her left brow. "Did my dad happen to tell you where they were going? Because I highly doubt that you're packing for Pennsylvania."

"Pennsylvania? No, he told me about the house in Missouri, and with everything going on, we needed a break. He did mention that they were stopping off to see some sights and would meet us there, but he didn't say anything about Pennsylvania. Regardless, it's the off season for the greenhouse business, and I think we should take a couple weeks to go out there for a little while."

Marcia frowned. "You agreed with him? You're willing to pack up on the spur of the moment and leave our business, all because of my dad's suggestion? Wasn't it last week he suggested you fill our pool in because he thought it was dangerous?"

"Um ..."

"Has everyone lost their minds?" Marcia turned to head back to the stairs.

"Wait, babe!"

"I'm not going to Missouri, and I'm not falling victim to my parents' crazy theories about the war between good and evil, either."

"OK, but listen to me first. Please."

"I'm listening."

"I've no idea what the good and evil thing has to do with this, but before we got married, Alexis and Rebecca had been through a lot because of your previous marriage. You were very cautious about moving forward. But I promised you then that I would always do what's right for our family."

Marcia smiled. "You are a great husband, and you've been an amazing father figure to them, but ..."

"It's only a couple of weeks, and we could use a family vacation."

Marcia sighed and shook her head. "I'm not going until Alexis is home."

Matt nodded and then pulled Marcia close and hugged her. "OK.

Maybe your dad should've stayed to talk you. It's surprising how persuasive he can be."

"I appreciate his intentions, and yours. I know you hope to take my mind off of everything. But do you seriously think a road trip across three state lines with us and a dog would calm me down?"

The two of them laughed and started putting back the boxes of decorations. Just as they slid the last box onto the shelf, they heard the crunch of gravel from the driveway.

"Rebecca's here," Matt said.

"Perfect timing."

Before Marcia could walk away, Matt wrapped his arms around her and kissed her cheek.

"I don't like to see you stressed, and I will do what I can to protect you from hurting."

"I know that." She pulled away. "Let's take Rebecca out for dinner tonight instead."

"Sounds good. After you, my dear."

Marcia and Matt hadn't made it to the top of the stairs before they heard knocking at the side door.

"Why is she knocking?" Matt asked.

Marcia chuckled. "Probably lost the key again."

The two of them made their way through the living room and down the hallway to the mudroom. Oslo, in the backyard near the gate, was barking. Marcia looked out the side window.

"Matt, that's not Rebecca's car. It's that little prick James Mitchell."

"What's he want now?" Matt muttered. He opened the door and said to James, "I don't know why you're here, but we ..."

"Mr. Zen, I apologize, but I'm not the one asking this time," James said.

"Oslo, quiet!" Matt shouted, but Oslo wasn't near the gate. "Stupid dog. Who's he barking at?"

“I told you he barks into thin air all the time.” Marcia stood next to Matt and glared at James. “What do you want, Mitchell?”

James stepped to the side. From behind him, Mr. Bekhor came forward. Marcia gripped Matt’s arm as she tried to keep herself from falling.

“Marcia?” Matt exclaimed as he turned to catch her.

James stepped forward to help. “Mrs. Zen, are you all right?”

Marcia was pale and her voice was shaking. “Tell me you see him. Tell me I’m not imagining things again.”

“See who?” Matt looked up at James, who just shrugged.

Mr. Bekhor took another step forward. “Marcia.”

“Hey, pal, I don’t know who you think you are, but don’t come any closer.” Matt put his arm in front of his wife, who was struggling to catch her breath.

“You’re supposed to be dead. How can you be here?” Marcia felt a pounding in her chest. “I’ve seen your ghost.”

Matt looked at her. “Who’s dead? Whose ghost?”

“Mikel’s,” she whispered.

James turned to her. “As in Alexis’s father? No, this is Mr. Bekhor, my associate.”

James glanced at Mr. Bekhor and remembered everything dealing with Alexis. But the man standing there appeared way too young to be her father.

“There is another time for explanation. Right now I need to ask you for something, Marcia.”

James stared at him. “Wait a minute. Are you really Alexis’s father?”

Bekhor glanced into the backyard where Oslo was still barking and growling. “Can we come inside?”

Marcia took a breath and stood up straight. “You come to me for something now? After all these years, you need something? I grieved for a long time over your death.”

"I apologize for leaving you without answers, but it was to protect you and Alexis," Mikel responded.

Marcia laughed. "Protect us? You see where your protection got Alexis? She's gone! And because of you not being there as her father she had to suffer through so much heartache and instability."

Mikel moved closer to Marcia. "Because of me? Are you sure about that, Marcia? I have continued watching Alexis since I left you, helping her to forget the things you allowed to happen to her."

Marcia clenched her teeth and shoved Matt's arm out of the way. "What did I do? I tried to get her help. Why didn't you protect her six months ago?"

"I came to the grave site that day. I watched from a distance, and then I paid my respects privately with her favorite flowers." Mikel softened his voice. "But you seem to have forgotten how amazingly she grew up and how she fought through all the trials in her life."

Marcia sighed and wiped away a tear. "I didn't forget—I just forgot to tell her. And according to your colleague, my little girl is out there lost and alone."

"I didn't mean to ..." James began.

"Mr. Mitchell tends to open his mouth before considering the audience," Mikel said.

"But you're not denying what he said," Matt responded.

"No, I'm not."

Matt looked at his wife and then at the two men standing before them. James was lost in thought, and Mikel stood with his arms crossed.

"Marcia has been through a lot this year," Matt said. "Too much death, not knowing whether or not Alexis is alive, and now you show up."

Mikel stepped closer to Marcia. Oslo began barking again. "Can we talk privately?"

Matt folded his arms. "You can say whatever you want in front of me."

"I planned to include you," Mikel said. "I meant in a more private area."

Matt looked at Marcia. "You don't have to do this."

"It's OK. Let them in."

Matt opened the door and stood to the side as James and Mikel entered. Just before Mikel stepped inside, he turned toward Oslo, who was still barking furiously but facing the backyard, not the doorway. The woods on the hilltop no longer had sunlight peeking through, and the thick brush blocked any view of wildlife. Everything appeared calm, with nothing obvious that might attract a dog's interest. Mikel turned away and went inside.

As he stepped out of sight and Matt shut the door, Cezar and a dozen other men in dark suits appeared at the corner of the Zen's backyard, near Oslo.

"Don't lose him!" Cezar commanded.

"Which one?" a dark being asked.

"Alexis's father," Cezar said. "I'll return soon."

The dark entities broke off individually and moved closer to the house. Oslo barked as they passed by.

CHAPTER TWENTY-FOUR

"MATT, PLEASE GO see why Oslo's barking or put him in the basement," Marcia said as she cleared the newspaper clippings from the dining table.

"Why? He'll stop in a minute. There's probably a few deer up in the woods." Matt put his elbows on the kitchen island and clasped his hands, glaring at the two men standing in the dining room.

"I'm having trouble hearing my own thoughts," Marcia said.

"All right," said Matt and he got up and walked to the sliding glass doors. He placed his hand on the latch to open it, but when he looked out, Oslo had stopped barking. Matt squinted at the two silver-coated fur legs poking out of the cedar-sided doghouse. "He stopped. Probably worn out from all that barking."

"That dog didn't like me whenever I stopped to see Alexis," James said as he checked his platinum watch.

"Smart dog," Marcia said. She wasn't smiling.

Matt sat down at the dining table and looked at Mikel. "So, Mikel, where have you been all these years?"

"No offense, but we both know you're not interested in my past or my present," Mikel said.

"On the contrary, I'd like to know exactly why you're here—and where you've been hiding."

"You in a hurry, Mr. Mitchell?" Marcia asked, causing a startled James to look up from his watch.

Mikel turned to James. "You can go ahead and leave, Mr. Mitchell. I will find you in a few days."

"I thought you would need me to drive you to ..." James began.

"I said I will find you in a few days. You have a plane to catch."

"You wouldn't be flying near England would you?" Marcia asked.

"No," James said.

"Why would you assume he was going to England?" Mikel asked.

"She's been wanting to take a trip there, that's all," Matt said.

Marcia sat down at the dining table.

Mikel sat across from her. "I thought you were afraid to fly?"

"I'm ready to take the risk. Alexis overcame her fear, so I should as well."

Mikel pointed to her hand. "Where's the ring I gave you?"

"I took all my rings off this afternoon when I was helping Baba with her dishes. I forgot to grab them before I left."

"Are you kidding me?" Mikel sounded aggrieved. "I'd like to have that back. It belonged to my family, Marcia."

Marcia shrugged. "They're probably gone by now. I helped her finish packing the RV for a ... vacation, and she was just waiting for my dad to return before they left." Marcia turned around and looked at the clock on the stove. "That was at least an hour ago."

"Where were they going?"

"Why do you care?" Marcia snapped. "You can get it back once they're home."

"Because that ring belonged to me, and it was to be given to Alexis when she turned sixteen. Why did you keep it for yourself?"

"I needed something to ..." Marcia looked at her husband as sadness and confusion filled her eyes. "They were headed toward Pennsylvania. I can call to see where they are, maybe they haven't made it that far. They'd probably turn around just to see you anyway."

"I don't have time for reunions right now, but could you call them?" Mikel asked.

"I can try." Marcia stood up from the table, picked up her phone, and went into the living room.

Mikel checked the time on his wristwatch and then looked at Matt. "Excuse me while I make a call."

He got up from the table and went to the sliding glass doors. He peered out at the backyard as he waited for the person on the other end to pick up. The yard was filled with dark beings watching him, but Mikel didn't notice.

"It's me," Mikel said into the phone. "I need a jet ready in an hour. Can you do that?" After a moment, he said, "Visoko. And, Colonel Logan, we need to delay Mr. Mitchell's flight for a couple of hours. He's going to be late."

He ended the call and slipped the phone into his pocket as he glanced back out at the backyard. Oslo was still lying quietly in his house.

"What is it about that ring that you don't want my wife to have it anymore? Or her mother?" Matt asked.

Mikel turned around. "It's nothing personal."

"Speaking of things being personal, how is it that you and the colonel are so close?" James asked. "It seems you haven't been very honest with me about who you know."

"On the contrary. I've never told you a lie." Mikel glanced at Marcia and Matt as he moved away from the glass door. "I've merely kept certain things private. As for the colonel, we met many years ago. We soon realized that we have a common goal."

"And what might that be?" Marcia asked.

"Uncovering the truth in the world around us."

"Good," Marcia huffed. "First truth you can expose is where our daughter is, and if she's still alive."

Mikel glanced at James, who blankly stared back. "If she's out there, she'll be found. I promise."

CHAPTER TWENTY-FIVE

DETECTIVES CARTER AND Lindsay were chatting with a handful of other detectives near the desk of the young new female in the department.

"Are you putting in for the lottery pool, Garcia?" Detective Carter asked her.

"Sorry, boys, I don't gamble," she said while filling out paperwork.

Her partner, Detective Negron, looked at her across the desk. "That's sacrilegious—we all put in five bucks a week."

"Nope, not me."

As the group continued to harass the rookie detective, one of the other male detectives loudly cleared his throat. When the others looked up, he tilted his head toward the hallway, where two men in suits were approaching.

"Did someone in holding ask for an attorney?" Lindsay asked the group.

Negron shook his head. "No, those look like federal agents. Check out the cheap suits."

The two agents were about the same height and build, but one was darker skinned, with thick eyebrows and a wrinkled forehead. As they approached, the group of six detectives pretended to be assisting Detectives Garcia and Negron. The agents entered the room to their left marked "Chief of Police, Steven Jenkins."

"Why would they be here?" asked Detective Phillips, a buxom female detective, as she leaned against the wall behind Garcia's desk. "There aren't any special cases, are there?"

"Not that I know of, unless they think you're ready for the academy," Detective Carter joked.

Laughter erupted. Everyone knew Detective Phillips was a year away from retirement.

Phillips was still considering her retort when Chief Jenkins's door opened.

"Carter and Lindsay, can you come in here please?" the chief called from his desk as one of the agents held the door open.

"Coming, Chief," Carter responded and made his way through the group.

"I thought you guys closed all your most recent stuff," Detective Negron said.

"We did," Lindsay said with a shrug. "But we took on something out of our scope, so I'm expecting forty lashes and a government flogging."

"Please close the door, detectives," Chief Jenkins said when Lindsay and Carter entered his office. He had a single document in his hand.

"Look, Chief, I'm completely responsible, not my partner," Lindsay said. "I encouraged him to help me pursue ..." Lindsay stopped when he saw Carter glaring at him.

"Responsible for what?" the lighter-skinned agent asked.

"They're not FBI," Carter said.

Lindsay glanced at the chief, who didn't disagree.

"Detective, they're here to ask you about a case you had over the summer. This is Agent Eldridge, from the CIA." The chief pointed to the lighter-skinned agent, who appeared to be the younger of the two. "And this is Agent Dristian, with ..."

"What case?" Lindsay snapped. "We worked more than one."

"The Ice Man," Agent Dristian answered.

Carter shrugged. "We didn't get anywhere with that one, and our lead suspect, or whatever you want to call her, is dead."

"Or missing," Lindsay murmured.

"What do you mean, missing?" Agent Eldridge asked.

"It doesn't matter," Carter said. "We have nothing that can help you. Some agents of yours came with their military guards and took everything we had on the case, including footage from the security cameras."

"The case file was wiped from our database," Lindsay added. "You guys have a lot of nerve asking us for help."

Agent Eldridge turned to Lindsay. "First of all, Mr. Lindsay ..."

"It's Detective Lindsay," Lindsay interrupted.

Eldridge nodded. "OK, Detective. The CIA never took anything from this building, and there is no record of anyone from our offices coming here. We're here now to talk about you helping us with new cases. We have some strange frozen bodies that are similar to your Ice Man."

"Frozen bodies where?" Carter asked.

"Cuba," Eldridge said. "Where it's way above freezing right now."

"And Israel," Agent Dristian added. He had a slight accent that indicated he was not a native-born American.

Lindsay and Carter glanced at one another. The chief stood up and closed the blinds.

"The past week or so has been anything but normal," Agent Eldridge said. "First there were the exploding pyramids, and now several black-site prisons have been breached."

"Black sites?" Carter asked. "Why would the CIA need our help with secret prisons?"

"Detective, I'm with Mossad, not the CIA," Agent Dristian said. "We shared our discovery with your government once we found that several countries had the same breach in security." He pulled out his cell phone and held it so that Lindsay and Carter could see its screen. "This is what we discovered."

The detectives looked at the pictures on the phone. Several were of inmates in small, dark prison cells lying on the floor with their eyes open. Dristian scrolled the images to the guard tower.

"They look like albinos," Lindsay said. He glanced at his partner. "Just like Pliate."

"All of them look albino." Dristian pulled up another picture of dead inmates and guards. "This was taken at Guantanamo yesterday in the middle of the day."

"How did you find out about our Ice Man case?" Lindsay asked. "As I said, it was erased from our database."

"Nothing put on a hard drive is ever completely erased," Eldridge said.

"Agents, my detectives will assist you in any way they can," Chief Jenkins said. "You will have the full cooperation of this precinct. Isn't that right detectives?"

Still staring at the images, Carter and Lindsay nodded their heads.

CHAPTER TWENTY-SIX

THE ZENS SAT AT their kitchen table talking with James and Mikel. Dusk had fallen, casting shadows onto the walls. James was staring into the living room, where the television was broadcasting a live news feed.

"Do you mind if I see what's going on?" James asked Matt.

"I don't mind," Matt said. "The remote is in there somewhere if you want to turn it up." He turned to Mikel. "So, Mikel, you were about to tell us where you've been."

"I've been a little everywhere."

The sound coming from the television increased in volume as James used the remote. "You guys need to see this!" he called to the others. Marcia, Matt, and Mikel got up from the table and joined him in the living room.

"What is it?" Mikel asked.

"Whoever blew up the pyramids is now destroying archeological dig sites." James pulled his phone out. "I don't understand how or why this could be happening. It has to be a radical group."

"What kind of radicals care about abandoned places?" Matt asked.

"Where are the dig sites?" Mikel asked.

"This can't be right," James said as he scrolled the online report on his phone. "It says here that all the Mayan ruins were turned to dust ten minutes ago. This has to be a very well-funded group of terrorists."

"Oh, my God!" Marcia gasped as she watched the replay of the video on the news. "I hope no one got hurt."

"It doesn't say anything on here," James said. "According to this, no one has been able to get close enough to see the damage or check for victims."

"They just said this is the start of a holy war, and they think these are suicide bombers," Matt said, staring at the television.

Mikel sat beside Marcia. "There have been a lot of earthquakes, too. And most of the pyramids and Mayan ruins are near"—he paused and concentrated on his ex-wife's face—"fault lines."

There was a knock at the door.

Matt looked at his wife. "Did you call Rebecca and tell her tonight wasn't going to work?"

"Yes, right after I tried calling my parents. But obviously people don't require an invitation to show up."

As Matt walked away, he glanced over his shoulder and saw Mikel quietly saying something to Marcia. He clenched his jaw but continued toward the side door, where someone was persistently knocking.

"Hold on! I'm coming," Matt called out before opening the door.

Ben stood there wearing a dark grey vintage Italian suit, black shirt, and narrow tie. The yellow porch light caught the tips of his blonde highlights and amber eyes. "Good evening Mr. Zen," Ben said.

Matt grinned and put out his hand. "Hey there, doc. I'm glad to finally see a friendly face."

They shook hands, and then Ben motioned toward the cars. "Is this a bad time? I can come back. I did notice Mr. Mitchell's vehicle and thought it would be OK to stop in."

"Depends. Are you here to take something or deliver upsetting news?"

"Is that what Mr. Mitchell is doing?"

"Never mind. Come on in, you can meet Alexis's father as well."

Ben stared at Matt as he stepped inside. "I thought her father was dead."

"Everyone did," Matt answered. "I'm still not sure how I feel about it."

Ben followed Matt down the short hallway past the dining area to the living room. James and Marcia Zen sat in silence watching the news. Marcia looked up and saw Ben, who smiled at her. Marcia got up from the couch and wrapped her arms around Ben. "I'm so glad you finally stopped by. Alexis …" She began to sob. "I know you were helping her through a lot."

"I'm sorry to show up unannounced," Ben said as they embraced.

"It's fine, really." Marcia wiped her eyes. "Can you sit for a while?"

"Where's Mikel?" Matt asked.

"He went out back," Marcia replied. "Said he needed to call someone."

Matt went to the sliding doors and peered out at the acre of fenced-in backyard. He opened the door and stepped out.

James was staring at the newcomer. "What are you doing here, Ben?"

"I thought it was time to come by and see Alexis's family," Ben said. "Why are you here? And how long have you known about Alexis's father?"

Before James could answer, Matt came back inside. "Marcia, he's not out there! What a jerk!"

James began to reach into his pocket. "Is my car still here?"

"Yes, I saw that German piece of crap from the back porch," Matt said.

"Then he's probably on the phone in my car," James suggested.

Ben joined Matt in the dining room and looked out at the backyard.

Matt turned to his wife. "Marcia, what did he tell you right before I went to answer the door?"

"Nothing really." She shrugged. "He just said it was great to hear I was considering a trip to England. Then he said he would be right back, same thing he said almost twenty years ago."

"I don't see how he could get past any of us." Unlike the others, Ben could see that the area was surrounded by dark figures, including Cezar.

"I think he should've stayed away," Matt said. "His visit was pointless. He should have come back when Alexis was still around."

Marcia shot Matt a harsh look.

"Sorry, babe, I meant when she was still here in the States."

Ben looked at James, who was typing something on his phone. "Mr. Mitchell. Why did you bring Mikel here in the first place?"

"He told me he needed to speak with Alexis's parents," James said.

Ben moved closer and waited. After a few seconds, James tilted his head toward Ben.

"How did you know him in the first place?" Matt asked from across the room. "You don't just taxi strangers around."

"It would seem Mr. Mitchell works for him," Ben said as he stared into James's eyes.

"Do you?" Marcia asked.

James swallowed. "Yes, but I didn't know he was Alexis's father."

"How long?" Marcia asked in a loud voice.

"I swear I didn't know he was Alexis's father. I'm as shocked about all this as you," James insisted.

"I asked how long?" Marcia said

James put his phone down and turned to the Zens. "A little over two years."

"The same time Alexis started at the base," Ben stated.

"I thought she didn't get promoted to your section until nine months ago?" Matt asked James.

"That's correct. I didn't meet her until June."

"You may not have formally met Alexis till then, Mr. Mitchell, but you were well aware of her," Ben said. "In fact, you live directly across the street from her apartment, am I correct?"

Matthew Zen crossed his arms. "Is this true?"

James looked at Ben. "How did you know that?"

Ben met James's stare but said nothing.

"Is what he said true, Mr. Mitchell?" Matt repeated.

"It's not what you think. I was told to keep an eye on her, that's all. I bought that building a month after she moved above the antique store to make sure ..."

"Did Mikel say why he wanted you to watch her?" Marcia demanded.

"He wasn't the one who told me to keep an eye on her. The only thing Mr. Bekhor ... I mean Mikel ... had me doing was research on certain artifacts. Alexis's work eventually became a part of the same research. As a matter of fact, he told me to steer clear of anything more than a professional relationship."

"Then who had you watching my daughter?" Marcia asked.

"The base commander, Colonel Logan," James answered.

Matt and Marcia looked at each other.

"Didn't Mikel just call the colonel?" Matt asked.

"Yeah, he said he was flying somewhere," Marcia said.

"Mrs. Zen, I was your daughter's friend. I'd never do anything ..."

"I think you should leave," Matt said, glaring at James. "You do nothing but cause heartache when you come here."

James stood up. "I'll leave. But understand I would never harm your daughter. I want her back, too."

"Just leave, Mr. Mitchell."

"I'll walk him out," Ben said.

CHAPTER TWENTY-SEVEN

BEN KEPT PACE WITH James as he made his way outside into the icy air. The only light came from the flickering yellow porch light, and it masked the uniformed ranks of dark entities surrounding the house that were moving in closer. As James stepped off the porch onto the gravel driveway, a sudden gust of wind rose up, pushing him backwards.

"Mind your step, Mr. Mitchell," Ben said. He was unaffected by the cold or the intense wind.

"What's your problem?" James said.

"I don't like being caught off guard, and trust me when I say it doesn't happen too often," Ben replied. "And you've never sat right with me."

"I've done nothing to you."

"James, I have a question for you. One that you failed to answer the first time we met in my office."

"What's that?"

Ben put his hands into his pants pockets and took a casual step forward. "Where is your family?"

"Why do care about my family?"

Ben stepped up close to James. "I'm trying to put together the pieces of how Alexis's father and the colonel both can control you separately."

"I told you then that I don't have any family, or least any blood relatives." James reached into his pocket and pulled out brown leather driving gloves. "I was orphaned at birth, and the colonel helped raise me, but I never called him Dad, if that's what you're wondering."

"I knew that much from doing a background check on you." Ben looked to his left, where Cezar stood in the shadows. "I'd like to know how Colonel Logan and Mikel know each other so well. Why would they both have you so close to Alexis without knowing each other?"

"What would that have to do with my family?" James asked.

"I'm eliminating all possibilities."

"Today was the first time I found out the two of them knew each other. Of course, some of it makes more sense now. But they each have separate agendas."

"And what would those agendas be?"

"Colonel Logan has been on a mission to find and open a portal ever since I can remember. He has wanted proof that there is a portal system between worlds. That's why he was so tuned in to Alexis when she was younger. Her amateur theory was beyond most made by people with advanced degrees, and that's why she was handed a blank check to go to whatever school she wanted, to fund whatever side project she wanted, or even to build the perfect lab for her own use. Just as long as she stayed at Wright-Patterson. That's also why he made me her supervisor, to make sure she was content and ..."

"Make sure she was finishing his little project."

"Yeah. He believed she was on the brink of creating an atmospheric device that could detect when alien ships came into range of our thermosphere and control where they could enter. He wanted to take control of one, and, I assume, access their portal system."

"Alexis didn't know about this, or she would have mentioned it in our sessions."

"You're right. She was only told that the device she was building was to protect the Space Station from meteorites or any other harmful debris. But since the incident that caused her disappearance, he's determined to find the ship we saw in Japan."

"Why do you think that is?"

James shrugged. “I have no clue. I’ve always chalked his random actions up to an obsession with aliens.”

“I’d say he has more than an obsession.” Ben stepped closer to James. “And Mikel’s agenda is what?”

“Finding a certain crystal, which happens to be the same one that showed up in Alexis’s lab, and the same one from Belize.”

“Why didn’t you take it?”

“At the time, I couldn’t understand why he wanted me to keep my distance from the crystal, because I could have taken it at any point, but now it makes sense.” James took the car key fob out of his pocket and hit the button to unlock the doors.

“Explain how it makes sense.”

“Because he’s her father.” James shook his head and then looked at Ben.

“That obviously has meant nothing to him all these years, so why pause when the one thing he is after is right in front of him?”

“At first he was looking into the myth of the twelve crystals, and then the one Alexis possessed, but now he says there is another one like what she had with her.”

Ben frowned. “How does Mikel know about the other one? Does the colonel know about it?”

“I don’t know, but neither Mikel nor the Colonel have any interest in finding Alexis or the portal she went through.”

Ben appeared intrigued as James shared his thoughts. All while his Watchers closed in around them. To James, it would only look as if the lights were dimming or the night was growing darker.

“Mikel insisted we solve the journal first, and Colonel Logan said he has a team working on the Belize data. He made it sound like it wasn’t that big a deal. I’d never guess they knew each other.” James opened the driver’s door. “Don’t get me wrong, finding the Garden of Eden or a hidden system of portals would be an amazing discovery, but I’d rather find Alexis.”

“Where are you flying to?”

"I'm supposed to be taking data from the pyramid sites, but now with all of them gone, I'm not sure where to start." James put his hands in his pockets and looked down at the steering wheel. "Alexis would have loved solving this mystery."

"Don't talk about her as if you know her," Ben snapped.

"I did know her," James shot back. "Maybe not intimately, like you, but I knew her well enough to know her interests."

"It's time you leave," Ben said. He was now nearly nose to nose with James.

"Seriously, what's your problem? You know I didn't mean anything by ..."

Before he could finish, Ben threw James ten feet across the driveway. "You never know when to shut up. And this family doesn't want you here. I don't want you here."

James picked himself up off the ground and wiped the wet gravel from his coat. "What did I ever do to you?"

"You should have let go. The portal would have closed, and Alexis would still be here."

James staggered to the rear of his car. "How was I to know she would try and save me?"

"Because she cared for you." Ben let out a small laugh, but his eyes held no humor. "But now Alexis is trapped inside a realm that is bound by a power I can't manipulate—at least not yet."

"What are you talking about? What power? Who exactly do you think you are?"

In a blink, Ben snatched James, lifting his feet off the ground. The dark beings watched as James tried to pull Ben's hands away from his throat.

"Master, let me take him," one being offered.

James's eyes widened as he saw the men surrounding him appear and begin showing themselves behind Ben.

"Who ... are ... you?" James struggled to get out.

Cezar came up next to Ben. "Master?"

Ben pulled James to his face. His eyes had flames of red circling the blackness. His tone was low and growling. "You won't be the first I make suffer, but you will be one of the few to remember your pain after death." Ben threw him into the side of his car leaving a small dent.

"Shall I take care of this for you?" Cezar asked.

"No, just take him away from here. I'll deal with him right after I'm finished with the Zens."

"What about his car?"

"Leave it. Someone needs to be responsible for what's about to happen here."

Ben walked back onto the porch and turned to look at James, who was coughing and trying get to his car. Right as Ben was opening the door to go inside, Cezar stood between James and his car. He knelt down and grabbed James by the shoulder.

"What are you going to do to me?" James asked Cezar.

Cezar smirked as the rest of the Watchers moved in, reaching out their arms. "We're going to make you disappear."

The moment Ben closed the door, Cezar and the Watchers disappeared with James.

CHAPTER TWENTY-EIGHT

DETECTIVES CARTER AND Lindsay had escorted the two visiting agents across the hall. A rectangular plaque marked Informational Technology Department was on the wall next to the door, and below it was a gleaming keypad.

"After whoever it was that confiscated our evidence, we had these installed to warn our techs before someone enters," Carter said before swiping his badge and entering a four-digit personal code.

When they entered the room, Eric Cruze was sitting at one of the three computer screens.

"Hey, Eric," Lindsay said as they entered.

Eric turned toward them. "What's up, guys?"

"We need everything from the Ice Man case," Carter said.

Eric swiveled around in his chair and noticed the two agents standing just inside the doorway. Eric shot them a quick glance. "You guys realize they took everything."

"It wasn't them," Carter said. "They're here because there are more bodies, and they need to see what we came up with on our end."

Eric frowned. "More bodies?"

"Over six hundred," Agent Eldridge said as he and Agent Dristian stepped into the room.

"Eric, let me introduce you to Agent Eldridge, with the CIA, and Agent Dristian, with Mossad," Carter said. "They need everything we saved from the Ice Man case."

Eric got up and went to the far corner of the room, where a narrow modular unit with shelving and drawers stood. Three ceramic coffee mugs were on the top shelf, and he took one down and plucked out a small, sealed plastic bag. He opened the bag and pulled out a flash drive.

"Everything is on there," Eric said, holding the flash drive out for Agent Eldridge. "It's the only one I have."

"We don't want to take it," Dristian said. "We want to compare it to what we found."

"Here?" Eric asked. "Now?"

"Yes," Eldridge replied. "And we need this kept completely confidential. We want to find the persons responsible without government red tape and without inciting widespread panic or another Internet catastrophe. And we need you to help us."

Eric stared at him. "Me?"

"Yes," Eldridge said. "We know you've created several facial recognition programs that surpass what we have available."

Eric nodded.

Agent Eldridge pulled out an inch-square device and handed it to Eric. "We only require that you share everything with us."

Eric took the device and stared at it, then looked up at Eldridge. "A Predator. I knew the government used these."

"I thought a Predator was an attack drone," Carter said, peering over Eric's shoulder.

"Or an alien with dreadlocks," Lindsay murmured.

"This Predator steals information without being detected," Eric said. "Watch."

Eric pulled the small square device apart, separating it into two halves. One had a clear plastic piece attached to the middle. He placed the clear insert into a USB outlet on his computer. Seconds later, he removed it and plugged the flash drive into the same USB port. "Their drive is wireless and requires only three seconds to access and piggyback a system permanently," Eric explained. "It will copy everything I have on this computer to its own cloud memory. And it's completely undetectable."

"Very cloak-and-dagger," Carter said.

"I'm syncing their info with ours, so I can go in later and isolate images to run facial scans," Eric said. He typed in several codes, and the screen brought up an access password window. Eric leaned out of the way to give Agent Eldridge access to the keyboard. Eldridge typed in a twenty-four-character password.

"Thank you," Eric said, and then he uploaded the CIA data.

Instantly, seven files popped up on the screen labeled with different locations. Eric clicked the one titled *Camp X-ray, Guantanamo*.

"Fast forward a little," Eldridge said. "There. Start it right there."

The thirty-inch monitor played grainy nighttime security footage showing prisoners screaming in the dark. Eric turned up the volume, and they heard the screams. Suddenly, the terrorized inmates began falling stiff to the ground. Eric replayed the last few minutes before the last prisoner died.

"This is unbelievable," Lindsay said. "This is almost identical to ours."

"Almost?" Agent Eldridge asked.

"Yeah, our guy was ranting like a crazy man, as if someone was with him right before he was taken," Lindsay said. "But these guys look like they're being tortured and then collapsing in place."

"Your guy was taken?" Dristian inquired.

"I'll show you," Eric said.

A few clicks later, a video screen appeared on the monitor. The screen showed the two security feeds from the night of George Pliate's death, one from an alley on one end of Fairfield, and the other behind the furniture store in the alley near Alexis's apartment. Eric pointed out the time codes, which indicated that Pliate's frozen body appeared behind the furniture store only seconds after he was seen in the first alley, miles away.

Agent Eldridge let out a breath. "Click 1391, please."

Eric clicked the file marked *1391, Location Classified*. A dark screen appeared showing several faint outlines of inmates in the corners of their unlit cells.

"Fast forward ten minutes," Agent Dristian said.

As the security footage scanned, it suddenly divided into four different areas of the prison. The top two quarters of the screen changed every thirty seconds, showing the recording of the interior hallways and holding cells.

"Stop," Dristian said. He pointed to the bottom left screen. "Watch this one closely."

"Are those guards or prisoners?" Lindsay asked as he watched around a dozen dark figures walking toward the stone edifice.

"Not possible. There is no way someone could get on site undetected," Dristian said seconds before the screen went blank.

"What happened?" Carter asked.

"I don't know," Eric said. He checked all the wires connected to the computer and then started typing codes and trying different buttons. "I'm trying to reboot the system."

"If no one can get there undetected, then how do you explain those men?" Detective Carter asked Agent Dristian.

"That's where you come in," Eldridge answered. He pulled his phone from inside his suit coat pocket and typed in something. "Who did you say took the files last time?" he asked.

"The chief said they were with the CIA," Carter replied. "One was named Cudder or something like that. I never saw a badge though."

"Did you have any leads or suspects that someone would want to cover up?" Eldridge asked.

Carter looked at his partner. "Yeah, Alexis Zen, a physicist over at Wright Patterson . But she died almost seven months ago."

"At least that's what the military is saying," Lindsay added.

"Zen." Eldridge started scrolling through his smart phone. "I've heard that name before."

"We hoped your investigation would help solve who or what is on that screen," Dristian explained.

"Ah, Alexis Zen," Eldridge said, staring at the screen on his phone. "In high school she won a scholarship from the federal government for her lunar-powered computer project."

"You remembered her name from a high-school project?" Lindsay asked.

"I was one of the panelists who reviewed project ideas," Eldridge replied. He showed the others a picture of a teenage Alexis and nine other high school students. "Needless to say, the projects where never built, but the ideas and plans were reviewed for the scholarship. I remember that her reasoning was to create a power source not reliant on ..."

Eldridge stopped talking as the floor vibrated below him. The five men stared blankly at each other. A moment later, the building shook, and people began shouting.

"Earthquake!" someone yelled from outside the room.

People streamed into the halls from rooms and offices, jostling one another as they headed for stairwells. The chief appeared from his office. "Stay inside," he called out. "Find an interior wall without a window."

Lindsay, Carter, Eric, and the two agents took cover under the three desks. A moment later, Eric crawled out and reached for his computer.

"What are you doing?" Carter barked.

The lights went out. Emergency lights flicked on, and alarms sounded.

Eric crawled back toward a desk, a flash drive in his hand. "I don't want to lose this."

The building shook violently, and computer monitors, keyboards, and towers crashed to the floor.

"Get back under here, you idiot," Carter commanded.

Eric scurried under the table as the coffee machine crashed to the floor.

CHAPTER TWENTY-NINE

WHISPERED SONGS SWEPT across the Realm of Light as Alexis lay peaceful in the tall grass of an open field. She slowly opened her eyes while taking in the sweet smell of clover and found that she was once again surrounded by people clothed in white.

"We've got to stop meeting like this," she said.

"Yes, we do." The soprano voice of a female Messenger called Giah came from behind Alexis. "You're lucky that this time your entry was aided by a guide. Made for a softer landing."

"The angel," Alexis whispered. "There was an angel with me."

"Yes, it was an angel that brought you back here. You were wrapped within his wings before he set you here to rest."

Alexis sat up, gazing at those who were standing nearest. Michael and Aharon were kneeling down in front, while Dathan stood behind Giah, staring at Alexis. She looked around. When she first entered this world more than six months ago, only a few were on hand to welcome her; today there were so many clothed in white that her eyes hurt gazing at them all.

"How do you feel?" Michael asked.

Alexis shrugged. "I feel great."

Aharon offered his hand. Alexis took it and started to pull herself up. She noticed everyone watching closely. Alexis rarely felt self-conscious, but this time the staring made her uncomfortable. When a cool breeze brushed across her bare shoulders, she looked down and saw that she was wearing a dress in place of her yoga pants and T-shirt.

"Who changed my clothes?" she asked.

A grey satin-like fabric fell from her neck and down across her chest. The dress fit close to her body until it reached her waist, where it swayed in the wind. Alexis slid her hands down the sides where there was a break in the flowing fabric. She slipped her hand into the pocket and took hold of the crystal inside.

"Do you remember what happened?" Aharon asked.

Alexis glanced up as she took her hand out of the pocket, leaving the crystal inside. "I … I remember walking through a portal. And …"

"And what?" Dathan asked.

She took another glance at those around her. The Messengers appeared the same, but something was amiss. Behind Alexis and beyond the white-clad Messengers a blood-red horizon was making its way across the sky.

"I was shown the worlds between mine and yours," Alexis said. "Why is the sky red again?"

"It's not important at the moment," Aharon asserted. "We first want to make sure everything is satisfactory with you."

"I said I was fine."

"What did you see?" Dathan asked. "Do you know where you were? Who was it that took you?"

Michael stepped into Alexis's line of sight. "Let's start with who came through to see you?"

"He said his name was Uriel."

Murmuring rose up from the white-clad throng. "Uriel?" someone said. "If he's here, who is watching the gate?"

Michael looked at Aharon and Dathan, uncertainty clouding his eyes. "The season is imminent for us to prepare."

"Season to prepare for what?" Alexis asked.

Michael wrapped his arm around Alexis and started to move her away from the crowd. "This way," he said softly. She turned her head back and watched the Messengers of the Light fade into the background.

"The time is at hand when the walls between us and the Darkness will become too thin, leaving the Earth caught in the cauldron of a war that has long awaited this universe," Michael said, his voice calm. "It will be a season for many changes on all sides."

"I have desired change since I came," Alexis said. "But not at the cost of war."

"Yes, but that time for you and everyone else has come. With the visit of Uriel and the walls between worlds thinning, it is the hour for you to go back."

Alexis shook her head. "If I hadn't experienced so many things, I'd say that this all sounds too much like my forced years in church with a side dish of Oz, and I'm not sure I see the point."

"The purpose, or point as you say, is not ours to hold in judgment."

Alexis pulled away. "That's my point. You've anticipated a war between the two sides, between good and evil. But I wonder why you think it makes sense to have a war. It sounds as if you want it more than you want to prevent it."

"It's the only way we can destroy the Darkness that besets the Earth. The outcome affects the humans from your world."

"You're making my argument easier." She pulled her golden hair to one side and swept her bangs away from her brow. "You have waited this whole time for the Darkness to make the first move just so you can eliminate them from Earth. If you have known since the beginning that a war was inevitable, why allow the Darkness to be on Earth in the first place? Why subject us humans to its evil energy?"

"Darkness has existed for a time on every planet that is or has been. Your Earth was the first of its kind to hold it captive." Michael started to walk away. "And humans don't have to be submissive to the suggestions of the Dark."

"Wait. How could Earth hold evil captive? Is it because Eve ate the fruit here and nowhere else?"

"In part, but who told you of this?"

"Aharon spoke briefly of it," Alexis said. "I'd like to know the rest."

"The laws and order of creation were first broken when Eve ate the fruit, but it was foreseen by the other Intelligences."

Michael and Alexis came to a natural rock bridge covered with clematis. They heard the sound of babbling water streaming under the bridge as they crossed over to a smooth dirt path.

"Regardless of my upbringing in church, my brain seeks tangible truth, and I can't calculate the idea of predestination," Alexis said. "Too many moving parts in the world. Don't get me wrong, I believe in a higher power. As I said, I have experienced enough that it would be crazy not to accept it."

Michael smiled. "There is a difference between the perception of what you were told growing up and the reality of what will happen. But know that everything is a product of choices, and we all choose our own destiny. Some choices affect generations until the very end."

"Obviously."

Michael looked away for a moment. "Aside from the choices of Eve, we should discuss the changes in you and how you have ..."

"How I have what?" Alexis interrupted. "I haven't changed."

He looked at her grey dress. "To begin, you haven't selected where you'll stand."

Alexis frowned. "Regardless of my weak faith in predestination, I'd never be a part of anything evil."

"You probably do feel that inside because your understanding of our existence is more clear, but your garments cannot lie. Faith standing in the middle can sway any of us to either side. That's why we wear white, while evil is clothed in the shadows of black."

She touched the satiny material that hung from her body. "Thermotropic fabric?"

Michael grinned. "Somewhat, but unlike the mood rings you're used to seeing, this only reflects what your mind and heart decide together. You must also agree to believe in what you want."

"Why is it grey right now? I believe what I see." She raised her arms, gesturing toward the trees behind her and then down to the ground foliage at her feet.

"Sight is not always a guarantee of faith," Michael stated. The grey shows the division between your heart and mind."

A strong gust of wind swept past, whistling near Alexis's ear. She walked past Michael and turned to the right, onto a separate path a few yards away.

Michael followed. "Where are you going?"

Alexis stopped and looked back at her attractive, youthful grandfather. "I know what I have to do next. I'm headed back to the cottage."

"We were already headed there."

"Uriel said that for me to figure out where I'm going, I must figure out where I started. I've realized that one answer to where I'm headed lies in the first thing Dathan showed me."

"Nothing we do is in vain," Michael assured her. "Uriel's guidance toward the cottage will surely show you the same, but I think he was referring to somewhere beyond the cottage."

"He never mentioned the cottage." Alexis turned away and continued into the thick forest.

"What exactly did he tell you that has directed your course back to the cottage?" Michael asked, keeping pace.

"It was more about what he showed me." She stopped again and looked at Michael. "The layers of realms between this world and my own are full of so much energy, living energy that is rapidly expanding and moving about my world—which explains the ghost-hunting fad of my generation."

"He took you through the realms? You passed through them?"

"Yes. Is that a problem?"

Michael blinked and looked at the distant horizon. The blood-red color was deepening, as if it were becoming more saturated, and it was rising higher above the trees and spreading out vertically. "We need to discuss your current state. If he took you through, then your garments are not the only things that need to change."

"Meaning?"

"You can obtain all the knowledge of this world and focus on your desire to leave, but you will die the moment you try to cross back." He took the lead toward the cottage. "There is a way you can survive, and that is why I was brought through after Dathan sought his question."

"Why are you only now sharing this information?"

Michael moved swiftly around the tall maple trees and down the hillside to the stream that ran in front of the cottage. As he approached the water, Alexis almost had to run to keep up. Then he stopped.

"We're here," he said, but his tone seemed unsure.

Alexis looked at the forest behind her. "That walk seemed to take longer than before."

"When you're distracted by questions, your thoughts will lead you off course, but when you focus, your mind can take you anywhere."

They crossed the stream running in front of the cottage and started up the short incline to the door. As Alexis reached for the handle, the wind picked up and a fierce gust blew past. She took in a deep breath and grabbed her chest.

"That was intense." She looked over her shoulder at Michael.

He was looking at the distant trees, where the sky was increasingly becoming smeared with darkness.

"We need not hasten any longer." Michael turned back to Alexis. "The atmosphere is changing more rapidly on your side."

"Michael, look," Alexis said, pointing at the stream. The water level was higher than before. "Michael, why not tell me this before? I'm talking about the way I can survive through the portal."

"I started to when we were near the beach, but someone came along and distracted me." He glanced up the hill to a loose stack of flat stones. "It doesn't matter."

Michael extended his right hand and lifted the stones from the ground. He levitated them across the stream of water.

"Why is the water so high?"

"Gravity is changing here." Michael positioned the stones in the stream to serve as stepping-stones. "We need to get to the cottage. It will take only a few days before the walls are too weak, if not gone altogether."

"If the walls are gone, then why can't I just walk through to my world?"

Michael gestured toward the stream and Alexis stepped onto the first stone. "You become more a part of this world with each passing second, but your body can't endure it much longer."

"So how do I survive?"

"You must forfeit mortality."

"I have to die? That sounds like a different plan."

They reached the other side of the stream and Michael stopped beside a large oak a hundred yards from the cottage. "You're not exactly dying," he said. "If you were to pass through the portal back into your world as you are right now, your body would freeze before the portal closed, and your spiritual body would be held within one of the realms Uriel took you through. And if you were to wait until the walls here were weak enough for you to cross through, your body would have enough energy to survive, but there is no way to know where you would end up. The Dark could claim your spirit before we could save you. To prevent that ..."

"My body needs to change."

"Yes. And that means your body must change permanently."

"How are you able to do that?"

"Because we are blood related, I'm one of the few who can take you through the marble wall inside the cottage."

CHAPTER THIRTY

MARCIA SAT NEXT TO Matt on the sofa, covering her face as she wept into his shoulder. Matt rested his cheek on her head while wrapping his arms around her, drawing her close.

"It's OK. I called your doctor and left a message," Matt said.

"Hopefully, he'll drug me, commit me, or knock me out. I just want to forget the past six months, because I don't know what to think anymore." She sniffed. "None of this makes sense."

"I know, babe," Matt said and gave her a hug.

Ben walked into the living room from dining area. "I made sure Mr. Mitchell understood his boundaries. He won't be coming back anytime soon."

"Good, because next time he was going to be met at the door with the end of my shotgun," Matt said.

Ben nodded. "Mrs. Zen, is there anything I can do to help you find peace of mind?"

"We called her physician," Matt said.

Marcia looked at Matt. "He did help Alexis overcome a lot in very little time. Maybe he has a quick remedy."

Matt nodded. "It's up to you."

Ben sat beside her on the couch. "Mrs. Zen, there are several things I can do to temporarily help you until you can see someone else."

"Please, it's Marcia." She looked into Ben's golden brown eyes. "Do what you have to do to help me forget."

"OK, but you must be willing to concentrate," Ben said. "In order to forget, one must first remember."

Marcia nodded.

"Thank you for this, and everything else tonight," Matt said.

"My pleasure," Ben said, and then he looked at Marcia. "Is there a comfortable place you would like to lie down while we talk?"

"My bed," she said as Matt gave her his hand and helped her stand. "The bedroom has a comfortable chair for you."

"That'll be just fine." Ben stood up and allowed Matt to lead the way.

Matt turned to Ben. "Are you sure you can take the time? We don't want to burden you."

"I'm sure. I'm only going to suggest something new to occupy her attention. She is the one who has to believe it."

Marcia sat down on the maroon duvet and then put her feet up as Matt situated the pillows behind her back. When he was finished, she lay back and closed her eyes.

"Marcia, I promise the memories that are painful will be brief and you will awake not focusing on the uncertainties," Ben said. He pulled the beige armchair up close to the right side of the bed.

"I'm just ready to find normal again." The dark circles beneath her eyes looked stark against the cream-colored pillow case.

Matt walked to the window and pulled the curtains closed. "Would it be OK if I sit in here with you?"

"If it makes her more comfortable," Ben replied. "But hypnosis is easier without distractions."

Marcia smiled. "Matt, I'll be fine."

"OK." Matt walked around the bed and kissed his wife on the forehead. "I'll be right outside the door."

Ben walked with Matt to the door. He touched Matt on the arm, releasing vibrations that instantly relaxed Matt's gaze. Ben's eyes were closed for a few seconds, but when he loosened his grip, Matt didn't notice Ben's eyes had become solid black.

"Mr. Zen, take this time to find your own rest."

Matt stepped out of the bedroom, closing the door and leaving his wife alone with the Devil.

CHAPTER THIRTY-ONE

THE EARTHQUAKE HAD torn across the states of the northeastern United States. Roadways had cracked, causing people to abandon their cars, and bridges had buckled, leaving people stranded in the cold night unable to cross toward safer roads. After thirty minutes, the vibrations had subsided, leaving a strange silence. One lone RV was teetering in the air on the broken road of Narrow Hills, two miles away from the Pennsylvania State Route.

"Baba, are you OK?" DziDzi called to the back of the RV from the driver's seat.

"I'm fine." The small white-haired woman pulled herself back up and grabbed a cushion that was starting to slip from under her. She looked through the bent blinds on her left. "But we need to get out of this before there are aftershocks."

The RV creaked as it teetered and swayed backwards.

"We're at least ten feet from the ground," DziDzi said as he glanced down at the broken road below the RV.

"Where is the cell phone?"

DziDzi looked around. "It's on the passenger seat. I think I can reach it."

He stretched his arm toward the cell phone, but it was just out of reach. He reached below his gut and released his seat belt.

"DziDzi!" Baba screamed.

It was too late. The RV lurched forward as his body released from his seat. His small frame had slipped out of the seat and fallen chest first onto the steering column. Baba grabbed the thin laminate table in front of her and braced her feet as the RV slid forward. The RV jolted when its back wheels caught.

Pots and dishes clanked and clattered inside the storage cabinets opposite Baba. She held onto the back of her seat as gravity pulled her downward.

"Are you OK?" Baba yelled up to her husband.

"Yes. And I think I can reach the cell phone now."

Baba could see the phone lying on the windshield. "Never mind, leave it. We'll find another way, you just stay put. Someone will see us and send help."

She looked back where the bedroom was and saw the luggage barely holding its position. The only thing keeping it from falling straight down through the RV onto her husband was the bathroom door that had flung open and got jammed with the bedroom door during the earthquake.

"DziDzi, sit still," Baba urged, but DziDzi was reaching for the phone again.

"I can almost reach it."

His left ring finger was touching the bottom of the phone. If he could get the phone over slightly to the left, he would be able to grab it. At that moment, a resounding vibration came from below. The asphalt that had buckled and thrust the RV ten feet into the air was rumbling.

"Brace yourself!" DziDzi yelled back to his wife.

Baba held tight to the bench and positioned her feet against the opposite bench. She peered out the window, watching the landscape wobble as the RV shook from side to side. The ground holding the RV in place gave way and tore apart beneath them. The vehicle tipped sideways, releasing the back tires. As it fell to the ground, the front windshield and the driver-side windows shattered on the pavement and slammed the console back into DziDzi. The RV now lay flat on its side.

"Are you OK?" Baba called out.

"I'm stuck." DziDzi sounded short of breath. "But I've got the cell phone."

"Dial 911 and tell them we're at the end of Narrow Hills and Rolling Rock Road."

Two lids on the jugs of water had broken off, and the water was pouring onto the wall where Baba lay. She looked at the food that had fallen out of the cabinets and the mess of dishes beside her face. Though the moon gave scant light, she could see through to the back window of the sleeping area, which had also broken out on the pavement.

"Hey, I see someone, a man," she shouted to her husband. "Probably from one of the nearby houses."

"Good, because the phone is dead."

"Can you help us?" Baba called out to the single set of shoes stopped at the back window.

The man crouched down and started to crawl inside.

"Is everyone OK?" the man asked.

"Yes, but my husband is stuck and we can't call 911." Baba was shivering in the small pool of water.

"I called for help twenty minutes ago. They'll be here soon," the man said kneeling down.

He started to make his way in through the bedroom and neared the doorway. He was wearing a thick coat that created a shadow over his face.

Baba adjusted her glasses on her face. "But we've only been stuck here for ten minutes."

The man had made it to where she was lying. "I know."

Their eyes met and Baba gasped. "Mikel?"

CHAPTER THIRTY-TWO

MARCIA SAT UP IN BED surrounded by darkness and heard the sound of a smoke alarm in the back of the house.

"Matt?"

There was no response.

She felt for her phone on the nightstand, but it wasn't there. She slid off the bed and made her way to the bedroom door. She tried the light switch on the wall, but nothing happened. The power was out, she didn't know where Matt was, and now a second smoke alarm was sounding from the kitchen.

"Matt!" she screamed.

Suddenly the alarms stopped. All that remained was a tingling echo in Marcia's ears as she opened the bedroom door.

The house was filled with rolling clouds of smoke and the distinct smell of wood burning. Through the smoke, she saw someone headed in her direction.

"Matt?" She fell to her knees and peered at the approaching figure, but everything was dark and every breath she took stank of smoke.

"Matt?" she said again as a bolt of bright orange burst into the living room near the kitchen wall.

Marcia stepped back and pushed the bedroom door shut. She crawled back toward the bed and grabbed the end of a sheet to cover her mouth. She heard flames crackling outside the room and felt the heat. On her hands and knees, Marcia made her way to the window next to her bed but she was barely able breathe. An intense orange light was starting to show under the door, and she saw smoke rolling in as well. If she went through the window, she'd have a twenty-foot drop to the concrete slab of the patio. She heard a male voice.

Open the window and jump.

"Matt?"

Jump, Marcia.

Marcia squinted, but the smoke had become too thick around her. She lay down on the floor next to the window by her bed, exhausted and weak, trying to find air. Marcia looked through the open space below her bed and watched the fire creep under the door—and then she saw someone walk into the room.

"Help me," she called out in a weak voice.

You should have jumped.

"Jump? Where?" Marcia tried to pull herself up to see the person talking.

Out the window.

The window exploded inward, and a shower of glass shards fell on Marcia's face and arms. The oxygen from the outside air drew the fire into the room. The flames licking under the door spread across the shaggy carpet.

Marcia.

She lay motionless.

The fire had climbed to the roof, and the ceiling was starting to cave in from the weight of the melted snow. Life was slipping away from Marcia, and each breath was harder to find.

I'll see you, Sarah …

Marcia, take my hand.

CHAPTER THIRTY-THREE

ON THE TORN ROADWAY off Pennsylvania State highway 32, Mrs. Prollofsky was wrapped in a wool blanket over her soaked clothing as she watched emergency responders hoisting her husband from the smashed RV.

"He's going to be all right." Mikel climbed up from the ditch near the RV and approached Baba. "They're waiting to pull him out. One of his legs got stuck, but he's free now."

Baba smiled and shook her head. "If you hadn't come along when you did, we probably wouldn't be so lucky."

"I'm sorry for everything. For leaving and not telling you why I left." Mikel wrapped his arms around her. "Some things are simpler without explanation."

"I'm thankful but it doesn't make sense," Baba said, adjusting the blanket around her shoulders. "You need to explain why you've come here."

Mikel stepped back and looked toward the east, where several hills were silhouetted in the distance, a quarter moon peeking over the top.

"Why are you headed to the Ringing Rocks?" Mikel asked.

"This isn't about me. You traveled over eight hours to find us, so you don't get to ask the questions."

Two paramedics were strapping DziDzi onto a board as a police officer assisted another paramedic with a gurney.

Mikel turned to her with one brow arched higher. "I came to get something that belongs to me—the diamond ring."

"What makes you so sure I have it with me? We came here to get away."

“I know exactly where you’re headed. I remember the stories of the mysterious Ringing Rocks, but why now?”

“To hide them. But I was a fool to think DziDzi and I would ever be able to carry them up there. I had hoped that Marcia and Matt would have came with us.”

Mikel looked back at the RV. “What were you planning to carry up there to hide?”

“My crystals,” Baba said.

“Why are you hiding your crystal collection? They’re just pieces of quartz, not even valuable.” Mikel’s eyes opened wide. “Wait a minute—how many crystals do you have exactly?”

“Minus the one Alexis took with her”—Baba looked around and then grinned—“all but one of them. Which is worthless without the rest.”

“You said those were hidden across the world and the Keepers were men,” Mikel said. “I heard you tell those stories.”

“Hush,” Baba whispered, and then she glanced at the RV. They were bringing DziDzi out from around the vehicle. “I married one of the Keepers.”

“The crystals from Eden were never to be together,” Mikel whispered. “Was everything you said a lie?”

“To hide them together has kept them safe all these years, but now things are changing, and evil has found my family.”

The fire department pushed the RV off to the side of the road, clearing a path for more emergency vehicles coming through.

“So the Rocks?” Mikel questioned.

Baba walked to the ambulance where the paramedics were loading her husband. “The pitches those rocks give off when they are hit are chaotic, and the crystal could easily be hidden within them. No one would be the wiser and the crystals would be able to activate their own frequencies.”

“Let me take them,” Mikel said. “I promise to protect and hide them.”

Baba shook her head. "I have a feeling your purpose here is not that of pure intent."

"True. I am trying to find Eden, and I have wanted those crystals for a very long time." Mikel pulled out a photo from inside his coat. "But I won't do anything to jeopardize her finding her way back."

He showed Baba a picture of him and Alexis when she was a baby. He was sitting in a rocking chair, smiling as he held Alexis in his arms.

Baba smiled. "You look surprisingly the same."

Mikel winked. "I knew there was more to all this than just kids' stories. But how long have you known about the diamond?"

"I didn't know it was the real thing until you showed up tonight. I had planned on hiding it with the others, waiting for a time when Alexis could have it," Baba said as Mikel assisted her into the ambulance. "Is it truly the companion of the *Poczatek*?"

Mikel handed Baba her purse. "The Immortalis and the Bereishit, or as you call it, the *Poczatek*, are almost identical in purpose, but like the marriage that forged their existence, they are totally different."

The ambulance driver turned on the lights just as one of the paramedics hopped into the back with Baba. The third paramedic began to shut the doors.

"You'll find what you're looking for hidden behind the passenger seat," Baba said. She leaned in to kiss Mikel's cheek and whispered, "But be mindful of those who are taking notice."

She sat up and turned away from Mikel and tended to her husband. When the paramedic closed the door, Mikel looked down at his hand. Baba had slipped a small card into it as she whispered into his ear. He turned the card over and read *Revelations 20.*

Mikel smiled as the ambulance made its way across the broken road. "Trust me, Baba, I want them watching."

CHAPTER THIRTY-FOUR

INSIDE THE COTTAGE, no air moved, no sound echoed. Though Michael and Alexis has just come in from the outside, they left no traces of dirt on the floor.

"So I was right about the walls becoming thin between the other realms," Alexis said.

"Yes, but it's more than that." Michael went over to the desk where she was waiting. "When planets begin to hold life, there are four main sources of energy that flow out from their Edens, but on Earth something changed the balance and only one of those remain intact."

"What happened to the others?"

"After the Garden of Eden was hidden from the humans, the other three sources were broken and released across the land so man couldn't find the garden. But somehow the people were led to the last remaining point, and they tried to build an idol structure over it to harness its godlike power."

"What do you mean *tried*?"

"They built the structure but were unable to use its power after being forced to abandon their temple."

"Who forced them out?"

"We did." He paused. "Though they left, they didn't stop building more temples and beacons of energy."

"Beacons? For energy? Who were they trying to signal, God?"

"At first they were, but then something else came instead, and they learned of life outside of this world."

Alexis frowned. "I don't see how this is a problem now—a lot of people believe in life on other planets. And how are those structures affecting the realms?"

"Because they're being destroyed. The potential of most of those structures has eluded modern man, but evil has always known about their energy, and they will soon realize how much power is held within the walls of certain places."

"Are we talking about pyramids, Stonehenge, or places like Gobekli Tepe?"

"If time were on our side, I'd explain further," he said. "But, yes, the pyramids were being targeted first for some unknown reason."

Alexis folded her arms and leaned back against the table. "My grandmother used to indulge me in her farfetched ideas about those types of places. That's probably what got me so interested in finding out the truth about those lost civilizations."

She smiled and remembered the soft voice of Baba telling her stories as a child, and how many farfetched stories were becoming too much of a reality.

"Alexis, did you hear me? I said evil is destroying those places on your side."

"So, did aliens teach them?"

He took her arm. "We need to get you out of here."

"Who is right about creation? Hindus, Catholics, or those nametag guys who ride bikes past my apartment?" Her eyes were glazed over and her skin drained of color.

Michael took her hand. "Alexis? You look unwell, and your hand is ice cold."

"Maybe I should sit down."

A white couch appeared in the corner of the room and Michael led her to it. She lay down and closed her eyes.

"I should take you away from here," Michael said.

"Not until you answer a few things. I have earned some answers, right?"

"The answers to your questions are not for me to reveal. And soon the Darkness will be able to control the elements, which will allow him to see through the veil of worlds. Then he will be able to control what gates he opens, and not only spiritual beings will be able to walk freely."

"Then what happens?"

"I told you. War between us and them."

Alexis shook her head slowly. "And the Messengers expect me to somehow stop war from happening."

Michael sat beside her on the couch. "No, the war will happen. You're here to end it so the Light can prevail and mend your side. I have faith in you, Alexis, but your state is weak, and I must take you through to my world."

"How exactly do you expect me to stop a power you can't control?"

He shrugged. "I have not been shown the how. That's why I know it's time for me to take you past this world through that wall."

"To Kolcep?"

"That's right," Michael said, looking pleased. "Uriel told you of this place?"

Alexis sat up and walked over to the solid white marble wall. She pressed her hand onto the cool hard stone. Light from the chandelier in the center of the room sparked tiny prisms within the specks of marble inlay, but the reflection cast light across the simple white room. She closed her eyes, took in a long breath of air, and then exhaled.

"OK, but before I go with you, I need to solve one mystery of my own."

"What would that be?"

"Where it all began." She opened her eyes and extended her hand up against the marble wall.

Michael joined her at the wall. "Your brilliance has impressed even my own thoughts, but to know the birthplace of life is ..."

"Is selfish, I know."

"No, it's beyond human gratitude."

"I may not be able to appreciate it, but I'm sure as heck going to try and find it." She pushed her hand off the marble where she had witnessed the Scroll of Realms float through when she was alone with Aharon. "Are you able to get me two maps from here?"

Michael looked uncertain but saw the determination in her eyes. "Which ones are you interested in?"

"I need the one that shows my Earth as it is today and the one that shows Pangaea." Alexis rested her hands on the table as her grandfather made his way to the wall. "I need to see what the land looked like in the beginning, before Eden was hidden."

Michael moved his hand across the marble and brought forth two large scrolls from the wall. They floated to the table where Alexis waited. At that moment, Aharon and Dathan entered the room.

"Is there something I can use to write on these?"

The three men frowned.

"Why would you want to mark them?" Dathan asked.

"Because of something I didn't recognize when I first looked at these, but now I do—this is a map of Pangaea." Alexis started to spread out the two maps, but they seemed to flatten on their own. "You've got to understand that when I first arrived here, I wasn't sure if I was on a UFO surrounded by aliens. So I kind of thought maybe these were from different planets."

"And now?" Aharon asked.

She grinned. "I'm still not sure if you're aliens."

The men smiled at her witticism but quickly refocused on what she was doing.

"I must heed what Uriel told me," Alexis said as she went back and forth between the two maps. "To know where I'm going, I have to see where everything started."

"And the maps show you this?" Aharon asked.

Alexis looked at him and then at Dathan, who was barely out of the doorway. "Yes. But you knew that already. Why else have them out the first day I came here?"

Dathan walked over and stood next to Alexis. "Yes, the maps have always been the key. I just don't know how to unlock it for you."

"I explained this to you, Alexis," Aharon said. "We can see, but we are kept blinded to protect sacred things."

"How is it that you're not curious about these things?" Alexis asked.

"Have you ever been distracted by something that wasn't your set task?" Dathan asked.

"Yeah, but the task still gets done."

"Our purpose is to be the Light and keep as many as possible protected from the Darkness. If we lose focus for one moment ..."

"I get it, and I'm fine with that. Being self-reliant has become second nature to me, so I can figure this out." Alexis turned back to the maps, sometimes pointing to a location on the present-day map then searching the other map.

"These are sacred scrolls," Dathan said. "One cannot trifle with these for personal gain."

"It's fine," Aharon assured him. "Alexis knows what she's doing."

Michael pulled a clear rod from the inner lining of his white garment and held it toward Alexis. One end was sharpened like the point of a pencil. "Each touch on the page with this will leave a trail of light."

Alexis accepted it with a nod and a smile.

"These maps can also be manipulated like the one I showed you," Aharon said.

"Perfect," she replied.

The three Messengers watched intently as Alexis gazed back and forth between the two different terrains. Then she touched the map of present-day Earth with her finger. The image on the scroll moved. She took the clear rod and began to place several dots on the map. Each glowing dot was about an eighth of a centimeter and illuminated like a small white LED light. When she was finished, there were two distinct lines across the world, the same lines she had placed on the map in Belize. The first line started in Alaska, went through Western Canada into the United States, and then went south through Central America and the western part of South America. The second line picked up in Great Britain and went into Europe, touching the northeast tip of Africa where Egypt is located. The line continued through into southern Asia and down to Australia where it headed back up to end in Japan.

Aharon and Dathan walked closer and stood behind Alexis as she put a few more dots onto the map.

Alexis put down the pen and pulled the crystal from a pocket of her dress. "I've been trying to figure out a connection to everything separately. But they're all one and the same. And given what Michael just told me about the original energy points, this is definitely the connection."

Michael moved around the table. "Show me."

"The journal my grandmother gave me had the same language that's written here on the corner of this map." She pointed to the words inscribed on both maps. "It was the first entry in the journal, and it's the same characters on the first inscription of the crystal."

"The language of the gods," Aharon said quietly to her.

"The language of the gods is to be spoken only in the presence of the Highest Glory. We don't even speak it here," Dathan said, looking at Aharon. "And I still don't see the connection between this and the pyramids anymore. Those structures were originally built to replicate a communication system the humans had taken too far, but humans on Earth no longer recognize how they work."

"Yes, and my grandfather here confirmed my thoughts about this when he mentioned the pyramids being destroyed on my side of the world."

Alexis used the tips of her fingers to move the continents around on the map. She pulled Europe, Asia, and Africa into the Americas. "And I don't need you to tell me what it says or how the pyramids work," Alexis said, looking at Dathan, who was focused on the maps.

"Then what are you doing?" Dathan asked.

"Some puzzles are meant to be solved backwards." She remembered her cousin Amanda speaking those words to her in her dreams. "I just need to see where they are located in reference to everything else."

"Why are you moving the continents into one?" Michael asked as he lifted the edge of the other map. "You have that map of the beginning land mass right there."

"Because I needed to see where the lines are now and where they would have been in the beginning."

Dathan hovered over the map. "I see the lines, but how are the pyramids connected?"

"When I was on my side and struggling to make sense of things, I found a small connection between some unique events and the places where the journal and crystal directed me. Like now, I sorted those places by making dots on a map, which created two lines that didn't connect." She moved Australia up with a twist and then moved all the other islands of the Pacific and Atlantic Oceans into the large mass of connected land. "But when I put everything back to the beginning, they intersect each other."

Aharon, Michael, and Dathan looked at the map Alexis had reconfigured. It was a solid piece of land with brightly glowing dots forming a staggered X across it.

"And the pyramids and mound-type temples that you say have been destroyed all lie on these exact lines as well."

Dathan looked at Michael. "Is this possible? She has located the four rivers?"

Alexis was staring at the point of intersection. "I don't know about any rivers, but something is at the center of these four points. That's either Kansas or Missouri."

No one spoke. A moment later, three female Messengers entered through the cottage door. They looked at Dathan and then to Alexis with sad eyes.

Alexis looked at her grandfather. "What's going on?"

"Michael, you need to take her through to Kolcep," Dathan said.

Michael nodded. "Yes. I can feel it changing."

Alexis moved around the table. "Is something wrong?"

"Nothing that can't wait until you return," Michael said. "Come, let me take you beyond the threshold of your world to where the angels rest."

Alexis glanced back at the maps and then took Michael's hand. The wall still appeared solid, but when she placed her hand into his, the blood began to rush through her body and the wall appeared to come alive.

Michael gripped her hand tightly. *Breathe and let me guide you.*

Alexis could feel her body being surrounded by warmth as an energy pulled her inward. She closed her eyes and stepped forward and felt a strange sensation as her body was pulled through the wall.

Alexis, don't let go, Michael whispered.

CHAPTER THIRTY-FIVE

DAWN WAS APPROACHING as Mikel continued along a narrow path leading eastward to an opening of pale orange light. He heard the sound of low-flying helicopters behind him, on missions to rescue others who had been stranded after the earthquake. The sound was accompanied by the unsettled growling of the Earth below. Trees stood fearful as dark shadows moved through them, following closely, watching Mikel. He heard downed branches crack and split under heavy footsteps, but he didn't hesitate, for he had made it to the opening at the end of the path.

Surrounded by trees, he stepped into an eight-acre field filled with boulders of varying shapes and sizes. It appeared as if the boulders had been dropped from the sky. Mikel glanced around. Dawn was breaking over the canopy of trees and across the field, leaving hues of pink and orange on the rocks. The sounds of the helicopters and the rumbling of the earth faded away. Mikel stepped onto the rocks.

He heard another branch break, and this time his focus changed for a moment. He wasn't alone, but he kept leaping from rock to rock. With each skip to the next boulder, a mysterious metal ringing rose up, and he heard the rustle of wildlife scurrying away through the woods. In the background, dark shadows glided invisibly toward the center, where Mikel stood holding the wooden box he had recovered from the RV.

Off to the eastern side, Lilith stood behind the cover of the trees, watching Mikel.

"What is he holding?" she asked one of the dark beings beside her.

"There must be great force in what he carries, because the box is protected from our sight," the being responded. "He seems to be taking it somewhere."

"Can you state something more than the obvious, you idiot?" Lilith snapped. "How is the box protected? We can see through almost everything."

The dark figures were inches from Mikel. All of them were clothed in long cloaks, and their faces were covered with hoods.

"The markings inlaid on the side of the box are from the language spoken only by the gods," the being said, a hint of disgust in his voice. "Humans have tried to create these contraptions before, but were never successful."

"Maybe a human didn't create it," Lilith said. "This might be what we've needed to gain control."

"We can bring him to you and force him to open the box."

"No. Not yet." Lilith motioned with her hand, commanding the beings near Mikel to move away. "I want to wait until his daughter is with him."

"How do we know Alexis is coming back?"

"She can't stay there much longer as a mere mortal. And when the others find out who she really is, Benjamin will quickly fall from his reign, leaving me to rule the Darkness of Earth."

"Why not tell them now?"

"Not all of them trust me as you do." Lilith hid behind the smooth gray trunk of a silver maple. "And I want to see Benjamin's face when he loses everything he holds precious, including Alexis."

CHAPTER THIRTY-SIX

EIGHTY-SIX MILES from London, in southwest England, the noon sun was blocked by gray nimbostratus clouds. Below the incoming rain, on a hillside in a low valley, stood the circular monument Stonehenge.

Ben stared at one particular dolerite stone. It was marked with three similar crosses that appeared to be etched into the stone.

Cezar came up from behind, pulling James by the arm.

"Stonehenge?" James said, trying to pull away. "How exactly did I get here?"

"You can leave, Cezar, I have it under control," Ben said, touching the marking on the stone.

Cezar shoved James to the ground and then disappeared.

"Why are you doing this?" James asked, his voice muffled by the cold, wet ground. "Why haven't you killed me?"

Ben turned around and knelt down. "You ask too many questions. And you never have any useful answers."

"It's not my fault I didn't know what Mikel and the colonel are doing or how they're connected. I was fooled."

"Then tell me, is this the same mark that was on the crystal? The one you proclaimed to Alexis and me in Belize to have seen before."

James's face was dirty and his clothes tattered. He looked at the stone and then at Ben. "Why does it matter?"

Ben didn't reply but he stared at James through black eyes. James quickly got up to peer more closely at the image.

"This is it," James said. "I've always thought it represented three daggers or swords. I figure Druids etched it onto the stone."

"Those are not daggers," Ben said. He moved away and headed into the center of the monument.

"If you know so much, why are you asking me?"

"I've kept you alive twice against my better judgment. I can't promise I'll show restraint in the future."

James inhaled as he rubbed his neck. "If they're not daggers, what are they?"

"A mark made to tell the future." Ben brushed his hand over the marks, and the three images shot out an electrical charge. "Three crosses to mark the coming Light."

"What light?"

"This place was built to control unimaginable electrical energy, and the people of this world have no idea how to access it." Ben took a step back.

"And you do?"

Ben smiled. "This is something you should understand quite well, Mr. Mitchell. And I know Alexis would definitely appreciate what's going to happen."

"What's going to happen?"

"Let's call it the reverse effect of the humans' Faraday cage."

James frowned. "I don't understand."

"An ancient microwave, to put it into terms you can understand. This was built to harness and keep the electromagnetic energy inside, in order to protect what is hidden."

"I know what a Faraday cage is," James said. "But how would ancient cultures understand this?"

"Humans live within the idea of theories and laws. Yet they can't solve something this simple." Ben gestured toward the monument. "Why build an enclosure if you weren't trying to trap or deter something?"

"Who exactly are you?" James asked. "How do you know so much about this?"

"Let me show you."

Ben closed his eyes and stretched out his hands. Instantly, the thick clouds above erupted with howling winds and streaks of lightening. The bolts of pale yellow and white electrical charges encased each of the stones.

James quickly stepped into the center as the dark clouds twisted down and around all of the rectangular stones in the circle. The outermost clouds dropped from the sky and appeared as solid walls surrounding the entire perimeter of Stonehenge. The howling winds whistled through the openings of the stones in icy bursts. James stumbled when the ground began to shake. The flat stones that lay atop the seventeen upright ones were tottering on the edge of their five-thousand-year resting place.

"What are you doing?" James yelled as three stones behind him tumbled to the ground.

The wind increased, screaming through the open spaces of Stonehenge. James dropped behind one of the stones and watched Ben in the center of the circle guiding the elements, his arms straight up to the sky. Two bright blue bolts of light flashed, and then a small glowing orb began to materialize at eye level with Ben. Instantly, the cold intensified into a deep freeze.

The two bolts of lightning wrapped around the orb clockwise, causing the edges to expand. The center began opening and growing in height.

"Is that what I think it is?" James cried. "Is that what took Alexis?"

Ben shook his head. "No. This is much worse."

"Then what are you doing?"

The center opening of the orb was a dark shade of gray that continued to expand. It was filled with moving figures trying to reach their hands out, but something semi-solid blocked them.

"Why isn't this portal trying to vacuum you inside?" James asked over the whirling roar of the cloud tunnel that had formed around them.

Ben looked at James with black eyes."Because I control who goes in and out of this one."

"Out?" James whispered.

Ben lowered his arms. His eyelids were barely open. "I call unto the keepers of Sheol and Gehinnon to bring forth the slave who serves me."

The clouds stopped rotating, and the winds died. James swallowed hard, looking for an escape. He was terrified but curious at the same time.

A growl came from inside the portal. "I am the keeper of Gehinnon. Your request can only be granted to the one who placed the slave within our realm. You echo the Master of Darkness. Bear true witness for your token."

Ben pointed in the direction of two tall stones erected side by side and one that lay flat on the ground below them. The three stones, weighing over thirty tons each, rose from the ground and hovered in the air. Ben motioned as if to turn a page, and the rest of the freestanding stones rose from the soil. He clenched his fists, and the stones imploded. Dust and debris twisted into the outer wall of clouds surrounding the area. Silence fell.

James could only hear himself trying to breathe as his heart raced. The scene was a nightmare, and he didn't know his part in it. He needed to find a way to survive.

"Master, it is thee, forgive my doubt," the voice roared. "Your servant has been brought forth."

The mouth of the portal expanded outward. No longer were hands or figures in the dark center trying to free themselves. Instead, a solid figure of a man came to the opening. He stepped through onto the frozen ground. His hair was blond, and his stature rivaled Ben's.

"Welcome back," Ben said.

The man bowed to Ben and then looked up with eyes of black. "Thank you, Master."

"Azure, my deeds were not for your benefit but for my own," Ben said. "You've seen parts of these humans that I cannot."

Ben turned away and started toward James, who sat motionless on the ground. The portal behind him had vanished, leaving no traces of ice, and the clouds had dissipated, leaving only broken fragments of Stonehenge.

"I understand," Azure said. "I also see why you kept Chuave and the others from opening that portal." Azure surveyed the rubble. "They would have become trapped."

Ben stepped over a piece of broken stone. "That is not why I stopped them. And it was never to trap, it was only to hold temporarily the creatures of Darkness per my command. Chuave and the others who attempted to open that gate in the past didn't possess the authority, and I needed to make an example of them because of their disrespect."

"But inside ..." Azure started to say.

Ben grabbed James by the shirt. "Mr. Mitchell, we have somewhere we need to be."

"How is this even possible?" James muttered.

"I control everything within the dark realms, which is unlike the ones Alexis discovered." He pulled James forward across the broken stones.

James pulled his arm away from Ben's grasp."Where are we going?"

"There are things you need to see." Ben glanced at Azure. "Unless you prefer I kill you."

"Nope, I'm good," James said.

"Master," Azure said. "Inside there I saw ..."

"Why is this guy calling you Master?" James asked.

"Because all that is evil sustains him as such," Azure said.

James frowned. "What do you mean, all that is evil?" A moment later, his face went pale. "The Devil?"

Azure grinned.

"If you're truly the Devil, which explains a lot, why were you pretending to be a shrink? And why am I still a part of this?"

Ben stopped and turned to Azure. "Azure, what has you thirsting for my attention?"

"There is something I realized," Azure said. "About them."

"Unless you have access to the Messengers, we're all headed to Spain," Ben said.

"Spain? No, this is about—" Azure stopped and glanced at James.

"Don't make me regret bringing you back," Ben said. "I haven't time for questions or guessing games. If you have something of importance to share, then do so."

"No games, I give you my oath of loyalty to your purpose." Azure stepped next to Ben. "While in Sheol, I could see the human subconscious, and it appeared as warm energy. And our kind as ..."

"Yes, I'm quite aware of how it all works, Azure. We appear cold and without life running through us."

"Exactly." Azure turned to make sure James wasn't close enough to hear. "But when you approached Stonehenge, he presented as neither."

Ben glanced at James. "Yes, I know."

Azure looked at James. "What does that mean?"

"Soon this will all make perfect sense."

He put his hand on James's shoulder and the two, along with Azure, disappeared.

CHAPTER THIRTY-SEVEN

THE EMERGENCY ROOM of St. Luke's Hospital swarmed with doctors, nurses, and volunteers helping to evaluate the injuries resulting from the earthquake. Rooms overflowed with the most severely injured, and the hallways were filled with those who needed only a dressing or a tetanus shot. Dim fluorescent lighting illuminated their efforts, and a diesel generator powered the surgical areas and the equipment that maintained life support.

"I'm sure the doctor will be in soon," Baba murmured to herself as DziDzi lay snoring. "Good thing you can fall asleep anywhere."

She walked away from the gurney and peeked through the peach-colored wool curtain. With nowhere left to sit in the waiting area, the hallways had become tightly packed arenas of disarray.

"Teresa! We have another bus coming in!" a silver-haired nurse called out to another.

"We have no place to put them," the nurse named Teresa said as she looked around. "How bad are the injuries?"

Then the ground shook, banging metal filing cabinets against the walls and spilling papers onto the floor. The already dim lights started to flicker. A huge aftershock struck, jolting Baba to the floor.

"I'm so sorry," she said to a man with his arm in a sling, whom she had bumped.

"It's OK," he said, holding his arm.

Three men appeared and helped Baba and the man to their feet.

After a couple of minutes, the vibrating stopped, leaving the outside structure in shambles and the inside barely standing. Ceiling tiles had fallen on top of many who were waiting in the hallways, and several light fixtures had shattered, leaving exposed wires.

"Ma'am, are you OK?" the nurse named Teresa called out from behind the nurses' station.

"Yes, I'll be fine." Baba picked pieces of cracked drywall off her shoulders. "I just wish someone could look at my husband. He's been lying there for two hours."

Teresa smiled. "I'll see what I can do."

"Thank you, he was ..."

"Code red!" someone screamed from down the hall. "Pediatrics."

Teresa's face went pale. She looked at Baba as she rose to her feet. "Fire in pediatrics. We need to get those kids out of there."

"Go," Baba said. "I understand."

"The phones are out!" one of the front desk clerks shouted.

Those who were physically able to help made their way through the knotted mass of injured, trying to assist with the electrical fire in the pediatric wing. Baba moved out of the way and headed back into the ten by ten room where DziDzi lay. She sat down in the chair next to the litter and took his hand.

"You're like an ice cube, Ghetta." She looked around the space. "Let me find you a blanket."

She opened a portable cabinet that had hospital gowns and sheets. She pulled out a couple of sheets and unfolded them, layering them across her husband's body.

"Is that better?"

"Uh-huh." He briefly opened his eyes. "Can you take me home?"

"Someone will be in soon ... I hope." She sat back down in the chair next to him. "Then we can go home."

Baba sat with her eyes closed and her hands clasped. A tear slid down her face and onto her shirt. She leaned back and rested her head against the wall behind her chair. She closed her eyes.

She felt a tap on her shoulder.

"Mrs. Prollofsky?"

She opened her eyes and saw a young man in navy blue scrubs.

Baba sat up straight and wiped the corners of her dry mouth. "Yes, that's me."

"We're going to take your husband down for X-rays."

"OK." She got up from the chair so the technician could maneuver the gurney. "What about the fire?"

"They got it under control about an hour ago."

Baba looked at the dainty gold watch around her wrist. "I didn't realize I had slept so long. Are the children OK?"

"Yes. It was a small fire, so they were able to control it fast."

"That's good."

"It may be easier if you stay here," he said. "The halls are very crowded. And if there's another aftershock, this room will be safer for you."

Baba nodded her head the pressed a kiss onto DziDzi's forehead. "I will see you soon."

"I love you, Annelise," DziDzi murmured.

CHAPTER THIRTY-EIGHT

JAMES SAT MOTIONLESS along the shoreline of southern Spain. Eroded stone pillars spread for miles in three directions. James's face was pale and his clothing was soaking wet.

"Answer it," Ben commanded.

"Huh?"

"Your phone!"

James took the phone from his pocket and stared at the screen until it ceased ringing. A few seconds later it started ringing again. His hand shook as he unlocked it and then held it to his ear.

"Hello."

Colonel Logan was on the other end, his voice loud but anxious. "Mr. Mitchell, where have you been? You missed your flight."

James wiped his forehead. "It's kind of hard to explain."

"The earthquake has destroyed most of the East Coast," the colonel said. "I need you back at the base."

James stared blankly at an enormous land mass ten feet in front of him.

"Mr. Mitchell?"

"Yes, sir?"

"Did you hear what I just said?"

"Something about an earthquake."

"The earthquake that tore across the Midwest, leaving millions without power, you didn't feel it?" There was a second of silence. "I was worried you were stuck in one of the buildings that collapsed in Dayton."

"I'm OK." James looked up at Ben, who was standing on what appeared to be eroded stairs. "For now."

"Then get to the base. Something else is happening, and I feel it's connected to this earthquake and all the pyramids being destroyed."

"I have some theories of my own."

"I'd like to hear your thoughts on all this, but first we need to confirm some strange reports," the colonel said. "Calls have been coming in that monuments like Goseck and Stonehenge are now piles of dust. You need to be on the next flight off this base heading overseas!"

James cleared his throat and spoke under his breath. "I'm here already."

"On base?"

"No. I'm ..." He looked at the broken pieces of stone surrounding him on the sand and gazed at the slowly rising dawn. "I'm somewhere on the west coast of Spain."

"We don't have any flights scheduled for Spain until next Wednesday. Why would you go there?"

"I didn't have a choice."

"Are you in some kind of trouble?"

"I don't know. But I can confirm the destruction of Stonehenge. I suspect another mega structure will soon follow."

"What do you mean? What structure?"

"I'm staring at an ancient piece of architecture and a land mass that was conjured from the ocean floor." James exhaled. "But don't ask me to explain."

"We received the intel about Stonehenge ten minutes ago," the colonel said. "How could you be in Spain. Are you sure you're not still in England?"

"I'm sure."

"Then how ..."

"Ben Asael brought me."

"The shrink?"

"Yeah. I don't think he's really a shrink."

"What in blazes is going on? What do you know about Asael?"

Ben and Azure were several yards from where James sat. Though they appeared to be unconcerned with James, he knew they were capable of hearing his conversation.

"Actually, I think it's time you tell me what you know about him," James said.

"I'm in the dark here, Mr. Mitchell. I don't know him personally."

"The last thing I need right now is diversion!" James said. "First you bring me into the top-of-the-line secret laboratory built for a second-year researcher and tell me to learn everything about her. And when Alexis gets close to Asael, you have me bug his office. I'm a scientist, not a spy. I want to know what was so important about her, and spare me the atmospheric device scenario."

"Where is Dr. Asael now?"

"Staring at me."

The colonel let out a breath. "Let me speak with him."

James stood up and motioned with the phone toward Ben. Ben came down from the massive structure and took the phone. He turned away but was close enough for James to listen to both sides of the conversation.

"Evening, Colonel," Ben said.

"Spare the pleasantries, Dr. Asael. What do you want in return for the safety of James and the rest of the places you plan on blowing up."

"Colonel, you sound distressed."

"I am. Especially for Mr. Mitchell, I've been a part of his life since …"

"Since his mother left him with you."

"How could you know that?"

"Colonel, I've always known about your arrogant acts of volition. As for Mr. Mitchell's connection to them, I had put some of the pieces together, but I didn't put all the pieces together until tonight." Ben looked at James. "I applaud your ability to separate your true feelings. It's hard for humans to disguise those things from my men, let alone me."

"What are you going to do?" the colonel asked.

"What I've been waiting to do—I'm going break this world apart. Except this time my fuel is to get Alexis back." Ben handed the phone back to James.

"And how do you propose to do that?" the colonel was saying.

James looked bewildered as he took back the cell phone. "Sir, what was that about? You said you didn't know my mother."

"It was for your protection. She didn't want anyone to find you."

"Why?" James asked. "Who was she?"

Ben started walking toward the massive structure. "James, follow me."

James followed and the call began to break up. "I'll call you back, and I want answers."

"No, wait, I'm coming to you, James. James?" The phone went silent.

James followed Ben and Azure through the structure. There were streets throughout the ruined complex, and they followed one to a framed building in the center, six hundred yards ahead. Ben knelt and picked a flat cobblestone out of the mud. He rubbed the surface. The color was olive-brown, with dark yellow edges.

THE WOMAN IN THE room next to Baba's was screaming. Baba peeked through the curtains and saw that the halls remained cluttered with people injured from the earthquake. Between the cries of the woman, Baba could hear someone else talking.

"Focus on breathing through the contractions," a woman was saying. Another woman said, "It's not time to push."

Baba pulled her coat tight and clutched her purse, and then walked to the next room. A pregnant young woman, a child in Baba's eyes, lay on a hospital bed, writhing. A nurse was trying to help ease the pain with warm compresses. A woman who appeared to be the young woman's mother was wiping perspiration from her forehead.

"You're doing great."

The nurse was at the young girl's feet, helping to keep them in place. "Alice, I need you to push for me."

Memories of giving birth to eight babies flashed into Baba's mind. The pain of childbirth and the struggles of raising eight children didn't keep Baba from smiling.

"Mrs. Prollofsky?"

She turned back toward the room she came from and saw a doctor waiting by the curtain. "That's me."

"I'm Dr. Ballard." The doctor, who looked to be in his mid thirties, was of medium height and had a slightly receding hairline. He took off his glasses and gave Baba a smile as he walked to her.

"How's my husband?"

Though his smile was comforting, Baba saw the sadness in his eyes. "Let's find a place where we can speak more privately."

"This is private enough," she said. "Is everything OK with Ghetta?"

Dr. Ballard grabbed the chair from the room and placed it behind Baba. "At least have a seat."

She sat down with her purse in her lap. Her hands trembled as she brushed her hair away from her face.

"Mrs. Prollofsky, the techs noticed your husband was losing consciousness and that his extremities were ice cold," Dr. Ballard said. "Mr. Prollofsky has some internal bleeding from his spleen."

"He was fine when you took him for an X-ray," Baba said, wiping away a tear.

Dr. Ballard took some tissues from the cabinet and handed them to Baba. "I'm sorry, Mrs. Prollofsky. I know this is hard to take, but we can't be sure how long he has left." He looked out at the packed emergency room. "All the phone lines are down, but we have satellite phones for emergencies. I can get one for you to use for any family that you need to contact."

"I need to call my children."

The doctor nodded. "I'll get a phone. In the meantime, can I have someone get you a blanket or anything else?"

"No, I'd like to see my husband please."

"I'll be right back with the phone, and I'll find someone to take you," Dr. Ballard said before heading down the hall.

Baba looked down at her thin gold wedding band and small diamond engagement ring. Ghetta had saved two months earnings from working for the local butcher to buy that ring. He waited until New Year's Eve, sixty-three years ago, to ask her to be his love forever. They married two months later.

A faint cry rose up from across the hall. A baby had been born.

CHAPTER FORTY

"MR. MITCHELL, do you know what this place is?"

"No. How could I?" James's eyes had dark rings, and his lids were barely open.

"A city so grand that humans of today believe it could only be built for and by the gods." Ben tossed him a round, smooth stone he had picked up earlier.

James felt the stone's raised markings, saw an image of a triangle and a circle overlapping each other with a sword between the two shapes. "This is a coin," he said. He flipped the coin over and saw the outline of a man.

"Correct, Mr. Mitchell," Ben said. "But, more importantly, whose currency?"

Still gazing at the piece, James shook his head. "I'm not sure."

"This place at one time stood as a haven for an evolved people. It flashed an aerial marker mocking the gods who looked down on them after they were scattered from their loved ones."

James glanced around the structure. Intricately cut stones that were perfectly laid out gave evidence of a once-spectacular city. He looked at Ben. "Atlantis?"

Ben nodded. "The lost city taken by pride and greed. My men helped bring these people to an understanding that they deserved all that was precious and desirable on this Earth."

"What happened to them?"

Azure stepped out from behind one of the columns. "Like every other civilization that succumbs to prideful greed, they fought against each other for power."

"They couldn't agree on who to serve," Ben said.

"Why bring it to the surface now after it's lain on the ocean floor decaying?" James asked.

"When we were going over the journal in Belize, one entry read, 'The mouth of the rivers will lead them away. Each divided with wealth but all brought together by death. Stand inside the bluestone circle to open a hidden gate.'"

"I recall that one went along with Stonehenge, which you've destroyed."

"With good reason," Ben said. "That entry wasn't only referring to Stonehenge."

James nodded. "Kind of makes sense, especially if we thought one of the markings also referenced ..." James stopped in mid-sentence.

"Referenced what?" Ben asked as he stopped in front of a tall stone beam. Ben motioned for Azure to remove a layer of ocean vegetation to expose marks made on the beam.

James was feeling the rough surface of the gold piece with his thumb as he watched Azure finish cleaning the beam, revealing an image that resembled the three daggers on the Stonehenge stone and the inscription on the crystal. "It appears that the inscription points and the direction of your rampage share landmarks, or at least the ones we've translated."

Ben furrowed his brow. "The crystal had a marking for Atlantis? This city was one of the first to be built after the destruction of Babel. This being a point of interest on Eve's crystal is unlikely. And viewed from above, many areas are laid out like Atlantis."

"The marking on the crystal did look lot like an aerial Stonehenge, but it was Mikel who thought it might be Atlantis," James said.

"When this city flooded, the survivors went on to build smaller shrines, like Stonehenge, to worship and offer sacrifices to their new gods, who helped them discover truths not offered before."

James touched an eroded column that displayed the mark similar to the three daggers. "Babel caused them to build this?"

Ben nodded. "Humans have never stopped trying to become like gods or find a direct line to them. It's been told that Babel was built to reach the heavens, and that's not far from the truth."

"So why did they build Babel?"

Azure stepped away from the pillar. "Babel was created to isolate an unseeable force so strong that it sent a powerful signal across the universe to the gods, but other beings also found the signal. Those beings were far more advanced than the humans of Earth, and they understood this planet's importance. They traveled here and helped build Atlantis and many other places across the globe. Their purpose was to create beacons that held the energy fields in place."

"So you're saying the people of Babel were building a huge lighthouse for aliens?" James asked. "And aliens responded?"

"He's saying they were building a communication device to talk with God and someone else heard the conversation," Ben said.

"And what is your purpose in destroying it now? You've demolished the Mayan temples, the pyramids, and now Atlantis. I don't want to be in the rubble this time." James tossed the piece of gold to the ground. "I'll take my chances finding a way back."

When he turned around to leave, he was face to face with Azure.

"I haven't destroyed all the pyramids," Ben said. "There is still one site left."

James reviewed what he had heard over the past two days. He knew all the pyramids were gone and that Ben had to be responsible. "Which one?"

"Babel," Azure said.

James frowned. "Babel was a pyramid? I thought it was tall, a kind of ancient skyscraper."

"It was the first pyramid built on this planet," Azure said. "Why do you think so many unconnected cultures built pyramids across the globe? Imagine a construction site that can no longer communicate and everyone scatters."

James thought for a second. "Chaos."

"Only the language was chaos. As they left Babel and found new homes with those who spoke similarly, they built what they already knew—pyramids, mounds, and smaller advanced cities." Azure looked around. "With a little help, of course."

"I hate to admit it, but all of this has amazed me," James conceded.

"Trust me, you'll want to see what happens next," Ben said.

"Do I have a choice?"

"Yes, but you will die without me."

They approached the center of the city ruins. The ocean-saturated streets had once been paved with smooth rectangular brick-like stones.

"Why now? Why destroy Babel?"

"I'm not going to destroy it. Once this city is gone, the forces that have flowed through here and through each structure I've taken down will make their way to Babel. It will again be at full power."

"Then what?" James asked, trying to keep an eye on Ben. "Why not destroy Atlantis now?"

They came to a stop at the base of another set of stairs. The leftover bones of what had been a grand complex showed the importance of this once-flourishing city. Twenty perfectly aligned columns were still standing, rising fifty feet in the air. The area was rectangular with a small circular opening into a courtyard.

"Because I need something first," Ben said. He headed up the stairs with James and Azure close behind.

"More gold?" James had noticed that the streets were strewn with mud-covered coins, and the steps they were climbing also had piles of loose gold.

"Gold is of no use to me," Ben said. "But feel free to take what you like."

James kept walking. "Then what do you want?"

"The Pearl of Gates," Ben said as he entered the courtyard.

"You mean the pearly gates?"

Azure shoved James and pushed him up the stairs."He said the Pearl of Gates."

Ben headed to the center of the courtyard and then turned around as James and Azure entered the courtyard.

"You think this pearl thing is still here after all these years of Atlantis being submerged?" James asked.

Ben didn't respond.

James turned to Azure. "What is he looking at?"

The courtyard's perimeter had six columns encompassing the outer court. The ocean had eroded the columns, but on each one, midway down, there appeared different combinations of lines carved into the hard stone.

Þ Ж Ψ Χ Λ I

"Don't you recognize any of these, Mr. Mitchell?" Ben asked.

James studied the individual markings. "A couple look like Roman numerals or Greek letters."

"They're Atlantian numbers," Ben said.

"I'm not seeing the point."

Ben turned and pointed to the first symbol, a vertical line with an attached directional right curve. He began to explain each number counterclockwise. "The first symbol represents five hundred, the second is one hundred, then fifty, and on to ten."

"Then five and one. I see the pattern." James looked at Ben. "And they add up to ... no way."

Ben directed Azure to a symbol that was a vertical line with what looked like a U intersecting the line midway through. "What I seek is inside that one."

James stayed in the center of the courtyard while Ben and Azure walked to the column marked with the ancient character for fifty. Ben waved his hand over the symbol, and the center morphed into a gravity-defying liquid surface. Beads of water crawled in all directions away from the center of the column.

"What's the significance of that one?" James called out.

"The number seven has always belonged to the gods. The number six is associated with the rebellion of man, who was created on the sixth day," Azure said. "And when man sinned against his creator."

James gestured toward the columns. "That's why the numbers add up to 666. The mark of the beast."

Azure pointed to the column. "He's neither beast nor a man. Subtract the human factor of fifty and you get 616."

"Why is fifty the human factor?"

"Throughout history, it has represented power, celebration, and the deliverance of man into freedom," Azure said. "Something we don't offer."

James asked no more questions. He turned his attention to Ben, who put his hand through the center of the column and pulled out a translucent inch-square cube. He held it in the palm of his hand.

"Ice?" James asked. "I thought you came for a pearl."

"I did."

Ben walked over to James, holding the cube between his thumb and middle finger. Inside it was a gumball-sized opalescent pearl. "It's not ice. This is a crystal."

"So that's a pearl inside a crystal?" James asked.

Ben looked at Azure then took hold of James. "We're done here. This talking is delaying my plans. We need to move on."

"Do you have to destroy Atlantis?" James asked.

It was too late. Ben had released his hold on the large land mass and pulled James and Azure through, all three disappearing moments before the ocean erupted. Waves crashed against the columns, knocking them over and crushing them instantly. Within ten minutes, the waters had swallowed Atlantis forever.

CHAPTER FORTY-ONE

"IT'S BEEN TWO DAYS." Dathan peered out from the cottage doorway. "Before long, this place will no longer be hidden from the human eye."

The sky from their side was more than half covered with blood-red streaks, and the Messengers could feel other dimensions of Light as they, too, began to tear.

"All will be visible in that moment, with no respect of either good or evil," Aharon said. "What will be has to be, and you, of all us, know there is a plan."

Dathan shut the door and watched the marble wall. "I do, but I hope she understands the weight of her sacrifice. If she hesitates for one second, he will let in doubt, and all will be for naught."

Past the marble wall and through the veil of worlds, Alexis had been standing in the presence of several beings that stood more than seven feet tall. A warm glow had wrapped around her, and the beings stood in such a profoundly bright light that she couldn't see their faces. She could see their torsos, which resembled humans', and they appeared to have feet like hers. Alexis looked down and saw that she was standing on stones that shimmered like antique gold grouted in crushed diamonds. Where exactly was she?

"We have shared with you the eternal progression for this universe and especially your world," a gentle male voice whispered. "And with that, you now must choose a side in which you have a future."

"I choose the Light."

"You must choose the Light because you have faith, not because you fear the Darkness," intoned a different male voice.

"Is it not the same?" she asked.

"We seek not allegiance or partial will." The voice seemed to be right in front of her. "When the time is upon you, you will know where your heart stands."

She shrugged. "Then why choose me if I'm not faithful enough?"

Alexis took a deep breath, and when she exhaled, the air ruffled her dress and the tint of grey evaporated. Her dress was left white and spotless.

"When you return to Earth, the Darkness will tempt your soul, and it will be of great importance to follow the path back to the tree whence that crystal came."

"How will I know where to find the tree?" Alexis asked. "I don't know how I alone can do this. Surely there is someone who has been more faithful."

"You have everything within your reach to find the Tree of Knowledge and to control the Darkness." Another whisper swirled through the room. "But we are not asking that you ever be alone."

One of the beings stepped forward. He was tall and muscular, like the others, and he knelt down before her, exposing his ivory face and neck. Below his chest and shoulders, he wore a white full-sleeved surcoat belted with a rope of gold. He had hair like driven snow and a beard of the purest white Alexis had ever seen.

Alexis gasped. "You're him!"

"I am."

Alexis studied the bearded being. "I ... I don't know what to say."

"My child, it's time for you to leave here and return to your planet," the omniscient being in front said in a clear voice. "But first we will give you one last gift."

"What is that?"

"We give you three rotations of the moon to see your loved ones before the pieces are aligned for our return to your planet," said another voice from somewhere behind her.

"Then what?" she asked, searching the room.

He helped her stand and then touched both sides of her face. Immediately her mind was awakened to her subconscious. Alexis closed her eyes and heard soft chanting voices that played like an orchestra. His hands warmed her face as he began to speak.

"Life bore you a destiny that can only arise with the entwining of your mortal flesh to your imperishable spirit. We place upon you the seal of Heaven to outlast the war, famine, and death. After the last great quake and the trumpets sound, you will put away the Darkness and bind his power away from the Light."

"What if he won't go?" Alexis asked. "What if I fail?"

"We all have the right to choose our destiny, but the Darkness can no longer rule the land. Failure is not your future, but know this—we all must step into the dark to be able to shine in the light."

"What's that supposed to mean?"

Alexis felt a strange sensation move across her body. Every fiber of her being was tingling and seemed to be filling with some kind of charge. The feeling slowed, and her entire body was filled with warmth. She knew what was happening. To travel further past this world and back into her own, she had to become one like them—an immortal. Alexis took in a breath of air just as a hand rested upon her shoulder. The room was silent as she opened her eyes to find that the beings were gone.

"Are you ready?" Michael asked with his hand on her right shoulder.

She turned back and put her hand onto his. "Yes. I want to go back."

CHAPTER FORTY-TWO

"WHERE ARE WE?" James shouted as a cold wind blew through the low valley where they found themselves.

"Bosnia," Azure answered.

James looked out at countryside that was surrounded by steep mountains and snowcapped trees. About a hundred yards from the base of the mountain, small houses filled the slopes of a valley.

"What do you remember about your mother, Mr. Mitchell?" Ben called back from where he stood.

James gaped at the two-hundred-meter-high mountain in front of him. "I don't, but you heard my conversation with the colonel. I was always told that he found me." He turned and looked at Ben. "Yet you sounded as if you believed he knew more."

When James turned back, he saw they were not alone. They had been joined by millions of men in black suits similar to Azure's.

"Who are they?" James asked.

Ben glanced at him. "Would you like to be reunited with your mother?"

"Is that a trick question? Because if she's dead, then the answer is no."

"No trick at all, and I'm certain she is very much alive. And my army is here to await her arrival."

As James pondered that, Cezar approached from the multitude. He glanced at Azure and paused, but only for a second. Seeing Ben's chosen favorite was not a pleasant experience for him.

"Master, there has been no sign of them," Cezar announced.

Ben nodded. "They'll be here. And once this is in position, the beacon will let them know who is calling."

He opened his hand to show the Pearl of Gates.

"Mr. Mitchell, this should be overwhelmingly exciting for you," Ben began. "After all, you are quite familiar with pyramids and alien lore. That's why the colonel chose you, correct?"

"Kind of. I'm versed in the tie between the two, but I'm on the skeptical side of believing this is a pyramid." James looked up at the twenty-three-hundred-foot-high snow-dusted, flat-sided mountain. "I've taken this to be nothing more than a flatiron formation. Top geologists, archeologists, and various scientists have all concluded that this isn't a pyramid because there is little sign of humans being involved with its construction."

Cezar and Azure shook their heads as they laughed.

"Why can't we rid this world of this moron?" Cezar asked.

"We need him," Ben said. "For now."

Around the base of the mountainside was evidence of ongoing archeological excavations. Because of the snow and unpredictable weather, the groups granted permission to research the site had left their recent findings covered with blue tarps.

"The Tower of Babel remains intact beneath this overgrowth of Earth," Ben said, patting James on the shoulder as Azure lifted one of the tarps to expose manmade concrete. "But tell us what you know about pyramids and their supernatural powers."

"I'm sure you know that stuff already," James said.

"Indulge me," Ben replied.

"Fine. It's been shown through tests that pyramids generate negative ions and that humans become more balanced when inside them."

"Go on."

The millions of Watchers smiled as they listened to James describe what humans know about pyramids. They bowed their allegiance to Ben as he walked past and moved closer up the mountainside. The men's eyes turned black when he went by.

"It's said that food can be stored longer inside a pyramid," James said before rambling on about changes in the taste of food and the slowing of microorganisms. "Some people have tested the idea of charging their water with negative ions by storing it overnight inside small modern pyramids."

Soon they came to a barely visible concrete stone path that seemed to follow the front of the base of the mountain. James continued to follow Ben until they stopped at a large mound of dirt in the middle of the path.

"And what about quartz crystal, Mr. Mitchell?" Ben held out the crystal cube. "How are they affected by pyramids?"

James frowned, his mind distracted by a tangible sense of evil. Why hadn't he put the pieces together? How did any of what Ben said make sense? "Unbelievable," he finally muttered. "Crystals can be charged by pyramids and even release their charge through a pyramid."

Ben effortlessly directed the removal of several hundred pounds of wet dirt covering a small area of the mountainside. James looked at the mammoth hole in the side of the mountain, and there it was—a doorway.

James's mouth dropped. "It's really a pyramid! I can't believe you were telling the truth."

"I have never lied." Ben grinned at Cezar and Azure.

A series of partially exposed, perfectly preserved stone steps ran next to the door. Ben knelt down beside the area, which was still covered by dirt and trees. He placed his hands on the ground and took in a deep breath of air. His eyes glowed red as a low growl came from somewhere within him. Soon there was a bigger audience. Down in the valley, less than a quarter-mile below where they stood, people were coming out of their homes.

"Looks like the locals are equally impressed," James murmured.

Azure turned to him. "Then they'll love what he's about to do next."

CHAPTER FORTY-THREE

ALEXIS AND MICHAEL came back through the marble wall with their faces aglow. Their trip to the center of the universe seemed to Alexis to take only seconds, but she knew that even with the wormhole it wasn't instant.

"I feel so weightless."

"Now that your physical and spiritual are one in thought, the gravity of your purpose is less complex," Michael said as he looked around the room.

"So this is what immortality feels like?" she asked, looking at Michael, who gave her a vague smile. She frowned. "What's wrong?"

"Before we left, there was someone here awaiting your return." He motioned to the crowd. "But it seems that she isn't alone."

The crowd inside the cottage had grown, and so had the cottage space. It seemed that as more people came in, the bigger the room became. But Michael was focused on the people in the front. Two women stood out.

"Aunt Sarah!" Alexis shouted. Then she saw her cousin. "Amanda!"

Alexis went to them and they all hugged. Then Alexis heard another familiar voice calling her name. She looked back at Michael, who stood silent.

"Alexis," a man said.

She turned back to find a short grey-haired man standing between Sarah and Amanda. "DziDzi?"

He nodded and took her hand.

"But if you're here ..." She looked at the others around her, and a tear welled in the corner of her eye. "That means you died, DziDzi."

"Yes, it does. But it also means we cannot stay." He wiped her tear. "No crying, you must be strong. We were given passage for only a small time so we could see you and let you know that we are here with you."

"Like other humans that pass, we are given another place to rest," Amanda added. "That place is where I was able to communicate with you in your dreams."

"Is Baba OK?" Alexis asked.

"My dear, she is fine and in safe hands," DziDzi assured her. "Don't worry about her or anyone else, they'll all be OK."

A couple of the Messengers from around them stepped in closer and whispered to Sarah and Amanda.

"We must move on, grandfather," Amanda softly said. "And Alexis must go back."

"Give me a second."

"All right." Amanda joined Sarah near the others.

DziDzi took Alexis to the side and spoke slowly. "Death is not easy from either side of things. And I will await the day I can be rejoined with Baba, but until then you must not be afraid to lose any of us when it's time. We are safe."

She took in a deep breath and hugged her grandfather.

"But will you do something for me?" he asked.

"Of course," she said.

"Tell your grandmother *To jest bardziej zielona*," the little man said with a pronounced Polish accent and a trembling smile. "She'll understand."

"I'll let her know." She put her arms around him and hugged him, and then she looked at her aunt and cousin. "I love you all, and it means everything that I was able to see you and see that you are with the Light."

"They really must go," Dathan said.

"OK." Alexis wiped a tear as she drew away.

Three Messengers came from the crowd and stood next to Sarah, Amanda, and DziDzi. The six joined hands. Just as they smiled, Alexis took in a deep breath, and then a warm beam shot across the room. Within seconds, her family was gone.

Aharon came up next to her. "You'll see them again."

"I'm not sure I will."

Aharon shook his head and was about to say something.

"Are you sure you're ready?" Dathan asked. "You sound less than positive."

"Oh, yes," Alexis said. "I'm ready."

"Good," Michael said. "Now that your physical body is immortal, you will be able to move with a moment's thought."

"How does that work? What if I don't know exactly where I'm supposed to go?"

Aharon explained. "When the mind and heart are in sync, you will find your destination. Both the Light and Dark travel this way, so remember this, because they can follow just as fast."

"Also, we are not to watch humans at every waking moment, thus allowing the development of free will," Michael added. "However, an energy is present during emotional changes of the heart and mind that will invite the beings of either the Light or Dark. This is how we learn to find our way. You need to tune into this energy and find your way."

"All of the crystals have stayed hidden from the Darkness for so long because there was no emotion connected to them," Aharon said. "But over the years, the Watchers found a way to track your family. We were able to divert them until they found Sarah."

Dathan was standing behind Alexis as he spoke. "They assumed she had the crystal you possessed."

"And that's why she died?" Alexis asked.

"Not exactly," Aharon said. "As you know, the same man responsible for her death came after you in your apartment. He was being controlled by two men, Watchers of the Darkness, and they could see inside Sarah's mind the night she was attacked. Her death is a result of human weakness."

"What did they see inside her mind?"

Aharon hesitated and looked at Michael, who nodded. "She had a vision of you holding the crystal with your grandmother. You were very young."

"I remember that day," Alexis said. "I was five and it was the day my mom told me we were moving to another new town. Baba was trying to distract me."

Alexis flashed back to that day. Her Aunt Sarah was temporarily living there because she had been evicted, and Alexis's mother was moving them out to live with her new boyfriend, Rusty, the man she later married and who abused Alexis when she was twelve. Her memories jumped back to Sarah, who was watching Baba show Alexis an amber crystal in a wooden box. *If you're a good girl, Alexis, I will let you have these crystals in my collection one day.* Years later, when Alexis was headed to her first college, Baba gave her the wooden box. The same wooden box she kept in her lab.

"Did my grandmother know what the crystal could do?" Alexis wondered aloud.

"She was aware of its purpose, but she tried not to understand more than she was told by her mother," Aharon answered.

"How did you see Sarah's last vision?" she asked. "Were you there?"

"Both sides are present when the spirit is separated from the body," Aharon explained. "And many spiritual beings carry their last thoughts and memories with them."

"That must have been why they came after you," Dathan said. "They saw your grandmother promise you, not your Aunt Sarah, that particular crystal."

"But why kill Sarah and not me?" Alexis asked. "She didn't need to die."

"We're not quite sure why they spared you," Aharon said.

The silence lasted only a couple of seconds before Michael motioned Alexis to join him near the door. She walked through the Messengers with her head held high and her gaze straight.

Michael pointed over her shoulder. "Giah has brought you something."

Alexis turned to see the tall goddess-like woman whom she had seen on two other occasions in this realm. Giah was present both times Alexis was found lying in an open field, but Alexis mostly remembered the angel's beautiful soprano voice that comforted her as she awoke.

"Depending on where you want to be, the seasons will be different," Giah said. She held out a folded piece of cloth and unfolded it to reveal a simple gold bracelet with etched details along the sides. "With this, your attire will adapt to where you appear and blend into that of your kind."

"What about the thermotropic part of my dress?" Alexis asked. "Are my clothes going to be white?"

Giah took the bracelet and unlocked the clasp. She opened it and wrapped it around Alexis's wrist. As she locked it into place, a surge of light shot around the inlaid markings of gold. "The power of your dress has now been sealed within this gold."

"I've never been much for jewelry, but I will take this over wearing a dress any day."

The women in the room laughed at Alexis's jest, and it brought a smile to most of the men.

"Just one more thing," Dathan said.

"What's that?" Alexis asked.

"You cannot give the details of this place, or reveal that you entered the gate to Kolcep."

"How am I to explain where I've been for seven months? Surely, you don't want me to lie."

"We would never ask you to lie," Dathan said. "But knowledge is everything, and you cannot chance the Darkness knowing how to find us."

Alexis pointed outside the door. The sky was almost fully covered with red streaks. "If this continues, there won't be a divide between you and them anyway. But I will keep its secrets."

"Don't worry about secrets," Michael said. "The ability to answer those questions will come to you. Right now, I need you to focus on where you want to be and let your body relax. Breathe in slowly and then feel where you want to be. Imagine your surroundings and feel the energy of those you've left on the other side."

Focus and be there.

She heard his voice repeating the instruction until it gradually faded away.

CHAPTER FORTY-FOUR

THE DIRT AND TREES had been stripped from the south and east sides of the mountain, revealing a gigantic pyramid in the valley of Visoko, Bosnia. Ben waited at the top for James to drag himself up the hundreds of steps.

"Why couldn't you just teleport us up here?" James asked Azure, who was ten paces ahead.

"Because this pyramid has a protective shield that keeps us from opening dimensions," Ben said. "There are four places like this on Earth."

James made it to the top. "Where are those places?"

"Eden was the first," Azure said. He stood next to Cezar. "Each time the gods came back here to reprimand humans, they'd leave another mark or protective shield."

The square platform was a little more than fifteen feet on each side, providing plenty of room for them to stand. A five-foot-square smooth stone protruded from the center of the pyramid. Remains of burn marks indicated that the stone had been previously used.

"Now that we're here, what's going to happen?" James asked. "Is my mother suddenly going to appear?"

Ben held up the crystal cube. "Once I put this in place, she will see that we are here."

James moved closer to the center. "Then what? Are you going to kill us?"

They all laughed.

"How is that funny?" He looked around and saw that the platform and the sides of the tower were filled with beings from the Darkness.

"I couldn't take your mother's life even if I wanted to," Ben said as he took the crystal and put it over a six-inch hole in the middle of the stone pillar. "She's the key to helping us get the Omiens to find Alexis."

"How does my mother have a part in this?" James asked.

Azure glared at him. "Because they might be interested in making a trade."

"Who's making a trade for what?" James asked.

"Is he joking?" Cezar asked Azure. "I thought Lilith's son would be more ... intimidating."

Ben placed the crystal and pearl into the center of the hole. Instantly, a loud hum arose and a bolt of energy rushed down the pyramid and across the land.

"Move away," Ben commanded his followers seconds before a stream of blue light broke through the hole and broke the pillar, shooting straight up and out of sight. The crystal floated amidst the light.

"Master, I can feel it," Cezar said with a grin.

"I, too, can feel the change," Azure said. "Your power will be unstoppable."

Ben walked past the two and looked toward the west. He put his hands out and looked at them. "It's impossible."

"What's impossible?" James asked.

"What is it?" Azure asked. "Is everything all right?"

Ben started to head down the pyramid through the Watchers. "Can you not see that?"

"The energy surge?" Azure asked. "We all can see it."

"Master, where are you going? Lilith and the Omiens will be here soon," Cezar called out.

"What did you see?" shouted Azure.

Ben turned and looked at Azure. "She's here, I can feel her presence."

Cezar looked at Azure. "Who? What is going on?"

Ben looked again to the west. "Alexis?"

As soon as Ben made it to the bottom of the tower, he disappeared.

CHAPTER FORTY-FIVE

MIKEL SEARCHED THE HALLS of the hospital and found the thin Polish woman asleep on the floor holding tight to her purse and wool coat. He got down on his knee and touched her shoulder. Baba was startled but smiled when she saw him.

"Baba," Mikel said. "Are you ready to get out of here?"

She raised her head and nodded. "Yes."

"I've got everything ready to take you home." He helped her to her feet. "But they need you to sign a few papers to release his remains."

"OK." Baba made her way to the nurses' counter, where a nurse was waiting with a clipboard. Each breath was slow and she tried to keep her emotions under control.

"I'm very sorry for your loss," the nurse said as she waited for Baba to fill in the lines of information. "Is there anything else we can do for you?"

Baba looked around and saw that the hospital wasn't as crowded as before. "How are the mommy and baby doing that were in the room next to us?"

"Great. She and the little boy are also going home today."

"So good to hear that blessings can come in the midst of all of this. I hope their home wasn't destroyed." She smiled and then handed the clipboard to the nurse. "But I guess that's not what is important here. It's knowing that life will find a way to prevail in the darkness."

The nurse stared blankly for a second but then saw a volunteer coming down the hall. "Hey, Shelly, can you help these two down to the morgue?"

The nurse gave the young woman the carbon copies of the signed papers. Shelly escorted them back through the waiting area of the emergency room and down a hallway toward the main section of the hospital. A few people who didn't have severe injuries had left and sought refuge in other places, while many others had remained, trying to stay safe from the elements outside.

"It's good you were able to contact your family to come get you," Shelly said. "I've heard the cell towers are going in and out. Plus, people have been talking about most of the bridges being damaged or blocked."

"One of the doctors let me use a satellite phone," Baba replied.

"That's good." Shelly guided them toward a set of stairs and then down a narrow hallway.

The lights still weren't working to their full brightness, but there was enough to see that the morgue was up ahead. Mikel kept pace with Baba.

"Did you contact everyone?" he asked.

"Almost everyone." Baba pulled her coat in close. "I wasn't able to get Marcia."

He pulled a thin cell phone from his coat. "This will work." He unlocked the screen and handed it to Baba.

They arrived at a white door marked *Hospital Morgue*. Mikel opened the door, letting out the smell of formaldehyde.

A nurse popped her head through the doorway. "Brent is on duty, he should be around her somewhere. Brent!"

Rustling came from the back of the room.

"Why don't you stay here and call Marcia while I take care of this," Mikel said to Baba.

"Thank you." She moved away from the door and dialed.

The basement of the hospital was cold and strangely quiet. The sound of the phone ringing through the earpiece seemed louder than it was.

"Matt! Finally." Baba exhaled. "I've been trying to get hold of you guys. What's wrong?"

"It's Marcia," Matt said in a tremulous voice. "There was a fire ... she was trapped inside for so long."

"Matt, what happened? Where is Marcia?"

His breathing was ragged. "They don't know if she'll wake up."

As Baba's heart sank, Mikel came out of the morgue carrying a small sealed container filled with DziDzi's ashes. He opened his other hand to reveal a gold ring.

Baba took the container and the worn wedding band. She gazed at them for a moment and then looked at Mikel. "Will you take us home?"

Mikel nodded. He saw the sadness in her eyes. "Is Marcia OK?"

Baba started toward the exit. "No. I'll explain on the way."

CHAPTER FORTY-SIX

BEN CAME THROUGH the thick woods behind his house, but he saw no one. There wasn't even a stir of animals as he searched the perimeter; everything was quiet. He walked up the paved path to the huge carved oak door on the side of the house and entered the living room, looking around the starkly cold room. Everything was dark and untouched. He trusted what he felt; Alexis was nearby. Yet that reality made no sense. Deep down, it wasn't until Lilith confirmed where Alexis had been taken that he truly believed she had survived being sucked through the portal in Belize.

He sat down on the bottom step of the large wooden spiral staircase across from the kitchen and dropped his head. What was he doing? Chasing his feelings? Sitting there was a waste of time. Alexis couldn't be there.

Ben had no sooner gotten up from the step when a ping came from the room above, followed by another. He cautiously made his way around the stairs, following the sharp pitched sound. When he neared the top, he heard the keys of the white grand piano being struck. He hesitated a moment and then took the last five steps up the staircase toward the open room and rushed into the room.

"Alexis?" He stood staring at the beautiful blonde sitting at the piano. "Are you really here?"

She stood up. "I'm really here."

Alexis's clothing had changed during the transferring of dimensions, and she now was wearing a loose-knit ivory sweater and beige linen pants. She stepped toward him and took his hand. At her touch, he dropped to his knees.

"I don't understand how you found your way back. I've been

doing everything to get you back. And I was ..." Ben shook his head. "And you came here—why?"

She knelt down on the floor and gazed at him. "You've been in my heart since I left. There was nothing you could have done. Where I went you wouldn't have been able to get to me."

Ben looked into her green eyes. "Alexis. I'm sorry for ..."

"Ben, there is nothing you need to apologize to me for." She ran her hands through his dirty blonde hair and down the side of his face. "Everything that has happened was meant to be. And I'm here with you now."

Ben locked his fingers between hers. "I guess the how can come later. I just want to enjoy you in this moment."

Alexis glanced to her side then back to Ben. "The journey we were on to find answers about the crystal has, well as much as I fought against it, it has led me to a greater cause to search for the truth. I had a great deal of time to think about what's important in my life, and the last thing I want is to see anyone else I care for get hurt."

"I don't understand," Ben said. "You're going to continue looking for answers about that crystal? The same crystal that opened a portal, sucked you inside and could have killed you?"

"I know how it works now, and I need to do this. I have to do this." Her eyes were filled with conviction. "And it didn't kill me."

Ben got up from the floor and went to the window. Seven months ago, he had initiated a chain of events to find Alexis, but even his immense power could not stop what was about to happen. Alexis would never forgive him.

"If you're still wanting to do this, then I'm a part of it, too," Ben insisted as he turned back to her. "Because you know I'm not leaving you."

Alexis sighed and got up and went to Ben, who was standing in front of the tall windows. The thick glass between her and the balcony was a reminder of the dimensional wall she had just come through.

"I don't want anything to happen to you," she said, looking out at the cloud-covered night sky.

"Alexis," Ben began. "I can keep you safe."

"When I was pulled through that portal, I thought my life was over and all I could think about was who I'd left behind. You were one of the ones I thought about most," Alexis said as the warmth of her breath fogged the glass. "I kept hoping that maybe you wouldn't worry about how to get me back, and that eventually you'd move on. I didn't know if I'd ever find a way back."

He stepped in behind her. His reflection was like a shadow against her angelic outline. "I won't be without you."

She turned and faced him. "The crystal that opened the portal in Belize and took me also saved me from something far worse."

"But you're safe here with me now." He smoothed his hand over her shoulder.

"No, I'm not safe anywhere until I take care of whatever evil has come after me and my family." She exhaled. "I'm sure this all sounds crazy, and you're probably thinking it's all in my head, but ..."

Before she could continue, Ben pulled her body to his and pressed his lips against hers. Alexis instantly gave in to the desire of his embrace and moved in harmony with his kiss. He pressed her back against the cold pane of glass and cradled her face in his hands. He slowed the pace and pulled away as Alexis caught her breath.

"I've never thought you were crazy." Ben moved a piece of hair from face. "And you're safer here with me."

"I wish it were that simple," she said.

"Tell me what's troubling your mind. Let me help." Ben placed his hand around the side of her neck and rubbed her cheek with his thumb.

"I was there for more than six months, and it took almost that long for me to convince myself what I was experiencing." She smiled and then walked back to the piano. "I couldn't explain it even if I tried."

"I'm overwhelmed by your presence here with me, but I will ask no more questions. When you want to explain it, I will be here to listen."

"Thank you for that." She sat on the bench.

She rested her elbows on the piano, thinking about the visit from Sarah, Amanda, and her grandfather. Seeing part of her family on that side of the dimensions was unutterably sad. It would be sad for anyone, even if they had faith that the dead were in a better place. How would she see her grandmother and not be able to tell her what she had experienced? How was she to explain any part of her absence? Alexis took in a deep breath and looked at Ben. "I'm glad to be back here with you. This was the only place I could think to find you."

"I have nowhere to be other than with you." Ben moved her long, wavy hair to her right shoulder as he kissed the left side of her neck. "Stay with me tonight, and in the morning we will go together to see your family, together."

"That sounds and feels good."

He took her hands and helped her up from the bench. "Is there anything I can get you? Maybe something to eat?"

"Strangely, no." He led her to a door on the other side of the room, a door she hadn't noticed before.

"Would you like to rest?" Ben asked.

"I'm not sleepy, but I would like to lay down and relax."

"Let me get you something more comfortable to wear."

Ben flipped a switch, turning on a dimly lit chandelier hanging from the center of the ceiling. He walked past Alexis to another door on the opposite wall while she stood back taking in the elegant rich mahogany wood floors accented by sheer white curtains and smooth slate fabrics.

"It's beautiful," she murmured. She turned to Ben and bit her lip. "Maybe I shouldn't ..."

"Shouldn't what?" he asked as he pulled a striped blue and white shirt from the closet.

Alexis walked toward him but stopped next to the king-sized bed, which was covered with a heavy spread and plush pillows. She rubbed her hand against the ivory duvet and pulled it down. Satin sheets that felt like cool water on the tips of her fingers.

"Maybe I shouldn't be just barging in on you."

Ben took a moment and gazed at her, taking in her glowing beauty. Her innocence was intoxicating, and he was quickly becoming overpowered by her presence. The shirt dropped onto the floor next to her as Ben took hold of her waist. Alexis instinctively wrapped her arms around his strong shoulders as he lifted her onto the bed.

"I said I wasn't leaving you," he said, crawling up on top of her. "And that eludes my wanting you here."

With only a breath between them, Alexis's heart raced as her desire to be with Ben trumped her purpose for being back in this world. She hadn't planned on staying, and now she struggled against what her heart wanted, but her mind was distracted by the sensation of his breath as it caressed the edge of her ear.

"I'm sorry." Ben started to get up. "I didn't mean to..."

She pulled him back to her and raised her head, pressing her forehead to his. "You what?" Alexis said as she began unbuttoning his shirt.

Ben stopped her and took hold of her hands. Alexis frowned. Maybe she had read him wrong.

He sat down beside her. "It felt like you were gone forever. And now that you're here ..."

"You just said you wanted me here, and you've definitely been leading this charade. Now you're having second thoughts?"

"That's not what I'm trying to say. What we have is like nothing I've ever imagined, but I feel the need to be honest with you about who I am and the things I've done."

"You're worried about your past?" Relief washed over Alexis's face. "It doesn't matter who you are or what you've done. No one in this world has ever made me feel as safe and secure as you have."

He took her hand. "If you knew, you might ..."

She got up from the bed. "If this was so bad, why didn't you tell me before I went through the portal? It seems you're finding another reason not to get close to me."

"It's not that."

"Then what is it? Why are you concerned about telling me now?"

"I wanted to then, but ..."

"But what?" She moved the tips of her fingers over the strong lines of his jaw.

A rushing sensation came over her body as the warmth of Ben's fingers began moving across her stomach toward her chest. She brought her body closer and let him pull her back to the bed.

"I feared you accepting me, but now I fear losing you." He kissed the side of her neck as he lowered her back onto the bed.

"Why are you scared?"

He stroked her hair and then whispered, "Because I'm in love with you."

Alexis embraced Ben and moved her lips against his, and they kissed passionately, and for a long time. Alexis finally broke off and pulled away, and then she took off her sweater. As Ben unbuttoned his shirt, she slid her hands across his perfectly carved abdomen and tugged the waistband of his black trousers.

"I wasn't scared," he whispered, and he began kissing her neck.

"Then what are you waiting for?" she said softly into his ear.

He got up from the bed. "Don't move."

"What are you doing?" she asked as he flipped the lights off.

The wall with the doors to the balcony was covered with sheer curtains. Ben pulled them apart, letting in the midnight sky. A brilliant filter of grey light was cast into the room and onto the bed, where Alexis sat with a sheet barely covering her breasts. The lights caught the sharp lines of her collarbone and the smooth waves of her blonde hair.

Ben moved into the light, and Alexis took in his bare silhouette as he approached the bed. He had observed mortals for many centuries, and he understood the human body and the attraction energy lovers often laid claim to, but he had never felt the craving that he felt now with Alexis.

Without restraint, between the layers of satin, Ben moved his body over Alexis's and began caressing her milky white skin. Ben lifted Alexis up, and their bodies entwined, her arms locked around his back.

As she held tight, something began to change. Like thick storm clouds taking over a peaceful sunlit sky, so did the darkness begin to fill the etching on the bracelet that dangled from her wrist.

FORTY-SEVEN

THE DASHBOARD READ 3 a.m., and the parking lot of University Hospital was packed with vehicles. Mikel parked along a curb, got out, and walked to the passenger side to help Baba out of the SUV.

He extended his hand and helped her out. They had to skirt a large puddle of water as they headed down the parking lot toward the hospital. "I can't believe everything is melting here."

Baba nodded. "It feels like summer instead of winter."

They entered the hospital, which seemed not to have suffered major structural damage, and saw that the halls were almost as crowded as the hospital in Pennsylvania.

Baba caught the attention of a full-figured woman wearing a hospital badge. "Excuse me."

"Can I help you?" the woman said.

"I need to get to the ICU. My daughter is there in room 325."

The woman looked at her watch. "Ma'am, visiting hours aren't for another five hours."

"I understand, but we drove straight from Pennsylvania, and I just lost my ..."

"Look, ma'am, it's three in the morning, and we're still dealing with the results of the rescue efforts of our local police department. And half of Dayton is still missing."

"I'm so very sorry. I had no idea." Baba looked up at Mikel.

"It's OK," he said.

"I'm sorry, it's been a long seventy-two hours." The woman sighed. "If you'd like, there's a waiting area for family on the third floor, down the hall from the nurses' station. You can wait there until morning."

"Thank you."

The woman turned and headed through doors marked for hospital personnel only.

"Come on, I'll take you up there," Mikel said. He took her arm, and they headed toward an elevator.

"Are you not staying?" Baba asked.

Mikel pressed the call button for the elevator. "I have something I need to check on," he said. "I promise I'll be back."

"You've said that before," she said, but she was smiling. They got on the elevator and the door closed.

The third floor was quiet as they exited the elevator. Mikel escorted Baba to the nurses' station.

A lone nurse sat behind the desk, examining charts. She looked up as they approached. "Can I help you?"

"My daughter is Marcia Zen," Baba said. "I was told I could wait in the family area."

The nurse, an older woman with short silver hair, nodded. "There are others in there as well. Let me know if you need blankets or pillows."

"Thank you." Baba went with Mikel to the door directly to their right.

Mikel opened the door. There were a couple of couches and a few chairs spread out, but only two people were in the room—Matt and Rebecca.

Mikel kissed Baba's forehead. "I will be back in the morning. I promise."

CHAPTER FORTY-EIGHT

THE BRIGHT SUN broke through the window onto Alexis as she lay slumbering between the satin sheets. She stretched out her upper body and reached across to the other side of the bed. She opened her eyes and saw Ben watching her.

"Good morning," Ben said.

She beamed and moved closer to him. "Yes it is."

He caressed the side of her face and brushed his finger across her lips. "I never thought I could find something to question my own decisions in this world."

"Are you regretting what happened last night?"

Ben put his arms around her. "Quite the opposite."

He kissed her and moved his strong hands along her bare back. She wrapped her leg around him, but suddenly there was a knocking sound. Alexis stopped and looked into Ben's amber eyes. "I think there's someone at your door."

Ben furrowed his brow, obviously not expecting anyone. The knocking came again, louder.

"Are you going to get it?" she asked.

"I guess I should if I want them to leave us alone." He smiled and kissed her forehead.

"You never know, with the sudden heat wave overnight, it could be someone stuck in the mud."

"You're right." He put on his pants and picked up his shirt from the floor as the knocking continued.

Once Ben had cleared the steps, Alexis grabbed the shirt he had taken from his closet the night before and put it on. Curiosity got the best of her, and she headed halfway down the steps, far enough to peer around the corner.

"Hello, Benjamin," said a tall brunette standing in the doorway.

"Why are you here?" Ben asked.

"The word is out that your human pet is back." Lilith tried to take a step in, but Ben stood in her way. "I wanted to see for myself."

"She's not my pet."

"So you don't deny that she's here." Lilith glanced up and spotted Alexis. "And it appears she has been here all night."

Ben stepped outside and closed the door behind him.

"Your presence here will get your son no mercy."

"My son?" She half laughed and then frowned. "What have you done with my son?"

"I have done nothing yet, but his survival depends on your willingness to make a sacrifice of your own blood." Ben looked out at the woods surrounding the house. "I've a gift waiting for you in Bosnia."

She glared at him. "What have you done?"

"Nothing." Ben cracked the door open. "Yet."

"This isn't over. Tell Alexis I can't wait to see her again."

"If you come near her, I will send you and your demon children to the outer realms," Ben said calmly before stepping back inside.

He shut the door and headed up the stairs. In the bedroom, Alexis was pulling her sweater on.

"What did that woman want?" Alexis asked. "She seemed to know you pretty well."

"She's someone I knew a long time ago." Ben went to Alexis and put his fingers through her hair. "She stopped by to be nosey."

"She's pretty. And she seems familiar somehow."

"I'm certain you two have never met." Ben picked up her shoes and handed them to her.

"Thank you." She looked outside. "Now I need to find a way to make showing up not such a big deal for my family."

"They love you, and having you back is going to be a very big deal." Ben sat on the bed. "I'm having a hard time taking my own eyes off you."

Alexis looked over her shoulder and smiled.

"I will take you wherever you want to go."

"I have a better idea." She held out her hand.

He grinned. "What did you have in mind?"

"I'll take us."

Ben was at a loss for words. There wasn't a trace of tire tracks or footprints in the melting snow. Until this point, he had assumed that she got back to this side through the instructions of one of the beings in the Fifth Realm. He figured they had opened a portal for her, allowing her safe passage. But they would never willingly bring her to the arms of the Devil.

"Wouldn't you like to see how I got to your house?"

Ben frowned and slowly nodded. "Yes, very much so."

Alexis took his hand. "Close your eyes."

His frown deepened. He realized she had come on her own, which could mean only one thing—Alexis was no longer mortal.

"Alexis, wait."

It was too late. She had already pulled them through the wrinkle of dimensions. A second later, they were at the bottom of her parents' driveway. Ben seemed thunderstruck.

"Alexis, I'm sorry," he said, looking off behind her.

"This won't be easy to explain but ..."

"Alexis." He pivoted her body around.

Alexis gasped and almost fell to the ground, but Ben held her tight. Up the wet embankment was the charred shell of her parents' home. It was gone, and there was no sign of anyone.

CHAPTER FORTY-NINE

IN THE EXPANSIVE VALLEY of Visoko, Bosnia, below the foot of the largest pyramid on Earth, billions of Watchers gathered, awaiting their Master's return. Those on the far western edge turned their heads as Lilith came down from a distant mountainside opposite the pyramid.

A tall Watcher blocked her path. "You vile painted woman. You're not welcome here."

Lilith sneered. "I'm here only to warn you."

"Warn us?" another growled. "You're here with a multitude of your enemies. Shouldn't you be the one taking caution?"

"You can't touch me without Benjamin's orders. So move out of my way."

"We can keep you from getting anywhere near the top of the pyramid."

The dark-suited men were like a solid wall staring at her. She didn't cower or show fear. Instead, she took a step closer.

"Your allegiance is founded on ignorance. If you knew what your Master was up to, you'd find no fault in me."

"We know where he is," the Watcher said. "Alexis is back."

"So you know about her father? And how she is of pure Light now?"

"What about her father?" an eerie voice asked from behind her.

She turned to see twelve Gatherers. Their eyes glowed red, with piercing black centers. They were demons from the darkest parts of the universe, and their loyalty to Ben wouldn't be easily shaken.

"Her father is the son of an archangel." She turned and scanned the crowd of Watchers, who appeared to be listening. "You already knew she was a direct descendant of Eve."

A full-throated laugh came from the Gatherer closest to her. "All that exists originally came from the Light. Even your mate Cain was one of the first two purely sent here from the Light, though he found the Darkness more to his taste."

"Why would the Light let her leave if she wasn't seeking to destroy the Darkness? And who was the first to be at her side?"

"He would never betray us. But you would take pleasure in leading us off course."

"How do you think I knew you were all gathered here?" She again looked around. "Because when I interrupted him and Alexis, he told me he had a gift waiting for me here."

The Gatherer grabbed Lilith by the throat and lifted her off the ground. "Maybe he led you here because he knew we'd eliminate you."

She glanced up toward the northern sky. "Then why are *they* here?"

One triangular black UFO approached from more than a mile away, its spotlights beaming across the night terrain. The Watchers who were farthest from the pyramid and nearest the incoming aircraft began disappearing. But for those who were within a hundred feet of the pyramid's base, it was impossible to jump dimensions and hide.

At the top of the pyramid, Cezar and Azure moved James toward the side of the pyramid still covered by trees, out of the line of sight.

"That's not an Omien craft!" Cezar said. He turned to Azure. "Those are Apexians!"

"Calm down," Azure replied. He peered around a thick covering of brush. "They must have seen the signal as well. Or ..."

Azure looked at James, who had gone pale. The aircraft was similar to the one he and Alexis had encountered in Japan.

"Or what?" Cezar said.

Azure nodded toward James. "Or they're looking for him, too. It makes sense. Ben said he knew there was something different about him, and I saw it. He is neither hot nor cold."

“How is that possible? He wouldn’t be human.” Cezar grabbed James.

“Hey,” James protested, breaking his focus from the Apexian ship as he stumbled across toward Cezar.

“Or half human.”

Cezar frowned. “You think he’s Lilith’s son? That’s how she hid him so well; the idiot doesn’t even know.”

“As I said, it makes sense,” Azure said. “But those words never came from Ben.”

Cezar took James and walked him closer to Azure, near the thick weeds. “Is this why he brought Mitchell here? To hand him over to them in order to save himself from the Apexians?”

“No, he wouldn’t dare harm Mitchell, because of Alexis, but it looks as if he did expect Lilith to show up.” Azure pointed down to the female making her way up the hill toward the pyramid.

“Brilliant, we’re defenseless against her.”

“Yes, but she is no match for the Gatherers now that Master’s powers have increased. And if we have her son and her servant ...” Azure nodded toward Cain, who stood in the far distance behind a house, watching the sky.

“That whore has no heart. She’d never give herself up,” Cezar said. “See ...”

Cezar and Azure watched as Lilith headed back in the direction she had come from. She vanished as soon as she cleared the edge of the valley.

“Why do you guys keep talking?” James said, sounding irritated. “There’s a UFO right there.”

“Have you not been listening?” Cezar was quick to respond.

James looked at Cezar and then at Azure. Both had been quiet as they spoke, and James was so consumed by the approaching craft that he had not paid attention to their conversation.

“That ship is here to collect someone,” Cezar said. “Doesn’t it seem strange that you would see the exact same ship months apart?”

"Yeah, that's why I was hoping to stay hidden this time."

Suddenly, the lights that were scanning the area shut off from the center of the aircraft, leaving only three smaller ones lit at each point of the triangular craft. All at once, the ship began to descend and emit a high-pitched sound. The quarter-mile-long UFO was landing. Billions of Watchers scattered, trying to reach the outer edge of the pyramid's hole in order to disappear. But as the Apexian ship neared the ground, many chose to hide in the shadows of the village.

"Now what?" James asked.

"We wait for Ben to return," Azure murmured, but the expression on his face showed doubt.

CHAPTER FIFTY

THE PARKING LOT of University Hospital was still overflowing with vehicles and people. Many were mourning the loss of loved ones. They paid no attention when the air became cold and Ben and Alexis spontaneously appeared beside a rusty brown van. Ben held onto Alexis as she rested her head on his shoulders, taking in the cool air and the smell of wet asphalt ... but her grandparents didn't have a blacktop drive.

Alexis opened her eyes and looked around. "This isn't Baba's house. How did I get us here?" She walked around the front of the van and headed toward the emergency entrance. "Maybe I did bring us here—he said to seek their energy."

Ben caught up with her and took her hand. "Alexis."

"I will explain how dimension jumping works," she said. "I promise." She wiped away her tears. "This emotional connection of teleporting is definitely not an understandable science for me, so I'm still trying to catch on."

"You don't have to explain anything. I'm well aware of the science behind it. I just want you to stay calm. If your family has led you here, then we'll find them together."

"Thank you." She slowed down and Ben could see her eyes were red and irritated.

"It will be all right."

"I wasn't expecting to see it all gone," Alexis said. "A lot has changed since I've been gone. I need to adjust."

"There have been many fires and building collapses because of the earthquakes," Ben said as they walked through the automatic door. "But that doesn't mean your family isn't safe."

The lobby was packed, every chair occupied. Parents held children, and the elderly sat quietly. Others stood along the walls or sat in groups.

"Alexis?" called a male voice from the crowd.

She turned to see Detective Lindsay standing ten feet away.

"You're really alive," he said, approaching her. "Your mother knew it, and ..."

"My mother, have you seen her here?"

"No." Lindsay stared at Alexis as she scanned faces. "Where have you been all this time?"

"I wouldn't know how explain it—no offense." She continued to take inventory of the crowd.

"None taken." Lindsay glanced at Ben. "What about you, Dr. Asael? Were you with Alexis?"

"Was I a person of interest?" Ben asked.

Alexis turned toward the detective. "No, he wasn't with me."

"Well, I can see you're busy, but it's good to see you again." The detective began to walk away.

Alexis touched his arm to stop him. "Is everything OK with you?"

Lindsay shook his head. "We lost a lot of good people this week."

"I'm sorry to hear that." Alexis leaned in and gave him a hug. "I've lost family this week as well."

Alexis was about to walk away when the detective said, "You know, the strangest thing happened before the earthquake. "And the fact that you're alive makes it even stranger."

"What do you mean?"

"That case over the summer with the guy murdered in your alley."

"What about it?"

Ben cleared his throat. "You know, Detective, I hate to be rude, but Alexis is looking for her family that she hasn't seen in seven months. Could this story wait for another time?"

"Yeah, sure," Lindsay said. He turned to Alexis. "I'm sorry, Miss Zen. I hope you find your people."

Alexis nodded and then headed toward the registration desk The detective began to walk away, but then stopped and glanced back at Ben. "Where have you been all this time?"

"Looking for Alexis," Ben said.

"Looks like you found her—I wonder where."

"If you'll excuse me, Detective," Ben said, and he went to join Alexis, who was nodding at the clerk behind the desk.

"Take the elevator up to the third floor, and the nurses will take you to your family," the clerk was saying.

"Did she say anything about who has been admitted?" Ben asked as they made their way to the elevator.

"No, it took forever for her to find anything on the computer. I guess the system has been slow ever since the earthquake." Alexis took a deep breath. "I just know what's on the third floor."

An image of her family gathered together and waiting for updates on her cousin Amanda surged through her brain. Remembering the sorrow and the struggle of her aunt's and uncle's decision to pull life support sent a cold chill down her body. Ben took her hand and twined his fingers with hers.

Alexis tried to smile. "Whatever happens, I have to trust that it's what is supposed to be, and that my family will be safe."

Alexis remembered the peace she felt when she saw her cousin Amanda, her Aunt Sarah, and her grandfather in the realm she had recently left. Knowing there was life after death gave great weight to how she would proceed, but knowing what her own future held gave a melancholy edge to seeing her family.

The third floor was noisier than expected. Several nurses were moving about as Ben and Alexis made their way down the hall. Across from the nurses' station and to the left were eight large glass windows separated by curtained entrances.

"Hello, Dr. Asael, haven't seen you forever," said a redheaded nurse who was standing behind the station.

"Good morning, Toni," Ben said. "Can you help us find Miss Zen's family?"

"Room 2, but you need to wait until visiting hours, 8 o'clock." She pointed to her right. "There's a waiting area through that door."

"Can you tell me who's in there and what happened?" Alexis asked.

"No, I'm not able to give out that information."

"Let's wait," Ben said. "Who knows, maybe the rest of your family is in the waiting room."

As Ben and Alexis approached the door, it swung open. Rebecca was standing there, and when she saw Alexis, her jaw dropped.

"Alexis?"

"It's me." Alexis wrapped her arms tightly around her sister.

Matt and Baba could see Rebecca being hugged but couldn't see who was hugging her until they came to the door.

"Oh, my God!" Matt cried out. "You're alive!" He swept up both girls in his arms.

Baba stood back, holding her mouth as tears streamed from her eyes.

"How did you get here?" Matt asked.

"It's a long story," Alexis replied. "Maybe we can talk about it later."

Matt and Rebecca finally released Alexis, allowing her to go to her grandmother. Matt shut the door.

"Hello, Baba," Alexis said. "*To jest bardziej zielona.*"

Baba's eyes lit up at those words. Alexis reached out and embraced her grandmother, happy that Baba knew her husband had safely crossed into the Light.

Matt looked at Rebecca. "What does that mean?"

Rebecca shrugged. "Something about it being greener, but my Polish isn't good."

"Thank you, my dear," Baba said to Alexis.

Alexis nodded. "He said you would understand."

Alexis realized someone was missing. "Where's mom?"

"There was a fire," Matt said. He looked at Ben. "The night you were there. Marcia got trapped inside our bedroom. I broke a window, but my ladder wouldn't reach all the way. I tried to get her to jump but she wasn't responding."

"I'm sorry," Ben said. "I had no idea."

"How did you get her out?" Alexis asked.

"The neighbors called 911." Matt said. "But she was inside for so long and ..."

"And her lungs took in a lot of smoke," Rebecca added. "She had a heart attack on the way to hospital."

"What's her status now?" Alexis asked.

"She's stable," Matt replied. "Her vitals have been improving." Matt glanced at Baba and heaved a sigh.

"But?" Alexis said.

"Mom hasn't woken up yet," Rebecca said.

Alexis looked at the clock on the wall above the door. They still had forty-five minutes before they could visit. Ben took Alexis's hand and pulled her toward the lime-green couches.

"Why don't you sit here with your family," he suggested.

"What about you?" Alexis asked.

"I still have privileges here, so I may be able to see your mom's chart." He kissed Alexis on the cheek. "And the nurse on duty used to be in the E.R., so she knows me."

Alexis nodded and then sat on a sofa next to her sister.

As Ben turned to head out the door, Matt stopped him. "How did Alexis get back?"

"Guardian angel," Ben said before heading toward the nurses' station.

CHAPTER FIFTY-ONE

AFTER BEN LEFT the room, Matt and Baba joined Alexis and Rebecca on the sofa, Baba between them and Matt on the other side of Alexis with his arm around her. Alexis tried to recall a happier time.

"Oh my gosh, what about Oslo?" Alexis said. She had almost forgotten about the silver-coated puppy.

"He's fine," Matt said. "Funny thing, though, he didn't bark during the fire. I thought he'd gotten loose from the backyard, but they found him sound asleep."

Alexis chuckled. "I'm not surprised. Who's taking care of him?"

"The neighbors are keeping an eye on him while we're at the hospital."

Alexis smiled and leaned her head against Baba. Ben came back, and they all sat up and awaited his news. He went to Alexis and knelt in front of her.

"I spoke with the doctors who were making their rounds, and I explained the situation." He stood and held her hand. "They're allowing you all to go in before regular visiting hours, one at a time."

Alexis stood up. "Thank you so much."

"They're in her room now if you have any questions," Ben said.

They trooped to Marcia's room and waited outside. Two doctors came out and explained that her vital signs had drastically improved overnight. Her oxygen levels and heart rate were cause for hope, but she still had to wake up on her own.

"You may go in one at a time, but if you don't mind waiting back in the room to respect the other patient down the hall," one of the doctors said before pulling the curtain halfway open.

"No problem," Matt said. "We thank you for letting us in early.

"You go first, sweetie," Baba said and nudged Alexis.

"Are you sure?" she asked, but she could see everyone else also wanted her to go first.

Alexis inhaled before entering. The room was no bigger than ten feet by ten feet and was nearly completely taken up by monitoring systems and a large hospital bed. She pulled the stool from the corner over and set it next to the bed. When she looked up at her mother lying peacefully, another woman stood on the other side of the bed. The woman was adorned in white.

"You can't be here, she's not leaving yet," Alexis said quietly.

"I'm here for you, Alexis," the angelic voice replied.

"Why?"

"Though family is one of the most important gifts you can have on this Earth, your time here is near an end."

"I know but ..."

"If you don't succeed, we cannot guarantee the safety of your family once the Darkness takes over," the Messenger said.

"I just wish I could tell her one last time that I love her." Alexis touched Marcia's hand. "And know that she will OK without me."

The woman in white leaned over and whispered into Marcia's ear. "It's safe now Marcia, you can awake."

The angel's words moved across Marcia's body, reviving her brain and heart. Marcia took in a breath and opened her eyes.

"Mom!"

Marcia looked confused. "Alexis? Am I dead?"

"No." Alexis got up from the stool and took her mother's hand. "We're both very much alive."

Marcia could barely get her arms up to touch her daughter's face. "Thank you, Lord!"

A monitor sounded. The nurse came in and saw that Marcia was awake and alert. "Mrs. Zen, it's nice to have you back with us. Can I get some vitals?"

FIFTY-TWO

ALEXIS TOLD THE others that Marcia was awake and they could see her once the doctors finished their exam. Alexis couldn't restrain the smile that lit up her face. After all the loss and stress she had faced in the past several months, things were looking up. She was back on her side of the world, and even though she understood things wouldn't stay this way for long, Alexis planned to savor it while she could.

"You're taking this rather well," Ben said.

"I've always been able to handle stress better than most," she said.

"That's for certain."

Matt cleared his throat. "Alexis, I'm not sure what your friend here has told you about, um ... recent visitors."

"I didn't want to throw that on her so soon," Ben said. "She's been through quite a bit."

Alexis frowned. "Throw what on me so soon?"

"While you were away someone showed up," Matt said. "And normally I'd keep him away from here but he ..."

"He who?" Alexis asked.

The door into the waiting room opened.

"Alexis?" a man called out. "Is that really you?"

She turned to see a casually dressed man in a brown leather jacket. She hadn't recognized his voice, but he looked familiar. A childhood memory flashed through her mind. Alexis could see her own eyes staring back at her. "You're my father?"

Mikel nodded. "Yes."

"I remember you from when I was little," Alexis said. She looked at Ben and then back to Mikel. "Why did you leave?"

"I never left you. Don't you remember me coming to you at night?"

She had always assumed that her visions of Mikel visiting her were the delusions of a young mind, but now the delusion was standing in front of her.

"I remember," Alexis whispered. She got up and hugged her father. She felt a jolt of energy pass through her. It was stronger than static electricity but not enough to cause pain. Then the lights flickered and dimmed. "What just happened?"

Ben went to her. "Are you OK?" A chill was forming in the air close to her.

She stepped back.

Mikel pulled Alexis between himself and Ben. "Alexis, stay here. I'll see what just happened."

The shadows on the wall were shifting and changing form. Thin faint shadow figures moved across the room, surrounding them. Only Ben seemed aware of their presence.

"Matt and Mikel, I think you two should stay here, and I'll go see what's going on with the power," Ben said as Matt started for the door.

"You can do that, but I'm going to check on my wife," Matt said.

"I'm coming with you," Rebecca insisted. "Baba, are you staying or coming with us to see about Mom?"

Baba got up and joined Matt and Rebecca.

"Guys, it's probably nothing," Alexis said, but it didn't take long before she saw the moving shadows. She tried to rationalize what she was witnessing, but she also knew what was searching for her. She wondered how she would explain this to Ben and Mikel.

"You two should go see what happened to the power," Alexis suggested.

"You're not staying here alone," Ben insisted.

"I'll be fine."

Unknown to Alexis, someone had opened the door and entered and was standing behind her.

"Why are you here?" Ben said in a voice that was sharper than Alexis had ever heard from him.

"Huh?" Alexis said.

"I told you before, and the reason is still the same," Lilith said, wearing a triumphant smile. "Except now there is someone else here I want to see."

Alexis turned to see the woman who had visited Ben earlier that morning. Alexis stared at her as she strutted into the room and brushed past her. With that simple touch, a flood of memories came to Alexis and she gripped Ben's hand.

"This isn't possible," she whispered to herself and then she turned to Lilith. "I know who you are now."

Ben shook his head. "I doubt you've ever met her."

"This woman is a psychiatrist," Alexis stated.

"No, she's anything but a doctor."

"Aw, Benjamin, that hurts," Lilith said. "But then again, neither are you."

"How do you know Ben?" Mikel asked Lilith.

Ben turned to Mikel and frowned. "How do *you* know her?"

Alexis's thoughts were swirling. She could see Lilith's face from when she was five. Back then, everything was innocent and Alexis didn't know what was about to happen, but after her journey through to Kolcep, she remembered exactly what was done to her.

"I know who she was to me," Alexis said in a strong voice, interrupting Ben and Mikel. "Dr. Gevira. She's the reason I could never remember anything from when I was younger. She drugged me to make me forget."

"What?" Mikel said. He looked at Lilith, who was smirking.

Lilith pointed at Mikel. "I did what was necessary to protect you."

"I didn't want your protection."

"That's why you could never go very far back in our sessions," Ben said to Alexis. He turned to Lilith. "You're the only other one who could have bound her memories to where I couldn't get to them. Why didn't I see that before? And what were you trying to hide?"

"It doesn't matter now," Lilith said. "And you're a fool to be blinded by your feelings for her."

Ben turned away, trying to hide his rage. He closed his eyes and began slowing his breathing, but the shadow images started to form behind Alexis. She didn't see them, but they were moving their energy upon her.

"Everyone stop talking!" Alexis demanded. "Would someone explain to me what is going on, and how you both know Dr. Gevira?"

Mikel turned to Alexis and let out a long breath. "She's my mother."

Alexis stared at him. She was about to say something when it dawned on her that the woman she had met more than twenty years ago showed no signs of aging.

Mikel took Alexis's hand. "I can explain. Her blood flows through me, but she is nothing to me. I have fought hard to keep her darkness from you, but it appears she knew all along who you were and used it for her own gain. I'm sorry."

"You don't have to apologize," Alexis said. "But when I was ..."

Alexis stopped and remembered her vow to keep where she had been a secret. She also knew that if Lilith was the evil she was to keep the information from, it was too late. Alexis stared at Lilith. If this woman was the great power set to destroy her world, she was showing scant proof of greatness. If anything, Alexis saw weakness.

Ben was nose to nose with Lilith, arguing with her. "Your secret wasn't hard to track down once I knew what I was looking for."

"That's a lie!" she snapped. "You think that putrid thing waiting atop Babel was my son, and that's why you tried to lure me there."

Ben snorted. "Though you had one of my men fooled into

thinking James Mitchell was your son, I knew it had to be someone who was trying very hard to steer clear of me."

"James?" Alexis said. "What about him? Is James OK?"

Ignoring Alexis and still facing Ben, Lilith laughed. "Then why leave him stranded? My men were barely able to get out of there. You left them all for dead."

"What is she talking about?" Alexis asked Mikel, but he was watching Ben.

Ben's eyes started to turn black. "Your men? They would never be willing to follow you."

Lilith put a hand on Ben's chest. "They would if they thought you had left them to find your human while the Apexians show up to take them captive."

Ben pushed Lilith's hand away. "I'm done with your games."

"It's too late." She looked over his shoulder at Alexis. "They're coming for her."

Ben pushed Lilith against a wall. He went for her throat but stopped when Alexis clutched his arm.

"What is going on?" Alexis demanded. "How do you know her? Who is she?"

Ben lowered his hand but his eyes were like onyx.

Alexis recoiled away from him. "Oh, dear God, what have I done? You? This whole time? You're the one to blame for all this?"

"Alexis, wait!" Ben cried out as he released Lilith's arm.

"Don't play dumb little girl, you've always known," Lilith snapped. "You just ignored the signs."

Alexis fixed an icy stare on Lilith. "There were never any signs. And you have no grounds for accusing me."

Lilith sneered. "Every time you touched him you felt it—something wasn't right. But your own selfish desires wanted more, and now you bear the blackness of his sin inside you."

Alexis glanced at the bracelet on her wrist. Its gold luster was consumed with blackness, and the markings were no longer visible.

Her heart was pounding. She could hear Mikel and Ben yelling her name. Lilith was right. Alexis had known there was something different about Ben when she was with him. There was no going back, yet it wasn't too late to do what she could to save the rest of her family. Alexis needed to find the location to open the gate to Eden, but first she needed to get out of there. She turned and fled, running past the nurses' station to a dead end of the unlit hallway. Mikel followed, running down the hall and finding Ben on his knees.

"Where did she go?"

"I don't know. She just vanished. I wasn't quick enough." Ben was breathing heavily, and his clenched fists were pressing against the floor. "But I'll find her."

"Is it true?" Mikel asked.

"What? Am I the Devil? The Master of the fallen angels?"

"I've always known who you were," Mikel said. "I want to know if you truly love my daughter."

Ben stood. "Why would you believe anything I say?"

"Because I have some of the same evil in my veins that you have, and I know that it can still find real love." Mikel looked back down the hallway toward the ICU rooms where Marcia was recovering. "But sometimes we have to surrender to a higher power to save the ones that mean the most."

Ben took in a deep breath and let it out slowly.

"If what has been foretold is in Alexis's hands, then she will be coming for you. When she does, and if you love her, then go willingly." Mikel gripped his shoulder. "And I'll take care of my mother."

"No need. Her fate was sealed when she gave birth to you." An instant later, Ben vanished.

CHAPTER FIFTY-THREE

NIGHT VISION SWEPT THROUGH the Bosnian valleys. Thick quilted mountainsides were covered with mature pines and the leafless branches of tall oaks. A U.S. military plane with Colonel Logan and a security team aboard began to descend next to the triangular aircraft near the pyramid. The cargo bay of the Apexian ship was open, and three men in suits that might have been made of leather were walking down the metal ramp. The men were very thin and their mouths were covered with air masks.

"Why are we not leaving with the others of your kind?" James asked Cezar. "We need to get out of here before those aliens find us."

"I agree." Cezar turned to Azure. "We need to get away from the range of this vortex."

Azure pointed to the Apexian ship. "It won't do us any good."

Six armed U.S. airmen walked behind Colonel Logan toward the lowered bay door of the UFO.

"That's the colonel. What is he doing?" James almost shouted, but Azure pulled him back.

"Let's find out." Cezar got up and started walking down the side of the pyramid until Azure got in his way. "Wait."

Cezar walked around Azure. "Ben said they could be persuaded just like humans."

Azure pointed toward another person near the military plane. "Look. She's back."

Cezar had no sooner focused on the slender brunette then the six-man guard surrounding the colonel had drawn their weapons on her. The three Apexians had jumped from the bay door and joined the airmen.

Cezar nodded toward James, who watched from behind a rock. "Maybe she came back for her son."

"Possibly. If so, we need to get off the pyramid." Azure pointed to a clearing in the distance.

"Are you not the least bit curious about what Lilith would want from them?" Cezar asked.

"Yes, but we need to get close enough to clear the vortex shield in case we need to disappear," Azure explained and started down the pyramid.

James pulled against Azure. "Hold on."

"What now?" Cezar asked.

"She's pointing up this way," James said. "Does she know I'm here?"

Lilith was saying something to the men below. Though the men had not lowered their weapons, the colonel and one of the Apexians had turned their attention to the pyramid. "She's pointing toward the beam of light," Azure said.

"I'm pretty sure the colonel and those aliens have noticed the huge pulsating light coming from this freshly uncovered pyramid," James said, his voice dripping with sarcasm.

"You're right. She's pointing to the Pearl of Gates," Azure exclaimed as he realized the crystal-encased pearl was floating in the center of the light.

"We can't go up there, they'll see us," Cezar warned. "We can't hide unless we clear that valley."

"What happens if she gets the pearl?" James asked.

"There's not much said about it other than its previous use to call the gods from this temple in the day of Babel," Azure replied. "Our Master kept it hidden for good reason."

"Maybe he was hiding it from your enemies," James said.

"The Light?" Azure shook his head. "No, they have a direct path to the gods. I think he was hiding it from her."

"And you two truly believe that woman is my mother?"

Azure glanced over the edge of the pyramid. "I don't know."

James headed back up the pyramid. He stayed hidden behind a small stand of trees near the top.

Azure grabbed James by the collar. "What do you think you're doing?"

"I may not be on your side of things, but it appears that whoever that woman is, she is trying to get them interested in what's causing the light. I think she's making a trade for someone else." James pulled away from Azure. "So I'm going to get it first."

"All right, but ..." Azure looked down at the houses beneath the foot of the pyramid. "Let me distract her first, then Cezar will make sure you're safe."

"I'm not babysitting him," Cezar said. "I'll distract her, and you watch the human."

"Fine," Azure said. "You need to hurry because they're headed this way."

Because of the vortex within the perimeters of the pyramid, no beings were able to teleport through dimensions, nor could they hide amid another realm. So Cezar was forced to run down the covered side of the pyramid and wait for a chance to distract the approaching forces. James and Azure waited at the top edge, five feet from the beam of light. Suddenly, Cezar jolted across the exposed stone of the front side of the pyramid and began to walk toward Lilith, who was leading the seven humans and three Apexians.

"They don't seem to care that he's there," James said.

"You're right." Azure watched the group head straight toward them. "Stop!"

Azure wasn't fast enough. James darted across the platform to the intense blue beam. When James looked, he hesitated only a second. When he saw Lilith begin to scale the side of the pyramid, he reached in and grabbed the Pearl of Gates crystal.

"Let's go!" shouted Azure.

As soon as James had taken the crystal, the beam of light ceased. He and Azure ran through the trees and brush on the northeast side of the pyramid. James looked back to see if they were gaining on them but tripped and began to slide through the mud.

"Come on, you fool." Azure pulled James up from the ground. "Do you want to get caught?"

"No."

"Once we are past the strongest of the vortex lines, we can cross the land undetected," Azure said, looking over James' shoulder. "We're going straight for those houses."

James nodded. "Let's go."

When the two of them reached the stone path that hemmed the perimeter of the pyramid, James stopped and bent over. Breathing heavily from the sprint, he looked back from where they had just came.

"Where are they?" he wheezed.

Azure looked in every direction. It wasn't until he stepped back and looked up to the top of the pyramid that he found the group with Lilith and something else.

Cezar came up behind Azure. "They've been there for a while. Their ship was hidden until he shut the light off."

Hovering over the enormous pyramid was a circular reflective mass, yet those standing below it didn't seem surprised. Even as it dropped closer to them, the colonel pushed forward in front of Lilith.

"Is that another UFO?" James asked.

"Yes," Cezar confirmed. "But those are the Omiens."

CHAPTER FIFTY-FOUR

MORNING WAS BARELY touching the ecru shores of Hawaii. Alexis took her finger through the cool wet sand, connecting lines to each other until the tide wiped the canvas clean. A shadow moved in, blocking the eastern sunrise that shined like honey on her hands.

"I can't believe you're the one they were warning me about." She wiped her eyes. "Yet I can see why they didn't tell me; I wouldn't have believed it."

Ben knelt beside her. "Who I am doesn't change how I feel about you."

"It changes everything." Alexis tossed a broken seashell into the ocean and then got up from the ground and headed toward the western shore.

"Alexis, wait!" Ben appeared in front of her and took her hand. "It doesn't have to change your heart. Tell me you don't love me."

"Are you serious right now?" She jerked away. "You are pure darkness, and you have sought to destroy innocent people, including my family. How can you expect me to ignore who you are?"

"Your understanding of my presence on this planet has been flawed. I cannot make humans do anything they weren't subconsciously already willing to do. My men only fulfill the free will given to all of God's beings."

"Killing people is not a part of free will," Alexis snapped. "My Aunt Sarah didn't need to die. She didn't even have the crystal!"

"I didn't kill her. She wasn't supposed to die, but I made sure the one responsible paid the price."

The security video of the back alley of her apartment played out in Alexis's head. Seeing George Pliate, the man who killed her aunt, mysteriously appear frozen to death next to the trash bin behind the furniture store sent a chill down her spine, the same feeling she had experienced when he had forced his way into her into bedroom.

"Those men, that night in my apartment, you knew what was about to happen to me? If I hadn't startled those men in black suits, would they have let him rape me?"

"You don't understand. It's different."

"Why? Because you say you're in love with me?"

"Yes. And I know you feel the same way about me."

"I doesn't matter how I feel. What matters now is that I finish this." She pulled the crystal from her pocket. "And take the punishment I deserve for what I've done."

She turned back to the east, where coral clouds hid the just-risen sun. Alexis felt cold saltwater on her feet and turned to look at the lines she had drawn in the sand. She furrowed her brow. Two lines that crossed each other had not been washed away.

"Alexis, please," Ben said as she walked away.

"I can't. I made a choice to follow the Light." She took in a slow breath. "I wish none of this was real and we could be together, but we …"

She paused a moment, tilting her head a little, and then disappeared.

Ben dropped to his knees and let out a scream of frustration.

An intense vibration rippled out from his scream, shooting across the Pacific Ocean and shifting the tectonic plates below the water, causing a divergence in all directions. Earth was on the verge of destruction and the forces of Darkness were growing in number as evil beings swept the through the rubble, taking what dead they could claim. But death wasn't the only scent they were scouring for, because now they sought to destroy Alexis and Ben.

CHAPTER FIFTY-FIVE

ACROSS THE WORLD, cities were beginning to collapse from violent seismic activity. Intense pressure along the fault lines in the center of the United States was ready to blow. Distress calls were being played across radio and television stations, warning people near the danger zones to begin evacuating.

The city of Dayton was one of the many where the homes had started falling like dominos and tall towers in the downtown area had begun to collapse from the top. To the northeast, most of Wright Patterson Air Force Base remained intact, and Alexis found herself in the parking lot of the research facility.

Why did I come here? she thought as she looked around for personnel.

The doors to the facility were open, but there was no airman at the desk. Without her badges, Alexis was stuck aboveground, because something kept her from being able to teleport anywhere inside the building.

"Are you lost already?" The voice came from behind her.

Startled that she had been followed, Alexis didn't turn around. "I told you we can't be together!"

A hand touched her shoulder. "You're safe, Alexis, it's only me."

She turned to see Michael, her young grandfather, and then thought about the other Messenger from earlier that morning. "I haven't forgotten. I still have two days."

He smiled. "That's not why I came. But maybe I could assist you. What is it that you're worried about?"

"I need the journal, but I have no idea if it's here. And something is blocking me from getting down to my lab."

"The only thing blocking you is yourself," Michael said. "Your mind has the journal stored, so retrieve it from behind the fog that has you distracted."

Alexis closed her eyes and slowed her breathing. As she blocked the hum of the backup generator, she listened to the rhythm of her blood pumping in and out of her heart and called forth her memory of the journal pages.

"Can you see it?" Michael asked.

"Yes, but I can't make out the words on the pages."

"Open your eyes."

"How?" She circled around the white soundproof room.

"You were able to focus on what you wanted and saw it." Michael pointed to the leather-bound journal sitting in a box on the table two feet from Alexis. "And I explained that the heart and mind must be in sync, or you will get off course."

She flipped to the beginning. "I just need this one entry and a map."

A soft tapping came to the lab door. Alexis felt her muscles tense, but Michael didn't hesitate to walk toward the door.

"The building has separate security watching from upstairs, and they probably saw us come into the building," Alexis said, grabbing the door handle. "Let me talk to them."

"I don't think it's military security," Michael said as she opened the door and saw Mikel standing there.

"How did you know where to find me?" she asked

"The same way you got down here," Michael said. "He set his mind and heart on his daughter."

"The abilities of my mother and the heart of my father," Mikel said as he stepped into the room. He turned to Michael and said, "Hello, Adam."

Alexis frowned. "No, this is Michael, your ..."

"I know who he is, Alexis," Mikel said. "But his name on Earth is Adam, isn't that right, Father?"

Michael nodded at Mikel and then turned to Alexis. "Michael is my angelic name, but when I came to Earth I was known thereafter as Adam."

"Please explain," Alexis said.

"Right now, there are more important matters to consider." He handed her the journal. "Then I promise to explain."

Alexis crossed her arms in front of her. "I'm done with waiting for explanations." She pushed the journal back. "And I'm done being in the dark. Either explain what's going on or I leave alone."

"If you don't finish this, you and yours will die," Michael said.

Alexis glared at him. "I don't think so. The god I met at Kolcep was a god of mercy, and he would spare the innocent. As for me, I'm already dead."

Michael took her hand. "No, that's ..."

"I'm in love with the enemy, and I didn't know before." She paused then, as if she had just realized something. "None of this would have happened if you had told me who he was. And I wouldn't have given myself to him so willingly."

Mikel looked at his father, who was equally shocked at hearing those words.

"Then you're right," Mikel said as he turned back to Alexis. "You deserve the truth."

"Very well," Michael said. "Where shall I start?"

"At the beginning," Alexis said.

"I will tell you what I can." He paced the room for a couple of seconds. "As your father said, my name while I was here was Adam, and I was the first man."

Alexis shot a look at Mikel. "Like in Adam and Eve?"

"Yes," Mikel said.

"But your mother isn't Eve."

"That's where it gets complicated," Michael said. "As you've come to understand, there is more life in this universe than on this planet."

Alexis nodded. "Go on."

"Each planet that has life also has a first man and woman," Michael said. "Each has a garden where they learn the nature of the elements. The fallen angel at one time was tasked with teaching the other first beings to know good from evil, but when he came to Earth, everything changed."

"This fallen angel—Ben?" Alexis asked still trying to make sense of this.

Michael nodded. "That's correct, but like me he was known by another name."

Her father put his arm around her shoulder. "You couldn't have known it was him. The Devil has never been the horned demon portrayed in Sunday school; he's just their source of power. But that's what makes him dangerous."

"Never mind that, tell me what happened on Earth that was so different from the rest."

"Earth was the promised planet," Michael answered. "Ben was promised that if he kept the balance between his dark followers and those of the Light, he would be given an eternal companion."

"My mother," Mikel said.

"This part I have heard more than once," Alexis said.

"From meeting her, you know that my mother is not one to play by the rules, nor does she care if harm comes to her own blood, as long as it serves a personal agenda," Mikel said. "And when she was placed in Eden to be Ben's companion, she found the one way to show that she served no master. So she sought out Adam before he was fully awakened and defiled his loin. I was born outside the gates of Eden after she was banished."

"When Ben saw what had happened, he blamed man and his descendants for denying him a companion," Michael added. "So when the gods gave me another, he changed the rules and tempted my wife. Alexis, you are a direct descendant of my firstborn, and that's why you were able to cross through the portal."

"But I'm also a daughter of Eve," Alexis said. "That's why I have to solve the mystery of the crystal and why I'm the only one who can control the evil that plagues this world."

"That's because you have more light than darkness flowing inside you," Mikel told her.

Alexis walked to where her desk once sat behind the white table. Three boxes sat stacked on the floor, with papers and miscellaneous items piled inside them. She rummaged through until she found an old dusty globe.

"Let me see the journal." She pushed two crates out of her way as she placed the globe on the table.

"What did you just figure out?" Michael asked, handing her the leather-wrapped pages.

"More light than darkness flowing," she said, spinning the globe. I think I know exactly which four rivers Dathan was referring to."

CHAPTER FIFTY-SIX

BOTH FATHER AND SON watched Alexis concentrate on notes she had dug out of the crates and boxes. She had cleared the white table of almost everything else.

Michael looked over her shoulder as she studied the first entry of the journal and compared it to the globe. "What are you doing?" he asked. "I thought you already figured out that those lines came together to make four rivers."

"But I didn't understand what Dathan meant by rivers, since there are no physical rivers where these lines lay." She pointed to the map she had created in Belize with the series of dots.

"Not everything is a literal interpretation," Michael said.

She pointed to the map again. "This was a literal interpretation. What my father just said about more light than darkness flowing got me thinking about rivers that might flow below the surface. And with all the earthquakes that have been happening on this side, it got me wondering."

She paused and flipped through the pages of the journal. Mikel and Michael leaned across the other side of the table, watching her.

She showed them a page. "When I first saw this entry, I thought it was a form of Eskimo, but it didn't entirely translate, because something was off."

Mikel pointed to a couple of words that appeared together more than once on the page. "That's Na-Dene. I recognize the combination."

"Exactly," Alexis said. "What I found unique about the crystal is that everything works backward geographically and not in the fashion of a timeline."

"What do you mean?" Michael asked.

"The cradle of life has always been thought to have originated in this general area because of the biblical references." Alexis turned the map so he could see it clearly, and then she pulled out the crystal. "But the inscriptions rotated back to this first marking. The same marking I saw on the maps in the cottage. It's a map in and of itself, back to Eden, and your wife, Eve, left this for us to find our way back."

"But Na-Dene is found mostly in Alaska and northern Canada," Mikel said.

She smiled and shook her head. "That's true, but when I studied the Native American language in college there had been some evidence found that suggested those ancient colonies migrated south into California and into the Midwest of the United States."

"How does this tie into the rivers?" Michael asked.

"Because of what it says." She returned to the journal and began reading.

Gods give us passage to return home safely through the waters that confine the land, but when angry lines from beneath growl as one beast, death will be filled from the rivers of fire.

Alexis looked up from the page of the journal. "I think the angry lines that growl is a reference to the fault lines and earthquakes. Which led me to what else falls along those same lines—volcanoes. And rivers of lava that flow beneath the ground."

"What's next?" Mikel asked. "Do you know what the first entry says?"

She turned the page and stared at the strange language. Two of the characters mimicked symbols of other languages, but the others repeated in a nonspecific pattern.

"Roman numerals," she said abruptly. "They're like Roman numerals, and these are coordinates."

She started scribbling notes on one of the pages next to the globe.

Mikel looked at the journal. "That seems too easy. If someone else got hold of this they might have figured that out as well."

"Even if these are coordinates, there is no way to tell whether it's a current location or from a time before the land of Pangaea split."

"What does your gut tell you?" Michael asked.

She looked over the page where she had jotted down a few numbers and then stared at the journal. "My gut tells me that Eve knew all along who would be receiving this in the end, and she inscribed the crystal based on how the Earth looks today." Alexis wrote something on the paper. Then she skimmed through the other entries but stopped when she heard Michael sigh. "What is it?"

"Benjamin tempted Eve out of vengeance and to persuade her to follow him after Lilith had altered their path together. And when we ate from the tree, we were given knowledge of that time but also of these present days, but we each saw something different. It frightened us to see what would become of this place, but we knew that everything would come together once the fruits we ate were brought back together at Eden's gate." He paused for a moment and smiled at her. "You bring new hope."

Alexis nodded. "Then I think it's time we finish this."

CHAPTER FIFTY-SEVEN

WRIGHT PATTERSON WAS swarming with military personnel. Armed guards were boarding trucks and other vehicles to head for earthquake-ravaged towns. Helicopters and cargo planes were landing with injured civilians from overflowing hospitals and then heading back out as soon as possible. Ben could feel Alexis belowground, toward the research building, but he couldn't go any farther than the airstrip a hundred yards behind a hangar.

"Why have you followed me here?" he called out to the seventy-two demon Gatherers standing in his path, glaring at him. "I freed you from Solomon, and now I have given you power over the dead."

"You did that for your benefit, not ours," one of the seven-foot beings replied in a husky whisper.

Ben walked toward them and stared at the one who had spoken. "What more do you want?"

"You know what we crave," the Gatherer said. "We desire to feast on the fear of the innocent, but you have blocked us from this!"

"I am not their creator, so for every spirit of the innocent we take, there is strength given to the Light. I've never deceived you in this." He moved through them and stood in the center. "You have been given freedom to hasten the wicked and the foolish to their graves, but your thirst must not be quenched by the blood of the pure. Those who have not turned their hearts away are the result of your lack of persuasion, not my nepotism."

The seven-foot beings glanced at each other. "You say this only because your human is of the pure Light."

Ben appeared amused. "That harlot speaks lies and you decide to hunt me down? What did you expect to gain when you found me?"

"We weren't looking for you," one of the beings said, his red eyes glowing. "Lilith told us of another way. Alexis's father, whose heart still beats, will be close to the daughter of Light, and when we take her, then you will accede to our needs."

Ben walked past them toward the research building. He acted as if their words did not bother him. "Her lies will not hold up. She failed to mention her relationship to Alexis's father." He turned toward them. "Because if you had known she was his mother, you would have brought her straight to me."

Their shouts rose up simultaneously. *Impossible! ... You lie to deceive us!*

"I have never lied. I have tried to show that freedom of will causes a corrupt species. This is because of her. Lilith has been our enemy since the day she was allowed to live. Her freedom has bound us here until our death!"

Thick, dark clouds, their edges tinged with red, began rolling in, looking as if they were on fire. Thunder pounded, echoing across the nation as Ben's rage grew.

"Our death may come sooner because of your lack of attention," a Gatherer said. "The Apexians are with Lilith and the humans. She has convinced them of her treachery. And they, too, seek Alexis."

Ben's eyes went wide, and fear clouded his face. "Leave me now!"

The Gatherers transformed into thin shadows and disappeared, leaving a foggy mist at Ben's feet.

"It is time this ends." Ben fell to his knees and the ground exploded around him.

CHAPTER FIFTY-EIGHT

SUBLEVEL 6 OF the research facility trembled, but within the soundproof walls of the lab, everything remained quiet.

"Uriel, he guards Eden's gate," Alexis said.

Michael nodded and then looked over his shoulder at a curious vibration coming from outside.

"He took me to the edge of the Garden's gate after we walked the other realms," Alexis said. "He said when I opened the portal again I would have to give him pittance in exchange for the gates to open."

She knew what was at stake and that the only way to stop the Darkness from consuming everything was to sacrifice the one she loved. A vision of Ben touching her skin and kissing her shoulders sent a chill through her body but left an ache in her chest.

"Alexis, do you feel that?" Mikel asked. "Alexis?"

There was a sudden crashing sound at the front of the lab. Alexis jumped back and saw that a piece of the catwalk had fallen into the room.

"What's going on?" she asked.

"It must be another earthquake," Mikel shouted as more beams began to buckle. "We need to get up top."

Alexis grabbed hold of the two men and focused her mind to take them away. A moment later, they were outside. Alexis released her grip on the men and turned around. All that remained of the facility was a huge crater.

They stared in silence for a moment, and then Alexis said to Mikel, "May I see your phone?"

"The towers won't be operational," he replied.

"I need to input the coordinates. And as far as we know, they're still orbiting us, right?"

Mikel pulled his phone from his pocket and handed it to Alexis. The touch screen lit up, and she accessed the mapping application, entering 39°59'2.05"N, 93°58'36.19"W. She waited for the rotating icon to finish its search.

"It looks like we're going to Missouri," She said, staring at the screen. She zoomed in. "Looks like it's right near a river."

Michael looked at the screen. "I remember where that is."

Alexis held onto his hand and smiled. "Then take us there."

CHAPTER FIFTY-NINE

THE MOON WAS NOT the brightest light in the Bosnian night sky. With the Apexian ship at rest in the western valley and the beam from atop the pyramid extinguished, the blazing light came from less than two hundred feet above the houses in the low valley. Cezar and Azure held on to James's arms as they watched from behind a cream-colored house.

"The Apexians look similar to humans," James said, peering around the corner. "But their skin is grey."

"We know," Azure whispered. "That's because they've lived in the deepest parts of the ocean for quite a while."

"How long have they been here? And are there more of them?" James asked.

"We have no idea how many are down there," Cezar replied.

"Quiet," Azure hissed seconds before a bright searchlight spanned the street in front of the house.

The three moved around the house, keeping to the shadows. As they passed a window, James glanced inside the house. Huddled under a table was a family of four, holding each other in the dark. James understood the fear that would seize anyone who had witnessed what was happening, and he was overcome with guilt.

"We need to protect these people," he whispered to Azure.

Cezar spun around and glared. "I'm not saving any humans!"

"It doesn't matter," Azure said. "They're not here for humans."

"Then why are they here?" James asked, keeping his voice low.

Once the tracking beam of light was further away, Azure and Cezar pulled James toward a white one-story home across the road.

"Come on!" Cezar urged. "A hundred yards and we'll be out of this vortex."

"Just wait until they're on the other side of the valley," Azure said, and then he turned to James to explain. "The Apexians have been here for thousands of years looking for Ben, and if they capture one of us they can find his frequency."

Cezar laughed. "That's why they abduct people in their sleep."

"I don't understand," James said.

Cezar glared at him. "We can enter the dream state of a weakened human mind."

As James tried to process what he had just been told, Azure tried to pull him along.

"I don't have time to explain the details, but they hold Ben responsible for their planet's destruction, and they will stop at nothing to find him," Azure said.

They pulled James along, ducking behind parked cars and sticking to the shadows. The searchlights were in the opposite direction, and the edge of the vortex was only ten feet away.

"Let's go!" Cezar said.

Azure joined Cezar but turned to see that James had stopped.

"What about these other aliens?" James asked. "What do they want?"

Cezar and Azure glared at him as they walked backward.

James started toward them. "Come on, give me something. What do they look like?"

"See for yourself!" Cezar said.

James spun around. The shed behind the house cast a long shadow onto the ground, but he could see five beings coming toward him. When he turned back around, Azure and Cezar had vanished. They had made it to the outside of the vortex and could leave.

"Please, I'm not the enemy," James said, his back to the five beings.

"James. It's OK to turn around," Colonel Logan said.

James turned around and saw the colonel standing next to four other men who looked very much like humans except they wore metallic body suits. The one standing next to the colonel had intense blue eyes that reflected like mirrors. The four with Colonel Logan approached James and examined him as if he were on display.

"Colonel, what is going on here?" James asked.

Logan smiled. "They're confirming who you are before you go with them."

"Why would I go with them?"

"Because you're one of them."

SIXTY

IN THE MIDDLE OF a one-lane road, an unusually warm breeze blew through the trees and across Alexis's face as she stood with her father and grandfather looking at the GPS.

"Where did you take us?" Mikel asked.

"This isn't the spot," Alexis said, staring at the map on the phone. "We're supposed to be about a mile that way."

"I didn't think we would be able to go exactly where you wanted," Michael said, and he started toward the trees. "This place is protected, so we'll have to walk the rest of the way."

Mikel looked back at Alexis. "When did you change your outfit?"

She glanced down. "I'm not sure. I didn't even notice."

Her ivory sweater had transformed into a thin, cream surplice three-quarter-length shirt made of a single piece of fabric that wrapped to form a loose V-neck. She also wore white Capris and form-fitting sandals.

"What's wrong?" Michael asked as she stared at her bracelet.

"Nothing," she said, but the bracelet's lack of gold color weighed on her mind.

"Let's keep going," Michael insisted.

Alexis stepped over the ditch running next to the road. "How is this place protected?"

Michael walked slowly and steadily, making little noise as he moved. "Across this world, at any given time, there are vortices influencing the way seasons change and ..."

"Of course, vortex patterns affect weather and all kinds of other things," Alexis said.

"Yes, but there are specific ones that have major magnetic

anomalies," Michael explained.

"Like the Bermuda Triangle?"

"Precisely. And the triangle you visited in Japan."

"Correct me if I'm wrong, Father," Mikel said. "But are there not ten of these so-called vortices?"

"In a sense, yes. But ..."

"Then I'm certain there isn't a vortex here," Mikel said, gesturing outward with his hands.

"Think of opposites attracting," Michael said, and he held his hands as if he were holding a ball. "If you could travel from the center of those ten vortices straight to their polar opposite you would find ten places like this. These are the vortices of the Light, the ones hidden from man."

"You're saying that on the opposite side of the world from here there's a vortex?" Alexis asked.

Michael nodded.

"If this is of the Light, then the others are ..."

"Yes, they're of Darkness. And because these areas are pulling against each other, it will block us from moving into them through teleporting. Originally, four were put in place to protect the four corners of Eden. One was inside the garden, and the other five, the opposites, kept things balanced."

"How did they multiply into ten of each?" Alexis asked.

"It was long after Eden was hidden from us, when the Earth flooded, that it began breaking apart the land and splitting apart the vortices," Michael said. He seemed about to continue but paused.

"What is it?" Mikel asked.

They had come to the edge of the trees, where the woods opened to a large field. Michael waited for Alexis. She joined him and checked the coordinates on the phone.

Michael put his hand on Alexis's shoulder as he looked at the GPS with her. "Are we close?"

Alexis pointed to the right. "It looks as if it's a little way past that farmhouse. But the farmhouse isn't on this map, so I won't be sure until we're on top of it."

Alexis took the lead and stepped out of the wooded area into the field. The three made it through plowed fields and past the house. Alexis followed the coordinates to a perimeter of pine and maple trees. "It has to be through there," she said and then looked back at Mikel and Michael.

"What are you waiting for?" Mikel said. "This is what you came all this way for. It's time to see what's on the other side of those trees, don't you think?"

She let out a long breath. "Yeah, I guess it is."

In the back of her mind, she feared what lay ahead and what she was there to do. It wasn't going to be easy, and she didn't have exact instructions for her next steps. The journal gave no more clues, and the crystal inscriptions no longer pointed the way. But she pushed on and made it through the ten feet of trees and brush to a clearing less than two acres wide. She looked around and sighed. "It's so ..."

"Peaceful," Mikel said.

The land was carpeted in lush green grass and surrounded by a dense forest. A broken boulder lay in the southwest corner. Alexis made her way toward the rocks, but before she could examine the large stones, the ground began to tremble, and she lost her balance and fell.

"Great," she said as she picked herself up. "Another quake."

"I don't think that was just another earthquake, my dear Alexis," Michael said. "I think someone else knows you're here."

"Ben? He won't hurt me."

"No, but his followers will. They fear he has betrayed their purpose on account of you."

Alexis remembered Ben's plea to her and knew her decision would be more difficult than she had first thought.

"His love for you has caused things to spin out of control for them, but it has played into the hands of prophecy," Michael started to explain. "He used his followers to find you and now ..."

Another tremor erupted along the fields, splitting the ground apart and separating Alexis from the other two.

"Hang tight, we're coming to you!" Mikel yelled over the shaking ground.

Alexis moved back and grasped the boulder. When she glanced back at Mikel, he and Michael were wrapped in a bright beam of white light shooting down from the sky. She hid behind the broken rock. Behind them, coming through the trees, a sea of shadow men were heading in their direction.

What would you have me do? You promised I wouldn't be alone, and right now I need you more than ever. Please, show me a sign.

A beam of light shined into her eyes, and her heart sank as she looked up and saw its source. A circular UFO appeared above her, sending down its bright light. Alexis turned toward Mikel and Michael, but they were gone. She closed her eyes and awaited her fate.

CHAPTER SIXTY-ONE

BLAZING STROBES OF light kept Alexis from seeing her surroundings, but the humming in her ears had ceased, and she could hear familiar voices nearby. She tried to block out the light with an arm across her eyes, but as she did, five strange figures started walking toward her. The heads looked very large, and one had dark oval eyes, but as they came closer she realized the light was distorting their size.

"Don't be afraid!" an unfamiliar voice said.

Then she saw that four of the beings were very familiar. Michael and Mikel were accompanied by three others. She ran to Mikel.

"What's going on?" she asked, looking from Mikel to Michael, but they just smiled and stared past her.

"I'm so glad you're really alive!" someone said behind her.

She turned to see James standing there, tears falling from his face.

"James!" She embraced him and began to cry. "I thought you were gone, and I thought that woman had ..."

"I'm fine."

"Wait." She pulled away. "If you're here, does that mean you were abducted, too?"

"No, I'm here because we were looking for you," he said, nodding toward the beings behind him.

"We who?"

"Alexis, these are ... well, these are the Omiens. And I am one of them."

"What?"

One of the beings in front of her raised his arm. The lights dimmed, revealing the inside of a round systems room. It was clear she was inside the UFO that was above her, and she also saw who was standing in front of her.

"Colonel? But how ... I don't ..."

"It's me, and I know this is confusing, but we don't have time to explain everything," the colonel said. "Those beings that were following you are right below us." He pointed at an illuminated screen showing the images beneath them.

"Please, Colonel. Please explain it to me." She noticed that none of the other people on the ship had strange heads, and the dark oval eyes were actually thin glasses. "Start with them."

"Alexis, we are not alone in the universe," James began.

Alexis raised an eyebrow. "No kidding, Mitchell. I asked for an explanation, not a statement of the obvious."

"Fair enough," James said. "Try this one on for size—I'm an alien."

Alexis folded her arms and stared at him. "If you're joking, Mitchell, I'm going to ..."

"Maybe I can explain," said an unfamiliar voice coming from the man standing next to the colonel. "My name is Keelan, and I am the commander of this ship."

He took off the thin glasses, revealing piercing blue eyes. Alexis looked at James whose eyes had the same blue color.

"We are from Omly, a galaxy a few million light years from here," Keelan said. "And we have been visiting Earth since the first beacon."

"The first beacon came from the top of the Tower of Babel," James added.

"The biblical Babel?"

"Yes, that's a whole story in itself," James said. "I'll tell you about it later."

"Fine, but how does this explain you being an alien?"

"After the first visit, we have come only in peace and curiosity to find an alternate planet if ours were ever to perish," Keelan said. "Yours is very much like our own, except for the constant sunlight.

But because of our advancements in galactic travel and altering space-time, we come often, and many of us have chosen to stay behind. A little over thirty of your years ago, one of our crew gave birth on one your military bases."

"I was a young officer then and brought her to the base to deliver," Colonel Logan said. "She gave birth to a healthy baby boy. James was that boy."

Alexis looked at James. "Where is your mother now?"

"She died during childbirth," Keelan said. "We left James here with your colonel in hopes we could monitor how well he blended in with humans."

Alexis glanced at James. "You did a good job fooling everyone, including me."

"That's because I didn't know. I only just learned the truth."

"I'm sorry," Alexis said. "It must be overwhelming."

"I'm trying to pretend it doesn't faze me."

"So this explains the close encounter in Japan."

James shook his head. "No, those were different aliens."

"The Apexians are neutral concerning us, and they seem to have their own agenda for the Darkness," Keelan said. "And they have no planet to go back to."

"Maybe they can help us," Alexis said.

"No," said Michael. "Though they are neutral as far as the Omiens and the humans of Earth, they are determined to find Ben and will not let anything stand in their way."

"So why don't we let them do it?" James suggested.

"Because it doesn't matter if he's on another planet, his power will still exist," Mikel explained. "He has to be in a completely different dimension in order to stop the evil in the universe."

Mikel directed Alexis's attention to the monitor. The field was consumed with Watchers and Gatherers. Alexis went to the three-foot illuminated image and scanned it, as if she were looking for something.

"Can they see this ship?" she asked the Omien controlling the panel of buttons below the image.

"No, we're able to cloak our ship to resemble any skyline," he said. "We only have to reveal ourselves when we fly over a certain vortex. It's the only way we can maintain our power supply in those areas."

"Or if we want to cause a stir with the humans below," another crewmember said, laughing.

Alexis shook her head and scanned the dark beings. "Aliens with a sense of humor—who knew?"

James knew who Alexis was looking for. "He's not there. Why would you want to find him after everything he's done?"

She saw Michael and Mikel over his shoulder. "Because I'm the only one who can stop him."

"That's not why," James countered. "You have the same look I saw in Belize. You're still in love with him."

"It doesn't matter," Michael said. "Right now Alexis needs to decide what she's going to do next. She is well aware of the stakes."

"Why can't we just kill him?" James asked.

"Because we'd be no better than him, Mr. Mitchell," Mikel answered.

Michael put a hand on James's shoulder. "It will all work out in the end, I promise. Trust in what is meant to be."

Alexis continued to watch the field become a solid black mass, and then she remembered the vortices below and the hold it had on her. Which meant the Darkness, too, would be trapped.

"How did you people find me?" Alexis asked Keelan.

"The crystals you possess give off a stronger frequency than normal ones," he replied.

She corrected him. "I only have one crystal."

One of the Omien crewmembers sitting behind her spoke up. "Are you sure?"

She turned and saw him gesture toward the holographic screen with three pulsating lights.

"What about that cluster over there?" she asked when she saw another faint grouping to the right of the radar system.

"Those have to stay hidden at all costs," Mikel said. "I took them to the Ringing Rocks to confuse their signature frequencies."

"You definitely have them hidden," the Omien sitting there confirmed. "When we flew over that specific group of lights, they disappeared. And if our system can't find them, no one on your planet can."

"But that doesn't explain how they saw three crystal signatures near us," Alexis said.

"We only saw two with you," Keelan explained. "The third signature was a crystal already aboard this ship before you arrived."

Mikel pulled a box from his pocket. It held the diamond ring he had given to Marcia.

"My mother's diamond ring?" Alexis inquired, recognizing the unique setting and large diamond.

"Yes, it's the only good thing that ever came from my mother," Mikel said before handing it to Alexis. "It belongs to you."

Michael took a closer look. "The Immortalis crystal. This is the same diamond I gave to Eve after we left Eden. It was formed from the fruit of which I ate."

"Yes, this is it. And my vindictive mother convinced Eve to give it to her since I was the rightful firstborn," Mikel added. "But I took it to keep her from growing an army of undead and to one day give it to Light. And that is what I'm doing."

Alexis examined the perfect diamond. "I never was able to see it this close since it was on my mom's finger. Why was yours transformed into a diamond and Eve's a piece of quartz?"

"Because each of the pieces of fruit on the tree was different," Michael said. "And that made them difficult to locate. I spent years seeking after them. I searched for diamonds and a single piece of quartz. It wasn't until I met someone years ago that I learned the truth about the crystals."

Alexis held the diamond up to the light, reflecting color everywhere. "Who else knew about this stuff?"

"Your grandparents," Mikel said. "Baba and DziDzi both came from the descendants that swore to protect the crystals. They vowed on their lives, and sadly DziDzi paid with his. So I promised Baba to make sure they were hidden."

"And I made a promise to finish this," Alexis said. She turned to Keelan. "Commander, with your permission I'd like to be taken to this spot."

The Omien commander seemed puzzled. "Where? In the heart of all that?"

"Yes."

"That's suicide!" James said. "You don't have to do this."

"Yes, she does," Michael said.

"When I crossed the universe I felt my body change, and whether I failed or not, I knew I had to try," Alexis said. She paused, and everyone turned to her, listening intently. "Standing in the presence of the Intelligences made me reflect on life's purpose. I know that knowledge is everything, but more important is what I do with that knowledge—that's what makes it all worth it. And before I left, they gave me a clear image in my mind of what I was to do in order to rid this Earthly plane of the Darkness."

"And what exactly is that?" James asked.

"The first thing I need to do is get to the exact coordinates from the journal."

Mikel took out his phone and opened it to the GPS coordinates Alexis had plugged in earlier. Keelan took the phone and handed it to one of his men, who instantly entered them in to the ship's navigation system.

"This exact point is right where that broken stone has been

placed," the crew member said. He handed the phone back to Mikel and then brought up an aerial view of the field where the boulder lay.

From above, the stone was split into four pieces, with one section larger than the other three. The lush grass of the field flowed through, delineating two lines crossing.

"X marks the spot," Alexis said, grinning at the screen.

"Ben will probably be looking for you, since Lilith has a bounty on your head," James said.

"I want him to find me. Especially since I have home field advantage on this one."

"But you'll be outnumbered," James stated.

"I'm aware of that, but they'll want Ben more than me."

"How can you be so sure?" James took her hand. "How can you trust anything with him?"

"His willingness to destroy this world to find me proves he would stand between me and them. And I'm going to make sure he has to choose."

CHAPTER SIXTY-TWO

AS BEN MOVED past the farmhouse and through the trees at the edge of the field, his followers bowed and parted to allow him a clear path toward the center, where two Gatherers held their female prisoner.

"Let her go!" Ben commanded.

Lilith jerked away, puffing her breast out as Ben got closer. "Have you changed your mind?"

"About you? Not a chance."

"Well." Lilith sneered. "You just missed your precious human pet."

As Ben approached, he glanced over her shoulder. "It's sad to think you were so wrapped up in me and what I was doing that you failed to recognize betrayal within your own ranks."

She expelled an airy laugh. "Whatever do you mean? There has been no ..."

Her words were quickly interrupted when Ben smiled and nodded to someone behind her. Cain, a hundred yards away, began to make his way toward them.

"I can know how they feel about you even when I'm not near," Ben said. "So your notion that you could convince them to turn on me was a waste of time. Especially since I had already put into place a spoil of my own."

"What are you talking about?" She frowned as she saw Cain walking toward her. He brushed past her while unwrapping the draping from his head. "My love what is he talking about? What have you done?"

Ben walked toward her with his hands in his pockets. "I give you some credit for getting them to fall for your half-truths and believe they had a chance against me. But it didn't take much to remind them of who you truly are and to have an advocate from your own bed side with me."

She glared at Cain. "How could you? I kept you safe."

Cain glared back at her with red eyes. "No, you kept me hidden. My appearance kept me safe."

The small childlike hooded beings moved through the suited men and closer to Ben. Their eyes, too, flamed red as they stared at Lilith, but Ben put forth his hand to stop them. He took Lilith by the arm and tossed her to the feet of the seventy-two-foot-high demon Gatherers.

"It didn't take long for them to be reminded of the sins you cast that bound them here," Ben said. "Why would you deny the truth of your relation to the human that you find jealousy with?"

A Gatherer whose eyes beamed black spoke. "Tell us the truth."

Ben grinned. "Tell them, Lilith. Tell them about your son and his daughter."

"He lies!" she shouted. "He led you to be caught by the Apexians while claiming he had possession of James Mitchell, who is not my son."

"She is trying to confuse us," a Watcher said. "He never said Mitchell was her son. Azure said that."

"Is it true that you have a human son?" a Gatherer demanded.

"It's true," Cain said. "Mikel is her son and he is Alexis's father. This I have known since I found her in the mountains."

There was an intense movement as the gathered beings started to growl. A moment later, an Apexian ship appeared over the horizon.

"Apexians?" a Watcher called out. "How did they track us here?"

Azure came through the crowd with Cezar. "It was her, she led them up the side of the pyramid, promising them us in return."

"No," Lilith said with a sneer. "I led them to the other alien ship hiding in the clouds, the ones who were called upon by the beam of light set in place by your Master. The Apexians are here to assist the Omiens, who are working to destroy all of you."

"Why? They have nothing in common," a Gatherer said.

"Oh, but they do." Lilith shot a glare to Ben. "They're both here to see that you all perish. And the Omiens have the crystal used to control the light atop the pyramid."

"Why do beings from other planets care about the Pearl of Gates?" Cezar asked Ben.

"Oh, he didn't tell you?" Lilith said. "Every planet has started with a Garden of sorts, which you already know. And you also know that each tree bore thirteen fruits."

A Gatherer took Lilith and gripped her throat. "Don't waste our time with a history lesson, whore."

She broke away. "I'm not! The Pearl of Gates was the fruit used to tempt the first man on Apexia. The Apexian astronauts returned and saw their planet had been broken. They searched for the signature of their crystal for years, hoping it could open a portal on another planet. They were lost out there until they found this forsaken planet bearing life, holding the signature of their crystal and the Devil himself."

"But he doesn't decide when a planet comes to its end," a Gatherer said, pointing to Ben.

"No, but all the evil throughout the universe is from his design. And his order of Darkness destroyed their planet."

All eyes turned to Ben. He gazed up at the triangular UFO hanging back near the western trees.

"Master, is this true?" Cezar asked.

"Yes," Ben confirmed.

Without warning, the Messengers of the Light began to move through the fifth realm into the world of the physical humans. All over the world, they made their presence known to those in the Darkness. And now they surrounded the fifty-acre vortex of the Missouri fields.

CHAPTER SIXTY-THREE

FROM ABOVE, ALEXIS and the others inside the Omien ship watched as the Light circled the ranks of the sea of blackness below. Both sides stood perfectly still, as if they were waiting for something.

"The land below is not safe," one of the Omiens stated.

"I agree," Keelan said before turning to Alexis. "I feel there is a battle about to happen down there."

"That battle is the reason I was brought back," she said, watching Ben move from the center toward a group of Messengers. "I have to take their power source away."

"It's not just that," said the Omien sitting at the controls. Everyone turned to him as he brought up a global map on his screen. "These readings I'm getting from below are happening across the globe."

"How so?" Keelan asked.

"Sir, I've been monitoring the dark beings since we entered Earth's atmosphere," the crewmember said. "They had been making their way here for the past hour, and, like the situation here, they have been surrounded by beings of the Light."

"That's not surprising," Alexis said.

"No, it's not, but this is." He pointed to another screen, with various colors. "I have also been monitoring the temperatures below the Earth's surface."

"That's how we maintain our power while we are on your planet," Keelan explained to James and Alexis.

"Through underground temperature?" James asked.

"No," Alexis said. She was looking at the screen with the temperature readings. "The temperature is caused from the magma below the surface, and ..."

"And it's about to be above the surface," the crewmember sitting at the screen interjected.

Alexis pushed back from the control table. "Then I need to get down there."

She took the diamond ring from the box and slipped it onto her left ring finger. Mikel took her hand and smiled. Alexis could see tears welling in his eyes. She pulled him close and put her arms around him.

"I'm sorry I never came back after that night," he said. "I didn't know your mom would send you away. I was the cause of a lot of your delusions."

"But I wasn't delusional." She pulled back from the hug, tears of her own streaming. "I may have forgotten that you were the one who taught me how to separate my mind and body, but when I needed to not feel the pain, it came naturally. So I think you saved me."

Mikel nodded. "Do you think you're ready for this?"

She gave him a reassuring smile. "Yes."

"Those things are everywhere Alexis," James said, looking out the window. "Hold on, can they see us?"

The crew member at the screen nodded. "I'm sure they can now. Our shields are down so your friend can go back. Which she needs to do now if she's going."

James turned to Alexis, who was speaking with Michael and Mikel. He remembered the first time he saw her at the base. She was no longer the same new girl under his supervision. He smiled, thinking she never allowed him to order her to do anything. Alexis had always been in control and always known what she wanted. He knew he had to support her.

"If something goes wrong, help my family understand," she said to Mikel. He nodded his agreement. "And keep them safe until we meet again."

"Are you coming back?" James asked.

She raised an eyebrow. "James."

"I understand. Someone has to do this, or they will overpower all that is good. And you're the most strong-willed person I've ever met."

"I'm glad you see that." She pulled him in for a quick hug.

"My eyes have been opened to more than enough today. It's not every day you find out you're an alien."

"It's not every day you find out your boyfriend is the Devil," she replied, and they both laughed.

"If you make it back, promise me you'll take a break from all this?"

"I promise it will be a great deal of time before I ever see that crystal again." She smiled at James and then glanced at Michael. "Now I must go."

Everyone got one last goodbye. As Commander Keelan escorted Alexis to the back of the bridge and led her to a shiny metal circle on the floor, Alexis whispered something to him.

"Yes, that is correct."

She nodded and whispered something else.

"Are you sure?" Keelan asked.

"Yes."

"Just give me a sign when you're ready." Keelan stepped back as Michael came into the circle.

"This is your token for the gates to open," he said.

"I have a token," she said, raising her left hand to show the diamond ring on her finger.

"Keep that, you may need it to return." Michael kissed her forehead. "I have truly enjoyed your presence."

She glanced down at her hand to see the pearl encased in the crystal. She looked at Michael, a question in her eyes, but he moved out of the way. Keelan waited for Alexis and then signaled his crew with a hand gesture. The lights inside the ship became blindingly bright. Instead of blocking it from her eyes, Alexis took in the white light warming her face.

The commander and his crew shielded their eyes with their oval glasses. "Transport on my count. And 3 ... 2 ... 1."

The room was illuminated by a cyclone of white light. Within seconds, the light was extinguished, and Alexis was gone. The ship was silent as they watched and waited.

CHAPTER SIXTY-FOUR

BEN AND HIS FOLLOWERS made their way to the edge of the vortex where the Light had them surrounded. Shoulder to shoulder and for miles around, the Messengers stood waiting.

"Why the theatrics?" Ben asked one of the Messengers, but he didn't respond. "You people knew you were outnumbered, and you invited peaceful aliens. Not that I'm surprised."

Cezar laughed. "They don't seem to have any clue."

"They know exactly why they're here. Probably more than you, Cezar."

As Azure grinned and relaxed his stance, a surging beam of light shot down ten yards from them. Dark beings tried to scatter away from the beam, but the sky was filled with nine Omien ships casting more beams of light down inside the vortex.

Ben turned to Azure. "I thought you said they left."

"They did, and they took Mitchell with them," Azure said. He moved back but there wasn't anywhere to go.

"You don't think he's stupid enough to fight us, do you?" Cezar queried.

"No." Ben looked up at the ships. "There is someone else up there with them."

He closed his eyes and clenched his fists. A fierce wind plowed through the trees and up toward the Omien ships. Clouds formed like cyclones, sucking two ships upward and taking them several miles off course. Growls of pride roared across the darkness.

Each of the seven remaining ships simultaneously released large balls surrounded by blue fire. When they fell, there was no explosion nor did the balls break into pieces, but an instant shock wave spread across the darkness, shaking the ground beneath them.

Cezar looked at Azure. "What are those?"

"I don't know. The Omiens have never shown signs that they were armed."

As the blue flames died down, many of the Watchers stepped closer. The only thing left as the flames went out was a clear glass sphere with a copper-colored center.

Alexis stepped out from the tree line ten feet from Ben. "Those look to be super-sized electromagnets. But I'm just guessing that my friends sent these as a precautionary measure."

Ben spun around and saw Alexis standing on top of the broken stone at the corner of the field. Unable to move through the dimension, he pushed through the beings to get close to her. She jumped down and was instantly swarmed by Gatherers and Watchers.

Ben stepped toward her. "Alexis, I want explain."

"You don't need to explain yourself to me," she said. "But you need to come with me so this can end. No more destroying the innocent."

Ben glanced at his followers, whose faces were stony, as if daring him to make the wrong choice, and then he turned again to Alexis. "I can't change. This is who I am, this is what my purpose has always been and will always be—to counter the Light. Yet I don't want to be without you again."

"And I can't imagine this planet's future if you stay." She kissed his forehead. "So you must allow your powers to be bound here."

Ben couldn't hide his feelings for her as her touch moved across his body. "I chose this life and all the darkness that came with it. I've always been prepared to take my punishment. And that would be an eternity without you."

"What if I gave you a way to stop it all and be with me?"

Ben cupped her jaw in his hand. "There's only way that could happen."

Alexis moved close and spoke into his ear. "I have the key to open portals to other dimensions, including Eden. Your power can be concealed inside."

One of the Gatherers, who apparently had overheard her, said, "To open Eden, you'd have to know where it is located. And you're in no position, human, to make offers."

Alexis stepped back and gazed at the seven-foot-tall being. "Actually, I'm in the perfect position."

She looked up to the Omien ship directly above her and nodded to Keelan, who was watching closely. The ship, along with the others, disappeared into the clouds. As if she had given them a signal, the balls on the ground started glowing from within. Pulsating beams shot out in all directions, making contact with the closest beings. One by one, Watchers were sucked into the balls.

"What's happening?" Ben asked her as he tried to use his energy to move the balls.

"What you've always wanted—a war."

"Why can't I destroy them?"

"When I was in the Omien ship, and I realized they were using Earth's magnetics to keep their ships operational, it reminded me of something James Mitchell said about where UFOs are normally found." She spread her arms. "I have also learned that many things factor into those areas as well, including where magma flows. So I asked the nice Omien commander to release their supercharged magnetic anchors—the core is made of iron."

The Gatherers laughed. "Iron?" one of them said. "Iron doesn't have any effect on us other than to draw us closer. It won't kill us."

"The plan was never to kill anyone. I'm not like you." She smiled and turned to Ben. "I sought only to weaken his power."

Ben watched as acres of darkness were consumed by the spherical charges.

Alexis took his hand. "Prove you love me before it's too late."

He looked over his shoulder at his followers, who were standing far enough away from the large iron pellets not to have been sucked in. Ben squeezed her hand. "Let's do this."

"I told you he would betray you!" Lilith emerged from the crowd of Gatherers. "He is going to leave us prey to the Light."

All at once, the Gatherers lunged for Alexis and Ben, but before they could grab them, the ground broke beneath them. Islands of land tore apart from each other, taking Watchers and Gatherers down to rivers of red magma. Alexis had quickly reacted and grabbed the boulder two feet behind her. When she was able to steady herself, she looked back. Ben wasn't there.

"Ben!" she cried out, but the noise of the terrain being ripped apart drowned out her voice.

But she could see perfectly and realized that the realms of both good and evil were being split apart. Quadruped creatures from the darkness emerged onto the land, some instantly falling between the broken ground, but many others able to stand strong and snarling toward the Messengers.

The wall of Messengers surrounding everything moved in unison, toward the field of darkness. They were joined by a force of large winged creatures, which soared in from above, grabbing beings of the Darkness and dropping them into the cracks in the ground to be consumed.

The war had begun, and forces of magic and battles of strength were being tested between both sides. With each side immortal, and the forces of Darkness only being trapped below, something needed to happen to help the Light. And now Ben was nowhere to found.

CHAPTER SIXTY-FIVE

As Alexis got up from the ground and gazed at the image before her, a memory of somewhere familiar flooded through her mind. The ground had tilted up as if she were standing on a hillside and the valley below was filled with beautiful flowers all the way to the tree line below. She was here, the place she had feared in her dreams, but this wasn't a dream and she was no longer afraid.

She pulled the Bereishit crystal from her pocket and the Pearl of Gates her grandfather had given her. How was she supposed to get the crystal to work? She searched the rock for a flat surface but noticed faint markings on the inside, which described a circle inside a square and an elongated hexagon attached to the square.

"Alexis!"

It was Ben calling her, but she didn't see him anywhere. "Ben?"

"Alexis, I can't hold on much longer!" His voice was strained.

Then she remembered what it was that made her fear her dream. The hand she would see coming over the edge as someone called out to her—and now it was happening. Ben's hand was barely over the brim of the surface.

Alexis rushed to him and saw the sea of darkness, many of whom were trying to take Ben below with them. She hesitated, knowing that letting him go wouldn't kill him but take him away from the surface. His power would remain but be weak enough to allow the Light to prevail.

"If you want me to let go, I will." Ben looked up at her as she weighed her next move.

She shook her head and Ben let go, but he instantly felt her grip inside his own. Alexis was holding on with all the strength she had. Ben pulled himself to where his arms and upper body were above the ground. Several Gatherers were attached to his legs, making it difficult to go any further.

"Alexis, I can't," Ben said. "If I pull them up with me they'll kill you."

She looked into his eyes. "You control them, remember?"

He reached down and grabbed the head of the Gatherer clutching his legs. Ben's eyes became black and his veins bulged. His hands released a bolt of black energy that not only crushed the skull of the Gatherer but also sent a surge down to all those trying to control him. When the beings below watched their own be destroyed by their beloved Master, they were enraged. Many turned and sought ways to get to Ben and Alexis.

Alexis helped Ben the rest of the way. "We need to hurry."

"How are you going to get the crystal to work?" Ben looked around. "There are no surfaces like in Belize, you can't guarantee that rock will work."

"I don't need a surface." She opened her hands, revealing the Bereishit crystal in one and the crystal cube with the pearl inside in the other.

"James took the Pearl of Gates and ..." He looked up at her, his eyes alight. "It was the key to this the whole time?"

"I think so." She pointed to the etching on the rock.

"That means you and I were always meant to come together?"

"There is balance in everything," she said.

"How are you going to open the portal?"

Alexis took the two crystals and struck them together. A noise like a trumpet blast echoed across the valley and throughout the Earth. Messengers who had been awaiting a sign began to increase their efforts against the Darkness.

A fierce cold wind blew where Alexis stood. Two orbs formed and began to open side by side. One was emanating warmth and light, the other was oozing cold darkness.

Ben frowned. "Two?"

She took his hand. "As I said, there is balance in everything."

A silhouette of a tall winged man came from the portal, blazing with radiance. As the gate to the Light opened wide, Uriel appeared, holding a sword. Alexis bowed her head before him and then looked up at his face.

"Do you have the keys that opened these worlds?" Uriel asked.

Alexis opened her hand, revealing the two crystals. Uriel took the Bereishit and the Pearl of Gates and placed them into the two voids of his sword. Instantly the world behind him opened, exposing a beautiful flourishing garden.

A growl rose up. A hundred feet away was a large group of Gatherers and Watchers. The only thing separating them was the broken ground, and they were already starting to join together to bridge their way across.

"Alexis, you must hurry," Uriel said. "I will take him into the Darkness myself. You go into the garden."

"No. I'm going with him," she said, looking over her shoulder.

"If you do, you can't return in the next millennium without a token of passage," Uriel explained. "You will be stuck there for eternity."

She put forth her left hand.

Ben shook his head. "Of course. Your mother's ring was the Immortalis."

"I have my token of passage," she said.

Uriel nodded. "Very well. This is your free choice, and I grant you both passage."

The dark beings had made it across to the raised portion of land where Alexis and Ben stood. The two of them hurried toward the dark portal and began to walk through it. As one of the Gatherers reached out, Uriel slammed his sword into the ground breaking off that piece of land and casting the dark followers to their doom.

Ben and Alexis entered the dark world, and Uriel returned to Eden, and both portals closed. The beings of the Light cheered and moved into the center of the broken field. The creatures of Darkness found that their power was gone and their efforts were in vain. Many fell to their knees and surrendered.

CONCLUSION

THE OMIEN SHIP was full of rejoicing and shouting. The crew removed their cloaking shield, revealing their presence to those rejoicing below.

"I can't believe it's over," Keelan said patting James on the back. "Your friend was very brave. She made a decision I could never have made."

James sat looking out the same window through which he had witnessed Alexis leaving this world into another. Replaying it through his mind, hoping the ending could've been different but it wasn't. He knew it would be hard, but mourning felt pointless when he knew she wasn't dead. He listened to the white noise of chatter going on in the ship, and it sounded like white noise.

Michael smiled as he hugged his son. "The only way that portal will open is if someone actually finds the other twelve crystals and knows where that portal took them."

"Exactly! And the beings of this here are about a thousand years from the technology to find them," Mikel said.

"Our tech was pretty close to pinpointing those crystals," Keelan said. "Yet, you're right that we are only starting to understand how the portals work and far from finding any particular one."

"It doesn't matter. The Light has a lot of work to do between now and then, starting with ridding this universe of its waste," Michael replied, referring to the followers of Darkness. "Now that they have no power here, all the Light can shine through."

"I sent a message through to our home," Keelan said as he and Michael started walking to the other side of the ship.

James waited until they were out of earshot before he approached Mikel. "What were you saying about the twelve other crystals and finding exactly where Alexis is?"

"I hid the crystals," Mikel said. "No one will find them for a very long time."

"Why didn't you just destroy them? I assumed you wanted to keep Ben inside. Isn't that why Alexis gave herself to that black portal?"

"James, you must understand that there is no beginning and there will be no end to Good and Evil. Both must exist to keep the balance of the gods. Ben and Alexis will only be displaced somewhere else for a time." Mikel sat down across from James. "She is not in Darkness, only accompanied by it."

"Where exactly would that be?" James asked.

Mikel shook his head. "I don't know. I only know that it's a place similar to Eden but without the sun. No mortal life can be sustained within. My guess is an alternate universe to this one, but it's only a guess. Only the architects of this universe have the answer."

James frowned then hung his head for a moment. "So Ben is coming back?"

"Yes, but not for a very long time, and by then this world will not be the same," Mikel said.

"What about Alexis? Will she come back?"

"Yes, that's why she has the diamond ring I gave her. It will keep her safe as she passes back through, and it will help serve as a beacon to find her one day. But unless someone collects all those crystals and knows exactly what they're for, it will be a very long time." Mikel patted James on the back. "She's my daughter, James, I know how hard this is."

"Then why are you and the others so nonchalant about her sacrificing the next millennium of her life to spend it with the Devil?"

"This is how it was always meant to be. No man could change that." Mikel stood up. "From the moment my mother betrayed Ben till the moment he met Alexis, all was meant to be. As hard as it is to accept, they love each other, and that gives me comfort in her choice."

James leaned back against the seat, no longer sulking. "Someone needs to keep a record of this, to help future generations understand what Alexis did, especially if someone does find those crystals."

"I think you will find your people are excellent at keeping records," Mikel said as he stood.

As Mikel walked away, Keelan approached James. "Are you coming back with us, James, or do you want to stay?"

James grinned. "I'll be going home with you." He took a final glance out the window at the ground below before heading to the group of Omiens, who had been joined by Mikel and Michael.

Inside the new world behind the closing portal, ash-white clouds obscured the moon giving limited light, but with what little came through it cast onto the silhouettes of two majestic mountains that rose up a mile from where Ben and Alexis stood. Then inches from their feet, a rushing waterfall poured over the sharp edges of a paynes-grey cliff.

"This place is almost like what I remember of Eden," Ben said. "The land is the same, the water flows in the same direction and those mountains ... all the same, except here it is devoid of life or light. It saddens me to know you have to endure this place."

She put her arms around him. "Feel no sorrow for my choice. I don't need to see the sun to know it exists somewhere—but you're wrong."

Ben frowned as she pulled away and walked around him. "How so?"

Astern to where he stood, was a leafless tree with thin, twisting branches reaching out. Alexis reached up to a branch that held one crimson apple. "This place is not without life, and where there is Darkness, so must there be Light," she assured him. "So goes the balance of the universe—at least that's how I have come to understand it."

Ben smiled and watched as her pale skin glowed through the gloom.

"There is something you must know," she said.

He took her hand. "I'm listening."

"Even though my feelings for you are clear, I didn't come here for you." As she turned, the moon appeared from behind a cloud. The light caught the edge of the diamond ring and projected a beautiful prismatic rainbow onto Alexis's chest. "I came to ensure that you were bound here while the others I love remained protected."

MAP OF THE WORLD PYRAMIDS AND MAYAN TEMPLES

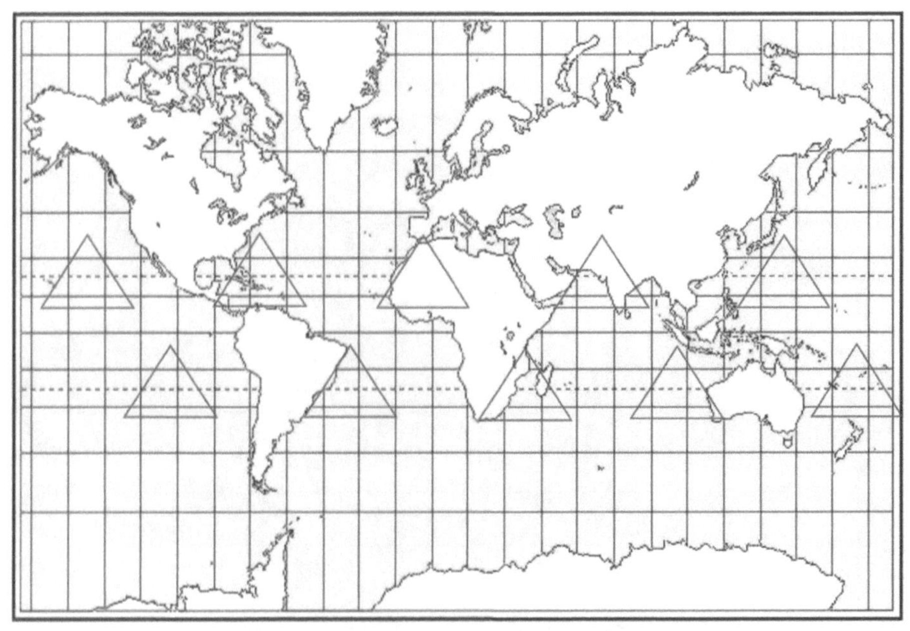

10 Vortices of Darkness

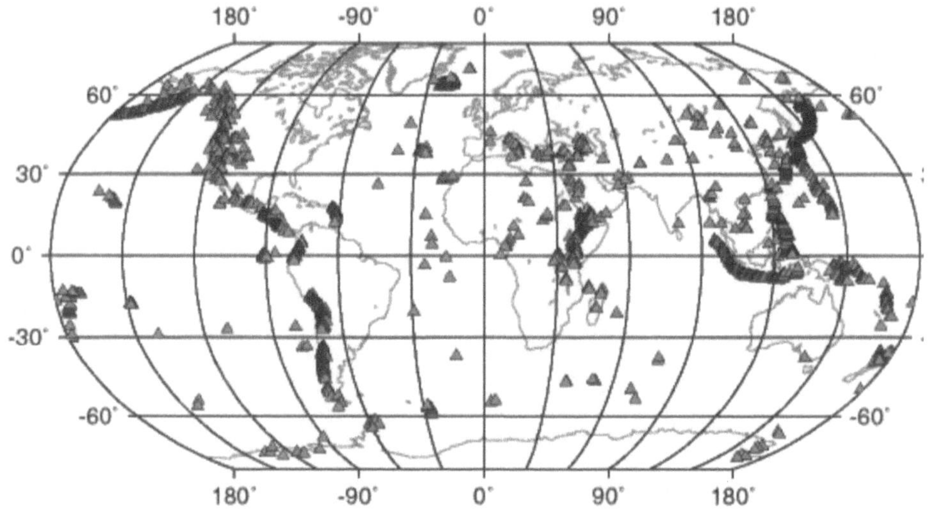

MAP OF THE WORLD'S VOLCANOES

VOYNICH MANUSCRIPT PAGE

www.ingramcontent.com/pod-product-compliance
Lightning Source LLC
Chambersburg PA
CBHW030424310726
48979CB00009B/1596/J

9781936307357